FLICKERING SHADOWS

A NOVEL BY KWADWO AGYMAH KAMAU

FLICKERING

S H A D O W S

AN OWL BOOK
HENRY HOLT AND COMPANY :: NEW YORK

Henry Holt and Company, Inc.
Publishers since 1866
115 West 18th Street
New York, New York 10011

Henry Holt® is a registered trademark
of Henry Holt and Company, Inc.

Library of Congress Cataloging-in-Publication Data
Kamau, Kwadwo Agymah.
Flickering shadows: a novel /
Kwadwo Agymah Kamau.—1st Owl book ed.
p.   cm.
"An Owl book."
1. Caribbean Area—Fiction. I. Title.
PR9230.9.K36F57   1997   97-27599
813—dc21   CIP

ISBN 0-8050-5472-3

Henry Holt books are available for special promotions and
premiums. For details contact: Director, Special Markets.

First published in hardcover in 1996 by
Coffee House Press, Minneapolis, Minnesota

First Owl Book Edition—1997

Designed by Chris Fischbach

Printed in the United States of America
All first editions are printed on acid-free paper.∞

10   9   8   7   6   5   4   3   2   1

Thanks to: my mother, who bore me; my aunt Rose, who raised me; Margaret (Thea) Jackson, who inspired me with the possibilities of college; Paule Marshall, my teacher, for your example of excellence and integrity; Faith Childs, my agent, for your faith and friendship; Talibah, my wife, for your patience and support; and my daughter Andrea and goddaughter Mataya, who are the future.

Above all, to Mama, my grandmother, whose love, guidance, and parenting made all of my accomplishments possible. I dedicate this, my first book, to you (please excuse the curse words).

I WAS THERE THE SATURDAY NIGHT the police raided the Brethren here on the Hill, with the lamps flickering in the lamp-holders up on the church walls, walls that my two old hands had helped put up with the other men in the village even though the rheumatism was turning my joints into knots.

The church wasn't no shack like the newspaper said. It wasn't big and fancy like the cathedral and them other big churches in town, but it was a church, we "own-own church," like Clemmie used to say, God rest her in her grave. The best wife I ever had, Clementina.

But like I was saying, even the shadows was dancing that Saturday night.

The drum skins feel tight and smooth. My hands feeling like they working by theyself, pounding out the rhythm. And the sound bouncing off the walls and echoing inside the church. The women clapping, dancing, singing. Their tambourines bupping and rattling. The men rocking and jerking. The women voices high and the men bass voices low, low, low—like oil flowing beneath clear water.

My grandson Cephus playing the drum with his head cock oneside and his eyes shut. Young Boysie, Cephus friend, leaning over his drum, working it, his hands in a blur, a frown on his face, naked to his waist, like the rest of young men sitting with their drums between their legs and the sweat glistening on their bodies.

Me? I had a robe sling over my shoulders, covering my old bones from the chill of the night.

Young Estelle collapse and fall down on the floor rolling around, in the power. And young Cephus eyes like two balls in his eye sockets, staring at Estelle puff-leg bloomers.

But Sister Wiggins pulling down Estelle dress to cover her nakedness. And disappointment pulling down Cephus young face.

I had to lower my head so nobody wouldn't see me smiling.

Sister Wiggins and Sister Scantlebury helping up Estelle, and Estelle reigning back and shaking; her eyes shut and her face screw up. And she talking in tongues, sounding like, "Ahumalumaluh . . . a-chimumalumaluh . . . hmmmmm!"

Sister Scantlebury is a tall woman, tough from working the ground by herself and raising a young boy-child ever since her man fall in a toilet pit and dead. She old enough to be Estelle mother. But the power got hold of Estelle, so Sister Scantlebury struggling, strong as she is.

Old Sister Wiggins, short and with the fat jiggling loose on her arms, trying to help Sister Scantlebury wrestle with Estelle. Sister Wiggins just like me, always complaining for rheumatism, but she grabbing on to Estelle right arm and en letting go. Every time Estelle shake, Sister Wiggins stumbling. But she determined. Her forehead crease up and her mouth set. One of her gray plaits unwinding from her head and hanging like thick rope, whipping back and forth every time Estelle move.

And Estelle big gold hoops glistening against her black skin in the light from the lanterns on the walls.

Brother Joseph, with his beard almost down to his chest, standing in front the drummers in his white robe, pounding the ground with his snake staff and stretching his other hand straight up in the air. "Yesss, sister! Yesss. . . ."

All of a sudden, *brug-a-dung!* Is like a hurricane battering the front door. People heads swing around. Even Sister Wiggins and Sister Scantlebury eyes fastened on the church door.

Estelle still shaking like she in a epileptic fit.

Old Brother Oxley and his wife still holding hands, moaning and rocking with their eyes shut, as usual, as if they in a world by themselves.

My hands stop. One of the drummers give a couple more beats—*whabap!*—on his drum and stop.

Look like the whole police station standing in the door, and the sergeant clomping down the aisle with his big-guts self. Big Joe.

Everybody quiet now. Everybody know Big Joe, with his two little marble-eyes, his small bullet-head, and his slant-back forehead. All Big Joe know to do is to beat people.

Big Joe standing up in front Brother Joseph, smacking the club in his palm, with his manager belly push out, his shoulders throw back, rocking backward and forward on his two bandy-legs.

"Unna can't keep no more meetings here," Big Joe saying. Big Joe got a small voice for such a big man.

Brother Joseph standing up straight, with his snake staff at his side. The snake carved on the staff, with the tip of its tail resting on the floor, the body winding up around the staff, and its two heads staring full in Big Joe face.

"WHY?" The voice booming deep, echoing in the church.

For years after that, people swear that it is the snake that ask Big Joe "why"—why they can't keep no more meetings in the church.

Big Joe jump; his eyes open wide; he gulp; he smack the club in his palm extra hard; he take a deep breath. "Cause the guvment say so," he say at last. "And *I* say so. That is all you got to know. The guvment say shut unna down, and I come to shut unna down." His little-boy voice is the only sound in the church building.

I throw a quick glance at Cephus. Cephus looking at his father and mother—Granville and Violet—standing couple rows back: Granville in his stiff-starch-and-iron short-sleeve white shirt—people say Granville is the image of me, but I don't know about that—I always thought he look more like his mother, Clemmie; Violet beside him in her white dress and white head-tie—she is a nice daughter-in-law. I can't complain.

Everybody eyes fasten on Big Joe and Brother Joseph.

Big Joe raise his hand and signaling the rest of policemen at the door to come in. "We taking the drums and all the rest of this," he say. He looking at the masks and the pictures of Garvey and Nkrumah on the walls, and the painting of a African woman holding a baby that hang up right behind the pulpit. And his face screw up like he smell a fart.

A young policeman coming for my drum, but I en letting go. I stubborn in my old age. I wrap my arms around the drum, looking up in the face of the young constable. The boy en even start shaving yet.

I see when he raise the club, but en had time to raise my hand to block before . . . *whacks!*

Is like something explode in my head. Talk about seeing stars! Is like the whole galaxy inside my head. I falling down off my bench, still trying to hold on to the drum; blood beginning to run down my forehead—warm; I crouch over and scrunch up to protect my head and my balls—I know this young generation spiteful; you never know what they would do even to an old man like me.

My drum rolling away. And my head hurting, hurting to rass.

My daughter-in-law voice bawling out: "Daduh! Cephus! . . . Oh Lord have 'is mercy! . . . Cephus!" And Granville deep voice saying: "God blimmuh! Unna hit my father!" He saying this like he surprised.

A bench tumbling over and women voices hollering,

"Mr. Cudgoe . . . !"

"Oh Lord Jesus . . . !"

"Hold he! Don' let he get heself in trouble!"

And a man voice: "Woman, shut up your mouth! Lef the man lone!"

And more benches knocking over. Blows raining, sounding like how bag flour does sound when you cuff it: *buff!* . . . *buff!* Heavy boots tramping down the aisle. Hands grabbing me up rough under my armpits and hauling me; my feet dragging on the ground. I open my eyes and the red carpet sliding past under my face; blood dropping off my head and making darker red spots on the carpet.

When they reach the front door and my shinbone hit the top step, I try to twist round so that they wouldn't drag all the skin off my old shinbones dragging me down the church steps. But I en as young as I used to be.

Through all the pain, I squint open my eyes.

A white inspector standing up longside the Land Rover in front of the church. A bony-face white man with a moustache, in a peak cap, khaki tunic, short pants, and long socks nearly up to his knees, standing upright like he got a bamboo spine, tapping the Land Rover fender with a cane, not doing a thing, while Big Joe and them in there busting people ass.

I en last too long after that—after police break in a church and beat up old people; Dolphus Blackman losing his finger when the police slam the door of the police van shut, and them brutes keeping him at the guardhouse with the blood dripping on the floor and Boysie just staring at his father finger hanging by a little piece of skin; Miss Blackman sitting on the bench between Dolphus and Boysie at the police station, big with child, and losing the baby later in the courthouse, with the judge banging his hammer and bawling, "Order in court! Order in court, I say!" and one of the Brethren jumping up and hollering "Order your fucking self!" and asking the judge if he en got a mother, and turning to the crowd in the courtroom and saying, "Look him! Look him! With a curly white wig on his head like a blasted sissy," and turning back to the judge and saying, "You lucky all these policemens in the court or I would come up there and knock that blasted wig off your kiss-me-ass head." And people gasping and their eyes popping open.

And the judge pointing his finger at the man and hollering, "Thirty days! For contempt of court!" and ordering the policemen, "Take him out! Take this man out of my court!"

And a whole gang of policemen rushing at the man right there in the courthouse and raining blows on him like peas, and the man bawling, "Loose me! Loose me! So help me, I go kill all you today!"

But his voice getting softer as the batons beating him down and the boots kicking him like he is a football, till after a while all you can hear is the kicks, the baton blows, and the man grunting and groaning like a sow in labor.

And the judge hunched like a vulture in his black robes, staring over his glasses and tapping a pencil on his desk.

My heart couldn't take it. It couldn't take it. I drop down right there in the courtroom. Dead.

Well, that cause a whole new set of commotion in the courtroom.

They buried me right next to my Clementina in the cemetery up on the Hill.

Things settle down on the Hill after I pass away, although life was never the same again.

The man that cause a disturbance in the court living in town now, roaming the street, walking up to people and barking in their faces, "ORDER IN COURT!" And people jumping with fright.

A lot of people stop going to Brethren meetings, and the few stubborn ones that hanging on with Brother Joseph peeping and dodging to hold their meetings down in the gully, with a little boy up in a tree looking out to see if the police coming.

Around that same time, Anthony Roachford, little brown-skinned Anthony that born and raised on the Hill, come back from studying law in Away, but he never set foot back on the Hill. He open a little law office in town.

Then the next thing the people on the Hill hear, he and a set of young lawyers start a political party—the People's Labor Party. People calling it the People's Lawyers Party.

Leaflets start appearing on electric poles, shop doors, even on the big evergreen tree in the square in town. The leaflets saying,

DOWN WITH COLONIALISM!

INDEPENDENCE NOW!

The Parliamentary Council in an uproar. The white men in the Council—plantation owners, merchants, the governor from Away—pounding the table with their fists and saying things like, "over my dead body," calling Roachford and his party "bloody upstarts" and "colored bastards."

Two black men in the Parliamentary Council: Dr. Bostick and Dr. Greaves. But all Dr. Bostick doing is standing with one hand in his waistcoat and playing with his watch chain and saying, "I object most strenuously!"

Dr. Greaves sitting with his gray-haired head down.

And through the windows they can hear shouts, glass breaking, running footsteps. People rioting.

A policeman catch a fella pasting a leaflet on a bench in the botanical gardens.

A crowd gathered around the policeman and the fella, and a rumor spread that a policeman kill a man just for handing out leaflets.

So now, people roaming the streets, breaking store windows and saying, "We want independence!"

But some fellas in the crowd only feeling up the white clerks in the stores. One of these fellas smelling his finger every couple minutes with a big smile on his face.

A bottle whiz through a window of the parliamentary building.

Dr. Bostick sticking one finger in the air, pushing out his chest and bellowing, "The day of revolution is at hand!"

Dr. Greaves still hunched over with his head down.

The plantation owners and merchants looking frightened and the president of the council—the governor from Away—a robust, red-faced man in short sleeves, striding to the door and bawling for the police. "I say! I say!"

Well, to make a long story short, the king in the Mother Country (that is what even the educated ones that should know better does call it) send down a man to investigate.

And the investigator going around asking questions, even going to the prison to talk to the people the police arrest in the riot.

The investigator gone back to Away. Things quiet in the country. But it is an uneasy kind of calm, like the stillness you get the day before a hurricane—a slow, heavy, oppressive passing of time.

Then the news is like sudden flashes of lightning—a big headline on the front page of the newspaper say, "Mother Country to Grant Independence"; the governor announce elections; the Council pass a law saying everybody over twenty-one can vote; and a delegation going to the Mother Country to make arrangements for independence.

Meanwhile Dribbly Joe, who does walk around town, sometimes with his fly open, with dribble dripping from his mouth and wetting the front of his shirt, having a flash of enlightenment and drawling, "How . . . anybody . . . can . . . give . . . we . . . in-de-pen-dence?" And he going on to say something about the king in Away tying a string to a bird leg, opening the cage door and flying the bird like a kite, and the stupid bird think it free because it en feeling the string around its leg, but if the bird ever try to fly too far it going get a sudden shock when the king yank the string.

Hearing so many words coming from Dribbly Joe is like hearing a baby fart. People mouth dropping open at first, then they laughing at the foolishness "that half-idiot" Dribbly Joe talking, forgetting what the old people always say: every fool got his own sense.

Not long after that, Roachford come back on the Hill. First time he set foot on the Hill in all the time since he come back from studying law in Away.

He and two carloads of men stop at Mr. Thorne rum shop.

A crowd gather. Inside the shop, Roachford done order rum. Two bottles on the counter. Estelle opening a tin of corned beef and setting it on a plate next to a packet of biscuits.

Roachford head towering above the crowd. "There's more where that come from," he saying.

Roachford slapping fellas on their back and talking about if the Lawyers Party win the elections, things going be different. "Massa days done wid," he saying. And it sound out of place the way he say it.

Ever since he come back from "my sojourn in the Mother Country," as he like to put it, he talking like he born and bred over there. So now when he trying to talk like everybody else, he en sound right.

The fellas laughing and tossing back the free rum and eating the free corned beef and biscuits. As long as Roachford standing the drinks and the eats, they don't care; he all right with them. So when he say, "Massa days done wid," everybody laughing and saying "Yeah!" Everybody except Boysie and Claude—Boysie with his full beard covering his face and looking serious, with one elbow resting on the counter and a bottle of stout in his hand; Claude, tall and lanky and leaning against the side of the shop.

"And what that mean in concrete terms? 'Massa days done with'?" Boysie asking.

Roachford turn to face Boysie.

"Give me some *specifics*, cuz," Boysie saying. "Some *specifics.*"

Roachford looking around at the crowd. Everybody watching him to hear what he going say.

He take a deep breath. "Well, for one thing," he say, "we plan to take away the land from the old plantocracy and give it to the people." He look around with this big grin, like he feel he do something.

But Boysie saying, "You forget where you come from? All of us up here own our own land."

Which is true. Years ago, when the plantation owner decide to move back to the Mother Country, he divide the land into plots and sell it out.

Some people only buy sufficient land for a house spot. Others, like Boysie grandfather (Roachford great-uncle), buy piece-by-piece till they got enough to support themself.

Roachford looking around the crowd, still confident. "Of *course* I know. Hill people independent fuh so. I is one of all you, remember? Gimme a break, man."

Somebody in the crowd snicker.

"He should stick to talking great," a low voice saying. "He sound like a real assbeetle when he trying to talk like we."

The crowd gone quiet.

Roachford start sweating, pulling a kerchief from his pants pocket and wiping his face.

He look around the shop, sizing up the people. Then he force a smile. "Anyhow, why spoil a good rum with talk, huh?" he say. He raise his glass. "Drink up, man. Drink up."

The other party, the Doctors Party, en do much better when they decide to hold a meeting on the Hill.

Dr. Bostick, the leader of the party, sticking his finger in his waistcoat and reminding people that he and his "colleagues have been fighting the colonial rulers" before these "young Turks" in the Lawyers Party were born.

But the people start booing and heckling, saying that since the governor give them two seats in the Council, they just like the plantation owners.

Somebody start pelting rocks, and Dr. Bostick and the other doctors in the party fleeing down the Hill.

Good luck for them a lorry driver spot Dr. Bostick as the doctor that take out his son tonsils. He stop his lorry and lean out the window, but he barely had time to say, "Hey, doc . . ." before all the doctors clamber up on the back of the lorry and Dr. Bostick jump in next to the driver, slam the door and hollering, "Drive, man! Drive!"

WELL, ROACHFORD AND THE LAWYERS PARTY win the elections big with the slogan, "SWEEP THEM OUT."

Dummy, the deaf-and-dumb fella that does plait baskets and make brooms, build a brand new house. The Lawyers Party symbol in the election campaign was the broom. And Dummy sell more brooms in the campaign than he sell his whole life.

People saying, Roachford is one of we. Things going be different.

Of course a lot of the Hill people en so optimistic. They know Roachford: Anthony Roachford who stop speaking to everybody on the Hill after he get a scholarship to secondary school; Anthony Roachford who win a national scholarship to study law in Away and en even come back to his mother funeral. The old wood house that he grow up in rotting and falling to pieces, empty since his mother dead.

Independence come soon after the elections. But all it bring is a new flag, a new anthem, and a prime minister, Anthony Roachford.

Independence night, big parade in the Square, bright lights, and I sitting on top of the flagpole looking down at the Duke of something-or-another that come from Away, dressed in a uniform with more gold buttons and decorations than you can count.

The old flag lower and the new one raise, flapping against my legs there at the top of the flagstaff.

Roachford waving a broom in the air and people bawling, "WE SWEEP THEM OUT!"

Big celebration let loose. Guns booming; the police band playing—the horn men puffing out their cheeks and reading the music sheets; the trombone man sawing away and rocking his body with the music; the little white man waving his arms and popping up and down like a jack-in-the-box, conducting the band. Fireworks lighting up people faces, and at the same time, plantation backras walking up the gangplank of a passenger boat that anchor in the bay.

For weeks now, the show window in front of the travel agency on Bay Street displaying posters that announcing steamship passages to Australia, New Zealand, South Africa, Argentina.

Every week the backras going up the gangplanks in droves, leaving after they done suck the substance from the land and the people. "Sail south," the posters saying.

South. It is like shaking up a cup of muddy water and watching the dregs settle to the bottom.

But funny thing is, it is like all these things happening in another world. Life on the Hill going on as usual, slow, easy—until the missionary and his wife come.

THE DAY THE MISSIONARY COME, the sun was hot for so, even under the dunks tree out on the pasture where Cephus was giving the sheep their mash.

Cephus. With his shirt open nearly down to his navel. His belly muscles like a jooking board. Stringy, with muscles like wire under the skin of his arms. Sweat making his forehead look like polished ebony.

The sun overhead, the whole place quiet, the men out working, most of the women and old people dozing off, and the children at school.

Even the shadows sheltering underneath the trees and houses.

But that day it was feeling more quiet than usual: not even the birds wasn't chirping; not a wind wasn't blowing; the tree leaves still.

And Cephus thinking he must ask Boysie if he hear anything about a storm pon the radio.

Even *I* was enjoying the scenery, taking a deep breath (that is only a figure of speech, of course), looking around: the sea glistening like a knife; the rickety wood houses scotch on the side of the mountain like ticks on a dog back; a girl walking up the track that is a scar on the green side of the mountain, balancing a bucket of water on her head; the housetops in the village down by the main road peeping through the trees; and the sky bleached light blue, with a few clouds fuzzing out and drifting, looking like if the big spirit just shake out his pillow and the feathers fall out in clumps, scattering and blowing away.

Cephus eyes taking in everything too, and his ears feel like a steelpan that just tune—every sound bouncing off his eardrums crisp, crisp in the stillness of forenoon: the sheep slurping their mash; Leroy hammer going *ping! ping!* in his tinsmith shop across the pasture, near Mr. Thorne rumshop. In the distance, Leroy, small like a jockey, with his navy blue cap on his head, sitting on a bench in the door of his little wooden shop, hunch over, concentrating and hammering.

A woman light voice drifting from over by the houses not far off, shimmering like the haze that hovering over the ground. "Cee-ciiiil."

"Yes, Ma."

"Boy, come in here out the hot sun. Right this minute. Don't lemme got cause to come out there and roast your little behind!"

A little wind blowing now, rustling the tall cus-cus grass. And the woman voice is like a echo of Cephus Gran-Gran Clemmie, calling him in as a little boy. "Ceeeephuuus!" And the breeze feeling like ointment against his skin, reminding him of the menthol crystal and vaseline that Gran-Gran Clemmie used to mix and rub his chest with when he had a cold.

Clementina. The best wife I ever had in all the last three hundred years. And the last one.

Here of late I find my thoughts wandering, back to Clemmie, back to past lives. And this worrying me, because usually this does happen when they preparing to send me back to the land of the living again.

"Th-that is a b-big mistake." Cephus muttering to himself.

My heart skip a beat, in a manner of speaking. Cephus voice jolt me back.

Cephus whittling a stick and thinking about this morning when Denzil little brother Courtney say, "First chance I get I moving to town." The boy piss only just start foaming and he talking about leaving the Hill.

And Cephus asking him why he in so much hurry. Things tight in town; work hard to get. "Y-you thi-think it easy?" Cephus asking him, and trying to explain that at least here on the Hill, a little forced-ripe boy like Courtney can live in his mother house, with a roof over his head, food to eat. In town he would be scrunting and catching hell.

But Courtney en listening. Till at last Cephus get vex and say, "Wha-what s-sweeten g-goat mouth d-does burn his a-a-ass. M-mark my w-words."

Now Cephus taking a deep breath and looking around. Let the rest of them move away. He going live right here, farming. Things hard, yes. But he can't see himself doing nothing else. Up here, he en working for nobody, en begging nobody for nothing. He staying right here. Life sweet.

And I saying: *You sure, boy? You sure?* making sure that my words echoing in his mind.

Because right then a motorcar engine droning through the village, getting nearer.

And Cephus vex because the car disturbing the quiet. A brown car, slow, big, like a hearse, metal and glass glistening, bouncing up and down in the holes in the road, easing past Mr. Thorne shop, nearly taking up the whole gap for itself, too big to go round the big rock in front Miss Wiggins board-and-shingle house.

The bottom of the car hit the rock in front Miss Wiggins house—*scrunch!*

But it too far to see who in the car.

Couldn't be nobody important, Cephus thinking. Otherwise that fart-frighten headmaster, Mr. Hutson, woulda had the schoolchildren line up out in the hot, broiling sun, waiting. And Hutson himself would be getting on like the boss-idiot that he is: standing up in front the schoolyard with his hands behind his back, in that heavy, gray flannel suit, with the beads of perspiration running down his face and his bald head shining in the sun, like he waiting for God self.

Could be tourists that get lost. Every once in a way that does happen.

Cephus walk over to the evergreen tree where it cool, and settle in his hammock. The sheep lying down in the shade. The heat got him drowsy. He dozing off.

And he got this dream: Doreen walking way from him; he hollering her name, but she en turning; she en stopping, only walking with her head straight. He running to catch her, but he en moving. And all he doing is bawling, "Doreen! Doreen!" but Doreen en taking him on, and the crywater running down his face. Big man like he crying like a child.

Same time, Doreen and Inez sitting down in Inez verandah cooling out. Inez fanning herself with a newspaper. Doreen watching Cephus lying down in his hammock with his hands fold across his belly and she can't help noticing again how Inez and Cephus is the spitting image of one another, especially with Inez hair cut short the way it is—same broad nose; same lips like somebody chisel them out. But Inez face a little broader than her brother face; more oval. Cephus face narrow.

Doreen eyes taking in Inez short hair, the hairstyle that always had Cephus dropping remarks, saying how good Inez hairstyle look. "Sh-She got a nice round head to suit it," he always telling Doreen, "J-Just like yours." That was when they was first courting.

Nowadays he coming right out and asking her why she don't wear *her* hair like Inez. Upwards to yesterday. Cephus must be drunk or foolish, one of the two, to think she would ever wear her hair like some picky-head boy. She would rather drop dead first.

And with that I pick up my hand and give her one thump across her head.

A sudden headache throbbing inside Doreen skull. She rubbing her temples.

Inez asking her, "What happen? Headache again?"

And Doreen nodding yes.

Doreen arms plump and brown like mahogany in the sleeveless print frock she wearing. She got these big, slanted eyes, sloe eyes, I hear somebody call them type of eyes one time. Is a pity she don't realize how beautiful she is.

Inez pick up the flowered glass of lemonade, let go this long "Aaaahhh" after she sip, then rest the glass back down on the glass-topped wrought iron table that Boysie bring back from Away.

And Doreen thinking that a little wrought iron table would look so nice under the tree in her backyard. But Cephus too damn cheap. Cephus en know how to treat a woman.

The big brown car that just passed stopping in front Anthony Roachford new bungalow.

"That is a funny looking license, ent it?" Doreen saying. Her headache easing away.

The licenses that Doreen accustom seeing is black with one letter and four silverish numbers. But the license on this brown car is ABG 639—a white license with blue numbers.

Inez fanning herself. The newspaper crackling and Inez enjoying the little breeze it making against her chest.

"Wonder who it is?" Doreen asking.

But Inez en saying a word.

The left side door of the car open and this tall white man

get out, wearing a light blue suit that look rumfle up even from where Inez is.

A woman get out the other side of the car, bareheaded, her hair the same color as dry grass, long, reaching down past her shoulders. She wearing a water-wash, flowered dress with no belt; sandals on her feet.

The man look up the gap and wave.

Doreen leaning forward in the chair and raise up her right hand by her shoulder, waving back at the man. She look at Inez.

Inez sitting back with her left arm fling over the chair-back and her right hand in her lap, staring down the gap. She en wave back.

Doreen hand ease back down. "Wonder if that is the missionary?"

"Look so." Inez serious as a heart attack.

The man rest the two suitcases in the road and start walking up the gap toward Doreen and Inez, then he stop, look back and call the woman with his hand. "Come on, hon," he say.

The woman standing by the car, en moving.

"Come," the man say again.

The woman move away from the car, slow, like she en too fussy.

"Hi. How y'all today?" the man say when he reach in front the verandah.

A tall man, hunched over as though he embarrassed to be so tall. A hard face and metal rim glasses giving his face an unfriendly look. The front of his shirt wet with sweat.

He dabbing his face with a handkerchief.

The woman reaching the man to his chest. Her arms and shoulders expose, dotted with brown freckles in the shapeless frock she wearing. Her collarbones look like they can hold soup. And her dark glasses nearly covering her whole face.

From afar, the woman mouth look like it bleeding. Up close, Inez realizing it is only lipstick and she wondering why the man let his daughter wear so much lipstick.

"I'm Pastor Rat. Billih Rat," the man say. "And this is Mahwaf."

A giggle bubbling inside Doreen. Mr. Rat. And what a funny name for a man to give his daughter—Mahwaf.

But then the man put his arm round the woman waist and pull her close, and from the look on his face when he look at her, Doreen realize the woman en his daughter. But Mahwaf still is a funny name.

"Howdy do," Doreen say. Doreen can't take her eyes off the woman hair. It is the color of straw, just like the hair on the dollies Gran used to bring home from the white people she work with in Belleville.

"I'm going to open a church in your lovely village," the man saying. "Spread the word of the Lord." He inhale deep and look around, like people does do when they go to the sea and smelling the sea breeze. "My, my (sound like "mah, mah"). This is one beautiful country you have here."

Doreen giggle, looking down in her lap, playing with her fingers.

Inez quiet.

Up the hill, the school bell ringing to let out the children for lunch.

"D'you ladies know Jesus as your personal lord and savior?" the man ask.

And suddenly it is like if Inez turn into board. She staring at the man. Her arm still fling over the back of the chair; her glass of lemonade in her other hand. If looks could kill, the man and the woman woulda drop down dead on the spot. Inez chest rising and falling; her nose holes flaring.

The man eyes shifting between Inez and Doreen.

Inez can feel the anger nearly bursting her chest, making

her fight for breath. She looking at the man skinning his teeth. His eyes en smiling.

Every skin teeth en a laugh, I whisper in her head, stirring her up.

She looking at the light bouncing off the woman dark glasses. She feel the woman sizing her up and she got five minds to snatch off the damn glasses and force the woman to look in her eyes woman to woman. She feel like pulling the woman stringy corn silk hair and leffing little holes in her skull, like them old dollies Doreen used to play with.

"Morning!" Inez say.

The man eyes open up wide behind his glasses.

Doreen head snap up, staring at Inez.

The man wife jump; her mouth open up, like somebody cut a slit in her face.

"I say '*morning*'!" Inez sitting up straight. "Where you manners? You get out your car, come right in front my house, see we sitting down here, and start talking and en even know to speak?"

"Ah, good morning," the man say.

His wife looking from side to side, like a mongoose cornered with a snarling dog in front of it.

"I, ah. I said 'hi'," the man say. "Didn't mean to offend y'all."

"Hai?" Inez say, "Hai? What kinda shit that is? . . . Hai. That is the way they does do it in Away? Hai? Well not here. You speak to me, is 'good morning' or 'good day' or 'good evening.' Who raise you?"

"Inez," Doreen voice real soft; she feeling shame. Because Inez en talking easy. Inez talking to the white gentleman like he is some little barefoot boy in the village.

Inez head snap round to look at Doreen, like she ready to tear loose in Doreen backside. "What you talking bout 'Inez'? This . . . this . . . (the word "man" can't come out of her mouth) en even got the manners to speak. Come talking Jesus talk. Just like them Jehovah Wickedness people." She whirl back and look straight in the man face. "That is what you is? A Jehovah Wickedness?"

"Billy," the man wife say. She looking round to see if anybody watching; she tugging his sleeve. "Billy? . . . The luggage?" She nodding back down the gap where the car is, with the suitcases in the road.

The man look at the suitcases then back at Inez and Doreen. His eyes going back and forth between the two women; en resting long on either one. "Uh, gotta unpack." The words rush out of his mouth. "Be seeing y'all soon." He make a back step.

He holding his wife elbow, looking back and waving. They hustling away, he with his shoulders hunch over and she making long, man steps, her long skirt swishing around her ankles.

Doreen and Inez in the verandah watching them, en saying a word, so quiet that you can hear the ice melting, going *"clink!"* in the two glasses in front the two women.

A fowl scratching underneath the house.

And Kwame inside hollering "Vroom! . . . Vroom!" playing motorcar.

And just then, Cephus wake up with his heart beating fast and water settle in the corner of his eyes and brimming over. And before he catch himself and know where he is, that he just wake up from a dream, he got this feeling like something wrong, like somebody just get lick down with a car or some tragedy like that. He looking all around him with wild, staring eyeballs.

A tall hunchback white man and a white woman walking past his house.

Inez and Doreen in Inez verandah watching them.

SAME TIME, BOYSIE AND CLAUDE CLIMBING the track from the main road up to the Hill. The minibus that he and Claude just get off of humming, heading up to the country.

From where he is, Boysie can see two of the black cargo boats that anchor out in the bay, waiting to come in the harbor. One of them is the Independence Maru. The water in the bay look calm, but Boysie know different. Today the waves were lashing the harbor wall and booming like cannons. Couple times, driving the forklift between the ship and the warehouse, the sea would gush over the breakwater, dousing he, the forklift, and the cargo on the pallet.

Overhead now, a flock of wood doves heading to the mountain, away from the dark clouds building up in the east.

Claude up ahead, a silhouette at the top of the track, tall, hustling to Mr. Thorne shop with the bag full of hair straightener sling over his shoulder.

How Claude can thief so bold-face, Boysie en know. Claude walking past the guards at the harbor gate with his bag sling over his shoulder and giving them a high sign—a little nod.

And when Boysie asking him if he en fraid he get lock up, Claude nodding his head back toward the gate and saying with a big grin on his face. "Who going lock me up? Them? They getting their cut, oui."

When Boysie reach by Thorne shop, Claude already got the bottles of hair straightener on the counter and Thorne gold teeth shining. Before next week most of those bottles will be off the shelf. They is the fastest-selling thing in the shop. If Boysie had his way he would take every bottle and fling it in the gully. But he only shaking his head. He keep walking.

Up the road, Doreen coming down the steps of his veran- dah and stopping to say something to Inez. Boysie heart pump a couple of hard beats.

Doreen standing up there on his front steps, looking like one of them statues that the fellas does carve to sell the tourists in town: broad hips, plump arms, and a nice, round ass. And the flowered dress that she got on en helping the situation, cause it en got no sleeves and it so light, it flowing over her hips like water. Man, if she wasn't Cephus woman, Boysie thinking.

Doreen watching Boysie coming up the gap, and when he getting near home Doreen can feel his eyes boring into her.

"Hello, Boysie," she say. "Just leaving." And her eyes tak- ing in Boysie full beard nearly covering his whole face; his bushy hair; the gold chain that showing through his shirt front open halfway down his chest; the gold rings on his finger; his gold watch; the big belt buckle with two guns crossed; his gab- erdine pants low on his hips; his black suede shoes. All of this she seeing in one quick glance. "See you later, Nez," she saying.

But Inez seeing the way Doreen eyeing Boysie from head to toe and her blood boiling.

Later, in Roachford bungalow, the preacher wife just finish unpacking her suitcase. She sitting at the edge of the bed smoking a cigarette with her legs crossed.

The preacher in the bathroom gargling.

When me and Dolphus enter the room, the window curtains flutter and a cold wind blow through the room.

Dolphus like to do things like that. Ever since Dolphus left in his fishing boat years ago and never came back, leaving Boysie fatherless, Dolphus roaming the place, bitter. Up to now, all he been doing is dramatic things like he just did. But lately, I have a funny feeling. For one thing, he got this new habit, all of a sudden, of walking around with a cutlass. A duppy with a cutlass. You can imagine that?

Now, the sudden chill in the room causing the preacher wife to shiver. She looking over her shoulder and walking over to the window to close it. But drumbeats drifting on the wind from the hills in the distance. She stop to listen.

Down the street—and then she correct herself in disgust, muttering, "What street? This is a goddamn dirt road, for God's sake"—children chanting a rhyme. The sing-song of their voices sound like music in her ears, and a little smile stretching her lips as she watching the children playing in a circle.

"Ring a ring a rosie . . ." their voices saying.

Dolphus stand right behind her and blowing a cold breeze on her neck.

She whirl around, eyes wide.

Dolphus chuckling.

"Billy." Her voice catch in her throat, soft.

And the loud noise of Billy gargling sound almost obscene in her ears.

"Billy!" Her voice louder now.

"Yes, honey."

"Are you going to take all night?"

"Coming, honey."

The bathroom door open, and before the preacher click off the bathroom switch, the light got him frame there in the door; a tall, bony man, naked as the day he born. He turn off the bathroom light and walk in the bedroom.

"What's the matter?"

She walk over to the bed and sit down.

"I've just had the weirdest feeling."

"What feeling?"

She shrug. "I don't know. Weird." Her cigarette end glowing in the dark. "Like we shouldn't be here."

"We're doing the Lord's work, Sandy. Where are my pajamas?"

"In your suitcase." Her voice irritable.

"You must have faith, Sandra," the missionary saying after a while.

"Huh. Faith." She sound real skeptical about this faith business.

Silence in the room. The missionary only staring at her.

She take a pull on the cigarette. "All I know is, this shit doesn't feel right."

My jaw drop. I en expect to hear a word like that coming from a missionary wife.

But the missionary eyes flicking at her with quick glances that tell me he afraid of her mouth. And his penis stirring. These people from Away is some strange people, I tell you.

And up the gap, Boysie, Inez, Cephus, and Doreen sitting in Boysie verandah. It is dusk time, and the bats coming up from the gully, swooping, whirling, nearly filling up the sky.

Boysie voice rumbling, ". . . said he had a vision. The Lord tell him go out and spread the gospel to the third world people. Convert the heathen souls to the ways of the Lord." Boysie imitating a foreign accent.

Cephus wondering aloud, "W-why somebody would w-want to come all the way from Away to open up a church up here behind G-god back?"

"What he mean 'heathens'?" Inez asking.

"And w-what he mean by th-third w-world p-p-people?" Cephus want to know. And he want to ask: If we third, who first and who second? But he keep his mouth shut on that one—Boysie might think he stupid.

The crickets chirping in the bush across the road.

Inez voice break the silence. "We should hold a council meeting."

"Why?" Boysie looking across the road as he talking.

"What you mean why?" Inez asking Boysie. "To decide what to do about the missionary coming, nuh?"

Boysie suck his teeth and want to know what council, if a bunch of old people sitting down talking stupidness is a village council. No power. Can't decide nothing. And who do that, uh? Who took away what little power people had? Roachford. Anthony Roachford that born and raise right here on the Hill. All-you Prime Minister. Cafuffling people, saying he centralizing. . . .

"Leave the man lone, Boysie," Inez saying. "Give him a chance."

"How much more chance he want?" Boysie vex.

Inez used to like to tease Boysie about Roachford, now she getting tired of hearing the same thing over and over.

Now Boysie going on, building up steam: "This is *four* years Roachford and them in power and up to now we still en got no electric on the Hill except for Roachford and Thorne houses—and the roads still en do yet. Nothing."

Then, Doreen voice come out soft, like she talking to herself. "Maybe if we did vote for the Lawyers Party, they woulda do what they promise." She didn't intend to say this, but the words just come out.

Inez and Cephus eyes snap toward Doreen. Boysie looking irritable, frowning at the interruption.

And the words tumbling fast and breathless out of Doreen, "If we did join the party and organize the women's and youth committees like Mr. Thorne was saying, maybe if we did do that, then maybe the guvment woulda do things for we."

Boysie and Inez look at one another; the two of them look at Cephus like *he* responsible for what Doreen saying. But Cephus staring at Doreen with his eyes wide. Nobody en saying a word.

But Doreen en care.

She find herself looking straight at Boysie, and Boysie looking back at her from behind his beard; all she can see is his two eyes boring into hers. It is as if only she and Boysie on the verandah.

She hearing Cephus saying, "Th-that is the stu-*stupidest* thing I ever hear." But his voice sound as if he in the distance.

And Doreen feeling good. Normally she don't get in the conversation when the rest of them talking politics. But now she building up courage. "I *tired* of all this talk about politics, politics," she saying. "Lawyers Party, Doctors Party; all of them is just politicians."

But just as sudden as her courage flare up, it deflate, leaving her feeling empty. She sighing. What is the sense arguing? What get into her this evening? But, she stun them? Good.

Everybody quiet.

Boysie look at Doreen real disgusted. At last he say, "Women." He turn to Cephus. "You ready to fire a rum, mate?"

Cephus stand up and stretch. "Yeah."

Inez look up at Boysie. "Why you don't wear a hat or something, Boysie? It look like it going rain."

Cephus looking down at Doreen, but Doreen only gazing off in the distance, not saying a word.

And Inez wondering what got into Doreen. But as Inez looking at Doreen through the corner of her eyes, she got to admit that she admire what Doreen just did. The men don't like nobody contradicting them, especially when it come to politics, *especially* Boysie.

Later, when Doreen shutting up the house, she standing at the front window in her nightie looking down the gap. A light on in Roachford bungalow where the missionary and his wife staying.

All of a sudden, she got a feeling like if somebody else in the room with her. She look around fast. A scratching and scurrying up over her head.

Two lizards up there. One of them scurrying off bird speed as if he just see a duppy—which he has. The other one poised stock still, staring straight in Doreen face. Eyeball to eyeball. Dolphus en like the way Doreen contradict Boysie earlier.

The flickering of the oil lamp making the lizard shadow dance in the rafters. And a chill shivering through Doreen body, putting chilly bumps on her arms.

Something in the way the lizard staring at her make her shut the window quick, hurry in the bedroom, hop in the bed, and lay down staring at the bedroom door, and she can swear she can hear somebody breathing on the other side of the partition.

Right at that moment, a beetle ping against the lampshade of the kerosene lamp and fall inside, killing itself.

Months later, when things start to happen, Boysie and Cephus remember passing Roachford house and walking to Mr. Thorne rumshop that evening when the missionary arrive on the Hill.

Everything was silent. No crickets, no frogs. Nothing.

They remember the heavy shadow that cover Roachford house when they pass by, and chilly bumps come up on their skin. All of a sudden the night feel cold and damp.

And Cephus feel like somebody behind him. But when he look around, nothing.

Boysie slippers slapping—*flup! flup!*—soft against his heels. Cephus bare feet scarcely making a sound.

A fragrance, like sweet-smelling flowers, filling their nostrils.

Ever since Anthony Roachford tear down his mother old house soon after he and his party win the elections and build a new bungalow on the spot, Old Miss Roachford, Anthony mother, got a habit of sitting in the verandah in the same dress that they bury her in. Just sitting there on the verandah rail and dangling her legs, staring into space and not saying a word.

But tonight, is only the smell of flowers filling Cephus nostrils.

The sugar cane blades on the other side of the road rustling in the wind.

"P-perhaps we shoulda sta-stay home, Boysie." Cephus head bowed down to keep the dust from blowing in his eyes. "The w-wind getting strong."

"Chuh, man." Boysie voice gruff. "Is only little wind." But his voice en sound so certain.

The rumshop around the bend up ahead. The men's voices coming from the shop.

Cephus glance back at Roachford bungalow and thinking that Old Miss Roachford never used to trouble nobody, but he coulda swear he see a shadow over the house only couple minutes ago. And that smell, like a funeral wreath.

But Boysie en say nothing. He could be imagining it. The shadow musta been a cloud passing over the moon.

But when Cephus look up, the sky is a black ceiling. No stars, no moon.

And down in the bay, in the distance, lights string out on a tourist boat like somebody pull down the stars out of the sky, leaving it black and empty, and string them out in the bay.

When boysie and cephus reach the rumshop steps, Leroy voice coming from inside.

"I hear for a fact that he come from a big, big church in Away, and the church they going build here going be even bigger than the Cathedral in town. And they going open a school and build a hospital."

Leroy. Short, with a small mouse face. Look like a jockey, specially with the navy blue cap he always wearing with the peak pull down, nearly covering up his whole face. People does call him Micey behind his back, but not to his face except they want to fight. Leroy small and spiteful.

"Man, what you talking bout?" Claude heavy voice booming.

Claude so tall that he bend over. And his woman Pearl always saying that he must have a tape worm in his belly, because with all the food he does eat, he won't put on a ounce of weight. Every time he go to the barber, which is every other week, it is the same thing: "Take off all." So he almost bald. Good luck for him, he got a nice round head that suit low cuts.

And he does shave every morning as God send—moustache and beard.

"That man belong to the CIA," Claude saying.

Leroy laugh out hard. "CIA?" He reigning back on his little bench, his head throw back and he laughing, kyah-kyah-kyah. "Man, everything is the kiss-me-ass CIA for you," he saying. "You does read too much. Full your head with shit. Kyah-kyah-kyah." He laughing and wiping his eyes.

And the rest of fellas laughing soft, "humph, humph."

Claude don't like nobody contradicting what he say. So now he looking round the shop with his face set up like rain clouds. The shop full—about ten fellas. Some of the men shoulders still shaking at what Leroy say.

"What all you laughing at?" Claude want to know.

Couple fellas pick up their glass and sip. Mr. Thorne put two glasses in front Boysie and Cephus.

Cephus wiping off his grin with the back of his hand.

Thorne standing behind the counter grinning with the gold tooth in the left side of his mouth shining.

"I en see nothing to laugh at," Boysie say.

Fellas looking at Boysie and their laugh beginning to cool down. Only Thorne gold tooth still exposed.

"CIA or not," Boysie say. "The government allowed him to come here. And we would be better off if he was *repatriated.*" Boysie showing off his big words again.

"Re-what?" one of the men asking.

"Sent back where he came from," Boysie saying.

Mr. Thorne en smiling no more. "Man, you people." He putting on the yankee accent strong. "What's your prahblem? Everything is a conspiracy. The guvment this; the guvment that. And what's wrong with somebody coming in from outside? Look at the schoolhouse. Dilapidated. Lord *knows* we need some help."

"That's why we have a government. That is why we paying

taxes." Claude voice booming. "Not for your politician friends to buy Mercy-Benz and live like big-shots. . . ."

Thorne butt in, irritable. "See? People in Away don't grudge politicians like that. They respect them. . . ."

"Man, what you talking bout?" This is Denzil—Estelle man, short and stocky, talking slow. En went no further than class five in elementary school, but you always got the feeling that every word that he say mean something. "Which Away?" Denzil saying. "I cut canes in Away just like you and I don't know about nobody respecting politicians. Where you get that from?"

Thorne frowning. He don't like nobody to remind people that he was cutting canes in Away.

Denzil still cool, leaning on the counter and rolling the glass in his two hands. "Besides, we talking about here, not Away."

Thorne open his mouth to snap back an answer, but then he stop, take a breath and say, "Same thing I tell Mr. Roachford. These people en going appreciate what you doing for them, I say."

"Which is?" Claude staring at Mr. Thorne hard.

Boysie admire Claude. Claude is a Garvey man. His father was a Garvey man, and his grandfather used to work in Panama just like Boysie grandfather. From the time Claude show up on the Hill and start living with Pearl, Boysie and Claude hit it off.

Boysie remembering how at first some of the fellas didn't fancy this man from one of the small islands moving into the village like it is his and living with one of their women. And some of the women, like big-mouth Sybil, used to say things like, "Who he is? Who his family is? Where he from? He could be a jailbird for all we know."

But Claude is a friendly fella, always willing to help a neighbor, so it wasn't long before Claude was like one of them, except for his accent. And even that started to change little by little.

Boysie resting one elbow on the counter and twirling the glass of rum on the wood that scrub so much times, it bleach out. The wet glass making dark rings on the board.

"Progress, man. That is what the Lawyers Party represent. Progress. They bringing we into the twentieth century. . . ." Mr. Thorne voice raise and he going on about "technology" and "industry" and "development."

And to Boysie, listening to Mr. Thorne is like listening to the union officials at the last meeting he was at.

They at union headquarters discussing the new container ships that coming to the harbor. And Branker, the general secretary of the union, sitting down at the head of the polished mahogany table, nearly busting his pinstripe suit, puffing a pipe.

The sound of traffic coming through the louvre windows from diesel trucks farting and belching, blackening the air with suffocating smoke that drifting into the room even from one story down; car horns honking; people voices; the metallic wheels of a donkey-cart on the road.

"We can't hold back progress," Branker saying.

"But what about the men?" Boysie say.

And the other union delegates in the room looking at Boysie like he commit treason. And Boysie regretting the day he decide to be a shop steward. Whenever you try to represent your men, somebody from union headquarters always saying, "Take it easy."

". . . Just like them Peace Corps people that you does see riding bout the place pon their bicycles them, looking so scruffy. Them is spies," Claude saying now.

"And you think the government would let spies come in the country so?" Leroy got a half-smile on his face.

Mr. Thorne frowning at Claude. "Claude, if you not careful, your mouth going get you in trouble one of these days."

The talk going on around Boysie, but Boysie en joining in. He reach out to the plastic bowl, scoop out couple ice blocks, pour some rum and a little bit of chaser and turn toward the door. Rum talk. Bare rum talk.

Boysie looking around the shop and it look like the rum beginning to go to the fellas heads. They making so much racket, they nuff to wake up the duppies down in the cemetery.

He feel like getting some fresh air. He open the door, step outside and sit down on the shop steps.

The wind blowing; somebody galvanize rattling. It late: people windows shut; the whole place quiet except for the rumshop. Light coming through a hole in the side of Miss Wiggins house next door.

Boysie take a deep breath. He feeling little bit numb. He en drunk; he en tight; just sweet. Got a good little buzz.

Tomorrow morning he got another union meeting, this time down at the harbor. He got to tell the men what the union decide. Compromise. That is the word Branker used. Compromise. The men not going like it.

Shoot. *He* en like it. *He* might lose his job. He en got no seniority.

They elect him shop steward because he was a seaman. "You traveled the world," one of the men said. "You know things." Besides, from the time he start working at the harbor he always talking about "exploitation" and "revolution." And with the big words he always using, the fellas figure he is the best man to represent them, even though most of them were working there longer than he.

As shop steward he sure that he can arrange something with the union if they try to fire him after the container boats start coming. But he don't operate like that.

Soon as a man start to get accustom to a job, something like this happen. Losing your job nearly as bad as going to jail. People does look at you bad, even if it en your fault.

The men voices coming from inside the shop.

Even some of them in there that drinking rum with him

going to be the first to talk behind his back if he lose his job. He can hear them asking him: "How come you loss your job and you is the union delegate?" And behind his back they whizzy-whizzying. Even if they don't know what happen, that en going stop them from licking their mouth, whizzy-whizzying to one another, talking bout how somebody musta catch him thiefing at the harbor, because union delegates don't get lay-off so. He know these people in the village.

Boysie sigh heavy, like he emptying all his worries out of his chest. "Technology." The word come out soft, rumbling low. His elbows on his knees; he rolling the rum glass in his palms. Back and forth. Back and forth.

People getting on like this new harbor is the best thing that ever happen. That is what the government saying. But they en telling the people that the new harbor going mean that they soon won't have no more blasted use for stevedores; everything will be machines. Containers. These big blasted containers that the ships will unload on the dock and lorries will come and hook up and drive way. Just like that.

He should never've come back here. He shoulda got off the boat in Away and send for Inez when he catch himself.

But he didn't know nobody in Away, only Uncle James that he never see, that went away before he was born and never set foot back home again. Boysie en know where Uncle James live, or even if he still living.

When Kojo say, "You can stay with me at my cousin's place in Brooklyn until you find a place of your own, of course," Boysie say no. Boysie frighten. Well, not frighten; a big, hardback man like he frighten? No, not frighten, just . . . well, you know. What would happen if he couldn't get no work? What would happen if, even if he got work and things began to work out, some spiteful person set immigration on him? Look what happened to Denzil: came back without even a grip, not even the suitcase he left with, because the woman he was living with set immigration on him after they had a noise about a woman that Denzil had on the side.

So when Kojo get off the ship in New York, Boysie stay on.

Kojo. Boysie en know when last he think about Kojo. They used to write regular—every month as God send—but then they stop. The letters start getting shorter, then they stop altogether. Boysie can't even remember now who stopped first.

Kojo. Short, a fancy dresser, with a soft voice. Joined the ship in Ghana. To get away, he say. "They say I am an instigator, a troublemaker."

Kojo open Boysie eyes to a lot of things: new ideas, books Boysie never heard about before.

"You've never read Franz Fanon?" Kojo looking astonished, as though Boysie'd just told him he was a virgin.

And from the tone in Kojo voice, Boysie shame to say no.

Kojo didn't like politicians at all. "They are parasites," he used to say.

It is funny how he took to Kojo right away, as soon as Kojo joined the boat when they dock in Accra. It is like he and Kojo was family, or grew up together.

Mr. Thorne voice interrupt Boysie thoughts. "You talking nonsense, man. Mr. Roachford. . . ."

Thorne talking politics again. Defending his prime minister.

Anthony Roachford is Boysie cousin. But Boysie could never stand Anthony from the day Anthony passed the exam for secondary school and start getting on like he better than everybody else in the village. Didn't even come back for his mother funeral when she passed away when he was away studying law. Serve her right, though. It is she who stop him from playing with the boys on the Hill—even Boysie, his own cousin—after he got the scholarship and start going to school with the brown-skinned and white boys at St. Christopher.

Brown-skin Anthony Roachford. Some say his father was the overseer at Walker Plantation up the road. His curly hair

slick down with grease. Come back from studying law over-
seas, with a scraggly white woman that nobody over there en
want, and everybody calling him Mr. Roachford. Now he is
prime minister. Who would've thought it? Prime Minister
Roachford.

The same Anthony Roachford who saw Boysie in town
one day the two of them walking toward one another on the
sidewalk. Boysie raise his hand to speak. And Anthony stared
straight at Boysie like Boysie is a stranger—like they en
cousins, flesh and blood—and walk right past, talking to the
man in the suit that he walking with.

Politicians. Boysie sucking his teeth. If he had his way he
would put all of them in a tar barrel and burn them.

A loose galvanize in Miss Wiggins paling flapping.

Boysie resting back with his elbows on the steps. His
behind feeling numb from sitting down on the cement steps so
long. Black clouds sliding over the moon. His glass empty in
his hand. The wind blowing cool through his shirt front.

The fellas in the shop still talking hard; the wind bate
down; Miss Wiggins fowls making them soft clucking sounds
that fowls does make at night.

". . . when the star boy say, 'Draw, yuh yella-belly
sidewinder,' the whole theater bawl for murder." Denzil
younger brother Courtney talking about some foolish-ass cowboy picture. That is all these youth doing nowadays—going to
matinee in town every Saturday afternoon.

". . . a storm coming." Cephus voice slow and slurring with
rum.

"You should get a job forecasting." Mr. Thorne making
sport at Cephus.

Cephus. Kojo was the best friend Boysie ever had, next to
Cephus.

"I saw my people turned stupid with that white man's reli-
gion," Kojo used to say.

And Boysie saw for himself when the boat stopped in Kojo country and Kojo took him around showing him the place. The minibuses with Bible scriptures paint on them in big letters; leaflets pasted on nearly every electric pole in town, advertising revival meetings.

That Sunday he and Kojo driving through the countryside and Kojo stopping the car. The engine idling. A breeze blowing through the open windows, and off the road in a clearing a small group of people in their Sunday best, some of them barefoot, singing hymns. Droning. No life, no spirit, no drums. It was like watching zombies in a graveyard.

Kojo shake his head slow, then drive off, silent. Then after a while, "They're like cats with their testicles removed," he said.

Boysie bust out with a laugh. He couldn't hold it back. It was the way Kojo said it—precise diction like an Oxford professor; a frown wrinkling his smooth brow.

Kojo staring at Boysie, irritable. "Is that amusing?"

Boysie wondering now why he thinking about Kojo all of a sudden.

Kojo would be a good man to have around now. . . .

But little does Boysie know that at that same moment, a policeman pumping a bullet in Kojo head. Kojo's body flying backward and he slumping to the subway platform like a rag doll, all because Kojo saw the policeman roughing up a man with dreadlocks.

"Sir. Why are you harassing this man?" Kojo voice was soft and polite. Kojo head reaching the big, red-faced policeman to his shoulder.

"Mind your fucking business and get the hell out of here!"

But Kojo standing his ground. "I *am* minding my business. Why are you harassing this man?"

And with that, the policeman whirl with his gun in his hand, shove Kojo, and as Kojo stumbling back and raising his hand to balance himself, the gun explode.

Now blood trickling from Kojo's mouth onto the subway platform.

And at the far end of the platform, people craning to see what happening, but nobody en moving.

Kojo joining me there on the shop steps and nodding, very polite. "Good evening."

"Good evening," I say.

The two of us watching Boysie sighing.

"Be careful, my friend," Kojo saying.

But Boysie en hearing him, en seeing him. He getting up from the shop step, slow, opening the shop door and slipping in next to Cephus at the counter.

"I was just thinking." Boysie looking at Cephus, but he talking hard enough for everybody to hear.

Cephus rocking back and forth; his eyes open wide and blinking slow, trying to focus on Boysie. "What?"

"I think we should throw that missionary off the Hill."

"How?"

"Put a beating in his ass. Send him back where he came from."

The talk in the shop quiet down.

"Oh." Cephus rocking. He staring at Boysie in that half-puzzle, half-earnest way that drunk men got when they trying real hard to concentrate.

Boysie look around the shop, in everybody face. "Or put out his lights." And he can see fellas jump when he say this, like somebody take a pin and stick them in their ass.

"Why?" Leroy looking at Boysie with this little smile like if Boysie is a babbling half-idiot. "What the preacher do you?"

Boysie look around the shop. "It's not what he do me, Leroy. It's what he going to do to the whole village."

Cephus still trying hard to focus on Boysie face, but the rum got him giddy. The whole shop rocking like a fishing boat. He getting ready to make a joke, but something in

Boysie face remind him of the time shortly after Boysie came back from sea, when Boysie told him about throwing a man overboard. "You ever see piranhas eat a man?" Boysie said then.

All Cephus could do then was shake his head. "No."

"Was like the river was boiling, m'boy. *Turbulent*. Like *soup*." Not an expression on his face.

Cephus noticing the fellas eyes touching Boysie and sliding off, because Boysie just say, "We going have to do something about him, you know."

Claude empty his glass and wipe his mouth with the back of his hand. His eyes lock onto Boysie face.

"I tell you what I going do right now," Leroy say.

The fellas quiet.

"I going fire one for the road and go home and get some sleep." Leroy say.

Everybody except Boysie and Claude laugh. But it is a nervous laugh.

AND WHILE THE FELLAS DOWN AT THE rumshop drinking and arguing, Inez lying down in her bed looking through the new glass window at the clouds skidding over the moon.

She miss the wooden jalousie windows and the fresh air that used to come in through the flaps. Sometimes at night she does wake up feeling like she suffocating. No fresh air. But Boysie say he want glass windows. They're more modern, he said.

But what is the use of modern if you uncomfortable?

Moonlight bathing the bed. It is a full moon. At least Boysie going be able to see where he going when he coming home tonight.

She can't get over that white man today: coming in the gap, en got the manners to speak, and talking Jesus talk. Wonder what demonation he belong to? Jehovah Wickedness? Baptist? She can see his long, bony face clear, clear like he right there in the room: the thick glasses, his ears sticking out like a rabbit, and his face shave clean, his goggle bobbing up and down in his throat. It call to mind the time when she was working at Wilkins store in town.

She was standing up at the counter with Gittens, the other girl that was working in the leather goods department, when this tall, white man in dark-rim glasses come up to the counter, put down the briefcase that he just pick up off the rack, take out a checkbook and start to write a check.

"You got any ID?" Gittens say when he tear out the check.

The man look at Gittens like if she mad. "D'you know who I am?" he say.

"That is the store policy, sir," Gittens say.

"Mr. Wilkins is a personal friend of mine," the man say. He putting away his checkbook inside his jacket, looking somewhere else in the store, like Gittens en even there in front him.

"I don't make the rules, sir" Gittens say. Gittens was real cool, though: slim; neat as usual in her bodice and skirt; little bit of lipstick, not much; fingernail polish; hair like it newly ironed.

All of a sudden, the man face twist up, like he catching fits. "You . . . you should be back on the plantation."

Inez giggle. Ever since coming up through school, that is something that they does tell one another when they get vex: "Why you don't go back pon the plantation," or something so. But they en mean nothing by it. It come like telling somebody: "Kiss my ass." You don't expect the person to get down and kiss your ass for true.

But Gittens serious. And Inez can tell by looking at the man face that he really mean what he say. That is the first time that Inez begin to understand what white people really like. All the years she growing up, she never had nothing to do with white people. She can't even remember even talking to one till she start to work at Wilkins. To she, white people is the people that own the stores, the plantations—everything—and live in Belleville in big houses behind walls with sharp glass bottle on top, and big dogs barking and snapping at the iron gates.

Anyway, the man went and complain to Wilkins, and Gittens lost her job. Just so. Even though she was right.

That is when Inez begin to look at white people different.

That thing with Gittens and the man really stick in her mind.

Even now she does still feel real foolish for giggling when he say what he say. She feel she shoulda know better.

And Gittens. Gittens never say a word when she get fire. She just pick up her bag and walk out the store with her back straight; every hair in place; a high school girl—a St. Catherine's girl.

Inez feel like running out the store behind Gittens and saying how sorry she is that Gittens get fire. But Inez feel shame. She feel she shoulda stand up for Gittens when the man say what he say. But it happen so quick.

From then on, Inez stop smiling with them when they come in the store. She always ready for them to say something that she en like.

Inez left the job soon after that and went back to working the ground. Her Mamuh and Pa was surprised. But they never say a word.

From then on, she can't stand these backra-johnny. The last thing she want is any of them living on the Hill.

Inez can hear the men voices down at Mr. Thorne shop raised in argument. Rum talk. Bet it is something bout the missionary. Hope they do something bout it. But most of them men got bare mouth. All they do is talk.

That Doreen. Inez does feel sorry for Cephus sometimes, cause she don't trust Doreen.

Inez want to know why Doreen always getting on like she different from everybody else. Ever since they was girls growing up together, they always used to be fighting. Inez would pick fights with her just to beat her. She never fancy Doreen. Doreen pretensive and sly. Everybody think she so quiet, but Inez know better. Look at the way she sizing up Boysie this evening.

She was so vex when Cephus start liking Doreen; she didn't want Doreen for no sister-in-law. But you can't tell people what to do, specially a force-ripe boy that smelling heself. He piss foaming, so he feel he's a man and want to start living with a woman. So when Cephus ask Pa for piece of land because he want to start living with Doreen, what she could do? She decide that she might as well try to get along with Doreen, cause by then she and Boysie was planning to live together, and Cephus and Doreen would be living right next door. "F-family sh-should be close," Cephus say.

Things start out good. She and Cephus pick out the spots where they was going put their houses. Cephus build his (Boysie was still at sea). And at first, she and Doreen was getting along good (not best friends but kinda like sisters), working in the ground together, going to market and Brethren meetings. But around the time Boysie come back from at sea, Inez start to notice a change in Doreen—Doreen going back to her old self: quiet; pushing up her face when Cephus ask her to do something and she think nobody en noticing how she reacting; unwilling, like she en satisfied with her life on the Hill.

Nowadays she en even coming to Brethren meetings like she used to. Always got a excuse: she tired; she robe want washing; she en feel good.

But Cephus en no better when it come to the Brethren. All Cephus doing these days is working the ground and going down by Thorne rumshop. He and Boysie stop coming to the Brethren meetings. They say big men shouldn't have to be peeping and dodging to go to no meeting. But they weren't even men when they said that, just force-ripe boys.

If it wasn't for the older men like Pa, only women would be at the meetings now.

Look at last Friday night. Brother Joseph call a meeting. He had a vision about two white men coming. One of them driving a bulldozer, digging holes in the ground, stripping the mountain naked. Peeling it like a orange. But you think Cephus would come? At least Boysie was working overtime. But Cephus sit down at Thorne shop drinking the rum till he foolish. En even went to the meeting that Brother Joseph call. Now, the missionary here—the first white man in Brother Joseph dream.

Boysie taking this thing about the fellas at the harbor getting lay off too cool. That en Boysie. Something en right.

Boysie been working at the harbor ever since he come back from sea: four, five years. She can't see Boysie giving up just so.

Hope he don't do nothing foolish. But that is another thing. Boysie en the same Boysie that he was before he went to sea.

Boysie left home with a boy-face—smooth, not a piece of hair; a low haircut, nearly bald, with his two ears sticking out the side of his head. But when the taxi horn blow in front her house a couple years later and Boysie get out, she scarcely recognize him: tall, bushy hair; a thick beard running from his sideburns and hanging from his chin.

And some of the things that he say he do, he woulda never do before he went sea. Like the white fella that he and the fellas beat and throw overboard in the Amazon.

Sometimes she look at Boysie and it is like looking at a stranger. Boysie kill a man. And he en feel sorry bout it neither, that is the thing. All he say is, "He think he could unfair Kojo just because Kojo small."

Boysie is a good man, though. Inez smiling in the dark, remembering when she and Boysie first start courting. They grow up together. But it look like all of a sudden she start to notice how good looking Boysie is. That is when Boysie was lifting weights and boxing in Mr. Thorne yard, little after Mr. Thorne come back from Away. Mr. Thorne wasn't so miserable then. He bring back weights and punching bags from Away. A lot of the fellas used to go in Thorne yard pon a evening. Boysie was one of them.

But now, all Mr. Thorne want to do is rob people. And it look like the more money he make, the more miserable he getting, with he face always sour, snapping and biting at people. He can only do that cause his shop is the only one in the village.

But who want to think about sour-face Thorne?

Boysie. When she and Boysie start getting serious and start thinking bout living together, Pa give her a piece of land. "I en want my girl-child depending pon nobody," he say. "Besides, I en able to work all that land anyhow—I en no more young yam."

They was out in the yard, sitting down under the mango tree heavy with mangoes weighing down the branches. She can remember like it is yesterday. Pa old felt hat stain with sweat; his toes dusty in his sandals; little bit of brown snuff powder under his nose. He waving his hand, like he throwing seeds to the wind, pointing at where Boysie father land butt-and-bound with his. "When me and Dolphus dead and gone, this going belong to unna. You, Boysie, and Cephus."

Inez looking down the hill to where Pa hand waving, and the cane blades on Boysie father land rustling in the breeze. The same canes she and Boysie used to go in nearly every night. The Blackmans house a good ways down the hill. If she holler they would barely hear.

Couple weeks after she and Pa talk, Mr. Blackman went out in his fishing boat and never come back. Miss Blackman take it hard. She en last six months.

And after his parents dead, Boysie decide he en working no land. And he sell his father fishing boat.

She can see Boysie face now—smooth, boyish.

"I thinking bout trying for a seaman job, Nez."

"But what bout the land, Boysie?"

"I leffing it in canes," Boysie say. "You father agree to keep an eye on it for me."

They in the cane piece and the canes whispering all round them, the stars up in the sky like silver jewels, the sky dark like velvet. And she can feel Boysie looking at her.

"That time I work on the schooner, although it was only between the islands, that was the best time I ever feel, Nez." His voice low like a bass drum.

She en saying nothing.

"Cept when I with you." He hugging her up round her shoulders.

She feel like asking him if he really got to go. She know sometimes seamans does spend two, three years out to sea. But she en want to prevent him from doing what he really want to do neither.

"There's so many places I want to see," Boysie saying.

The night before Boysie get on the ship, they spend nearly the whole night in the cane piece. Although Boysie got the house to himself now his father and mother dead, it wouldn't look decent for anybody to see her coming from Boysie house late at night. To besides, she did always like it better outside.

When she get home, she find out that the back of her dress was dirty-up. She had was to hide and wash it next day.

Inez getting excited now remembering that.

When Boysie come back from sea, he bring back all sorts of things that she never see before: gas stove; big fridge; stereo set; even saucepans that the food don't stick to—even when it burn. He build a nice wood bungalow with a nice gallery where they can sit down and cool out.

Only thing is, she wish Boysie would help her work the land instead of working down at the harbor. He buy a new fishing boat when he come back from sea and he en even working that neither. Denzil working it for him.

"Is something about those big boats," he say. "Even though I'm not working at sea, I like being around those big vessels."

Now, it look like he might get lay off. And he taking it so cool. That en right. That en like Boysie.

But sometimes she feel like she en know Boysie, like she living with a different Boysie from the one that she first start courting.

The men voices still coming from down at Thorne shop. They singing now. Loud. Like donkeys braying. Rum singing.

She got to give Kwame some castor oil in the morning; clean out his insides. She can hear the cold rattling in his chest in the next bedroom.

Hope Boysie make haste and come home. It getting late. Although the moon out and Inez can't see no clouds right now, the wind outside sound like it stirring up.

A loose galvanize sheet on the fowl-run flapping. One of the branches of the mahogany trees scraping against the house-top.

THAT NIGHT AFTER EVERYBODY GET HOME from the rumshop and the whole village sleeping, a storm hit. And looking back, it seem to people that from that moment, time start spinning faster on the Hill.

Inez wake up and hear the wind like a duppy outside moaning and trying to get in, whistling through the crease under the back door.

The branches of the tamarind tree in the yard rubbing against one another. Every once in a way, a branch cracking and hitting the ground. These en no little twigs that breaking off; big branches bupping heavy when they crash to the ground.

The bedroom dark. The wind done blow out the lamp that usually burn low throughout the night on the dressing table.

Inez raise up on her elbows, then start shaking Boysie shoulders. "Boysie . . . Boysie." She keeping her voice low, cause she en want to wake up Kwame in the next bedroom.

"Hmmm?"

"Wake up, Boysie." Inez shaking him some more. "A storm. I think we got a storm."

Inez eyes getting accustom to the dark now. Boysie raise up his head, look at Inez. "What?"

"Listen." The wind moaning like somebody in pain. "We got a storm."

Boysie raise up himself, and now he sitting up in the bed. "Jesus Christ."

He swing his feet on the ground and start dragging on his pants.

"Jesus Christ!" He buttoning up his fly.

The wind whistling through cracks in the house that they didn't know was there. The trees making bacchanal outside, like stick lickers in the yard fighting: blocking *(whacks!)*; cracking open one another head *(whup!)*. Just then, *Craacks! Bruggadung! Craaash!* Sound like somebody house blow down.

Boysie hauling on his shirt.

"Where you going?" Inez voice screeching with fright.

"To nail up the windows."

"To do what? You mad? You making sport? You know how dangerous it is out there? Look, lef the windows. Too late for that now. Everything in God hands. Pray that God spare we."

Boysie en put up no argument. "Put on some clothes," he say. "In case we have to run out."

Inez light the lamp and look in the next bedroom at Kwame. Kwame sleeping, curled up in the bed, like nothing en happening. The light inside the lamp chimney darting up, down, in every direction, like a lizard tongue, and the shadows dancing on the wall.

Inez putting back the lamp on the dressing table, telling Boysie, "He sleeping," when she hear the bamming at the front door.

"Inez! Inez!" Sound like Doreen voice, but the wind blowing so hard that the voice faint.

Bam! Bam! Bam! Pounding at the door again.

"B-boysie! Hey! Boysie! Nez!" Cephus voice.

When Boysie open the door, the wind pulling he and the door outside, big strapping man that Boysie is.

Cephus jump back. If that door had hit him, Cephus would've been out cold.

"Jesus Christ!" It look like them is the only words Boysie can say.

Cephus and Boysie wrestling with the door, backing in, and Doreen squeezing past.

When the door shut, the storm-sound quiet down inside the house.

"What happen?" Boysie buttoning up his shirt.

Doreen and Cephus soaking wet.

"Siddown. Siddown," Inez say, pushing a chair toward Doreen. Doreen sit down. Cephus standing up.

"The huh-house bluh-blow down," Cephus say.

"Wha?" Boysie and Inez say it the same time.

"One minute we s-sitting down at the d-dining table praying that nothing wouldn't happen; next thing you know, the roof t-tear off, just so . . . like somebody opening a s-sardine can. W-we en even had time to grab nothing, c-cause the whole house start w-w-wobbling and the rain s-soaking we."

"We en get outside good before the whole thing collapse." Doreen got back her voice. She hugging herself.

Inez come out of the bedroom with two towels in her hands. She hold them out to Doreen and Cephus. "Huh. Dry off unnaself." Then she walk in the kitchen and put on some water to make tea. When she come back in the front room, Cephus and Doreen sitting down; they got the towels wrap round their shoulders, shivering.

"I making some tea to warm unna up," Inez say. "It soon done."

Boysie thinking that it dangerous to be lighting stove the way things is. Bad enough that the lamp burning. They taking a chance. But he keep quiet. The tea soon done anyway.

The wind making this low humming sound like somebody tapping a giant tuning fork. Then it change pitch and it whistling and whooshing through the creases, drowning out every other sound so that all you can hear is the wind.

And the tree branches scraping against the side of the house like a hag trying to get in.

Everybody got a cup of hot tea. Cephus and Doreen still shivering, but it is hard to tell if it is from fright or cold.

Doreen wearing one of Inez dresses; it fit right. Boysie shirt hanging down off Cephus body like a boubou, and the only thing that holding up Boysie pants on him is the belt that got the waist wrinkle like if it is a drawstring instead of a belt.

The steam rising from the cups of tea and the warmth hitting them in their bellies; they feeling good, sheltered, close. Even Inez and Doreen got their heads close together, talking.

Then a wind blow through the house like a spirit and blow out the lamp.

Everything gone dark; sounds magnified. It is like if they trap inside a engine or something and the noise all around them. Coziness gone from the house.

A couple times, it sound like somebody voice hollering somewhere outside, but Boysie and them en sure they hearing it. The sound so tiny next to the noise the wind making that they en sure if it real.

They hearing other things too: cows mooing; sheep; a jackass braying; fowls; everything that got a voice; all sorts of noises underneath the wind. The wind. Like a parent bawling and painting children backside with lashes and the children little voices underneath all that commotion.

Nobody en talking. Doreen, Cephus, and Inez sitting in the mahogany armchairs; Boysie sitting down on the floor in the corner with his knees draw up to his chest.

Their eyes accustom to the dark now.

The wind pushing against the house like a bulldozer; the

house creaking; the galvanize sheets on the roof flapping at the edges—one time a nail screech overhead and one of the sheets give a *fwup!* like it ready to go and they expect the whole roof to blow away and leave them staring up at the sky. And every time something like this happening, Inez and them hearts thudding and hurting them inside their chests, and they can scarcely breathe and their ears fastening on to whatever little sound it is that frighten them, and they praying. Whenever the sound bate down, they realizing how tense they was; they scrunch up in all sorts of funny positions with their fists balled up.

Some time in the night, water gurgling, rushing past the house, sounding like if a river right outside. And things passing by real fast: a pig, squealing like if the butcher just stick it; fowls squawking; a cat scratching against the front door and meowing, then all of a sudden it gone.

The house lightening up. Foreday morning.

Kwame come out rubbing his eyes and asking what happen. And they look at him standing up there, rubbing his eyes, still sleepy, and all they can do is laugh. Kwame want to go to the window and see what happening, but Inez and Boysie say "No!" at the same time. Good thing. Inez was in the bedroom getting clothes for Kwame to put on when this big noise crash in the front room and glass tinkling on the floor.

"Oh sh-shight!" Cephus voice loud and high with fright.

"Oh God! We dead!" Doreen bawl out, and start one loud wailing.

"Come!" Boysie voice.

And Inez look round and see Boysie holding Kwame under his armpit, with his shoulder hunch over, heading for the dining room; Doreen right behind Boysie and Cephus last. Doreen got her two hands on Boysie back, pushing; Cephus shoving Doreen shoulder, trying to hustle her along.

Inez run out the bedroom to look in the front room. One of the front windows smash in; nothing en there no more—

the wind rip the whole window off it hinges and roaring in the front room, celebrating. While she standing up there looking, the chairs start moving; look to her like they moving in slow motion, but then, *whoom!* everything rushing to the open window, smashing against the window casing, breaking and then disappearing outside. Even Boysie bookcase flying through the air and going through the window clean, clean. Boysie grabbing on to Inez, hollering "Come back from there!" and she holding on to the door jamb, looking at the things flying through the window like she mesmerize. It feel like the wind want to rip her hands off the door jamb and pull her outside; her nightgown whipping round her legs, flapping like a flag; the wind howling, angry, mad; Boysie arms feel like bands round her chest, and it sound like Cephus grabbing on to Boysie, cause she can barely hear two sets of breathing behind her above the sound of the wind.

"Leggo!" Boysie holler. "Leggo the door!"

But she frighten. Coconut trees outside bending like grass. The sky is a gray slate. Rain whipping in through the open window.

Just then she smell the fragrance of flowers. She feel as though somebody resting a hand on her shoulder, calming her.

Miss Wiggins. Up to today Inez can't tell you how she knew. But she standing there with the wind whipping around her and she know that Miss Wiggins just dead and trying to calm her, to get her let go the door jamb so Boysie can pull her back in.

A sadness sweep over Inez, brimming her eyes with tears. She leggo, and her heart nearly jump through her mouth as she feel herself pulling into the front room. Is like a tug-of-war. The wind tugging her to the window; Boysie and Cephus pulling her back. Her body bend forward; her head snap past the door jamb; the wind feel like a sea current whipping at her face. Oh Jesus God! Something whiz past her face and smash on the wall: the picture of her and Boysie and Kwame that was lean up on the bookcase in the corner.

Through the open window, it is gray daylight, rain lashing like a solid sheet of water. The gutter in front the house is a raging river.

Inez glimpse a galvanize sheet sailing through the air like a paper plane. Coconut trees bending like they make out of rubber. Through the heavy rain, she glimpse what look like a little kitten in the middle of the road, soaking wet, hunch over in a ball and looking all around. Then it lift up off the ground, it feet kicking, hanging about a foot off the ground for what look to Inez like a long time; then all of a sudden, it en there no more; it disappearing into the distance, kicking and twisting in the air.

A sudden pull from Boysie and she feel herself moving backward. The pull from the wind slacken off. They back-back all the way to the kitchen, slow, like they fighting to walk through molasses, and although the wind en pulling as strong no more, Inez still bracing herself. Boysie still holding her.

"All right," he say, when they reach the kitchen. He blowing hard like he just run a mile.

Before the window blow out, the noise outside was loud. But now, it inside. The noise in the front house sound like duppies in there fighting.

Inez look round. Doreen standing up in the corner, holding on to Kwame shoulders.

Boysie let go Inez and he and Cephus drag the larder from the kitchen and, with the wind pulling them and the larder and trying to suck them through the front window, they lodge it in the door to the front room. Then they turn the dining table on its side and put that against the larder, making a barrier to keep the wind from sucking everything in the house out through the front windows. Cause by that time, they could hear two of the other front windows breaking away. They realize after the storm done, that that is what save the roof from getting blow off. The other windows blowing out allow the wind to rush right through; otherwise, it woulda bottle up in the house and blow off the roof like a cork.

"Come!" Boysie say to Cephus.

And the two of them hustle into the bedroom and Inez can hear them in there dragging something. They come out and go into Kwame bedroom. More noise of things dragging.

The two of them come back in the kitchen, blowing hard. "We put the mattresses up against the bedroom windows. The way that wind blowing, the safest thing is to go in the bathroom and shut the door," Boysie say.

All this time, Kwame sitting down on the floor, bouncing up and down, going "Yeah" whenever he hear a loud noise; he think it is sport. He never see a storm before. Doreen helping Inez carry sheets and spread in the bathtub and on the floor.

Then Boysie and Inez and Kwame squeeze up in the tub; Cephus and Doreen lay down on the floor next to the tub, holding one another.

The noise en as strong in the bathroom; at least they can hear one another talk without hollering.

"Miss Wiggins just dead," Inez say.

"Woman, what you saying?" Boysie sound irritable.

"Is true." Inez voice firm. "Is she calm me down sufficient to let me let go the door jamb so you could pull me in."

"Sh-shit, Nez. A ch-*child* in here. Y-you want to f-frighten K-Kwame?" But it is *Cephus* voice that shaking with fright.

For a long time it quiet inside the bathroom.

But the wind tearing up the trees outside. Things smashing against the side of the bathroom. One time they hear a loud thump, then a cow mooing weak, like it having calf. But the mooing soon stop. Inez thankful that the bathroom and kitchen make out of cement wall.

All of a sudden, the sound start to die down; then it stop altogether. They can hear one another breathing.

"That is the eye," Boysie say. "Bet some foolish people going go outside to see what happen."

"Mommy, I want to see. Lemme see the eye," Kwame say.

"No, Kwame. It en nothing to see. The storm going soon start back."

Kwame sulking.

"You want something to drink, man?" Boysie getting up out the tub as he saying this.

"All right." Cephus sitting down with his back prop against the wall.

Before you can say buff, Boysie come back in the bathroom with the bottle that he does keep in the larder in case somebody drop by, or for emergencies. "Unna women en want none, right?"

He en wait for a answer. He pour couple drops on the floor for the ancestors them, then pour a shot for himself and hand the bottle to Cephus.

They only get about two shots a piece before the wind start back, soft at first, then building up fast. Howling again. This time, Boysie and Cephus passing the bottle back and forth between them.

Over in Roachford bungalow, the preacher and his wife quarreling.

When I hear this screeching I bop over to see what happening, but her voice really grating on my nerves. "WHAT'D I TELL YOU, HUH? WHAT'D I TELL YOU?"

And he trying to pacify her. "Take it easy, Sandy. Take it easy."

"I should've *never* listened to you! Then I wouldn't be in this shithole in the middle of a *goddamn hurricane!*"

"Sandy! For God's sake! Take it easy."

"Don't you 'take it easy' me, you *goddamn hypocrite!* You goddamn missionary goddamn hypocrite!"

And she scream, cause something heavy hit the roof. A tree limb, sound like.

"Smack into a goddamn *hurricane,* for Christ sake!"

"Will you shut up, Sandy? Huh? Will you?"

"Don't tell me to shut up! Don't you EVER tell me to shut up!"

"Take it easy, Sandra, will ya?"

"Take it easy? Take it easy? This wasn't part of the *goddamn* deal! You never said anything about a goddamn *hurricane!* Not a goddamn word!"

"You're hysterical, Sandra. Calm down."

The wind whistling, rattling the windows.

"Calm down?" She shrieking now. "Calm down? In the middle of a fucking hurricane and that's all you have to say? Calm down?" Her hands straight down at her sides; she clenching her fists; her eyeballs glaring. And she speechless.

And the missionary just staring at her.

And Miss Wiggins standing up next to me and shaking her head from side to side. "Where he get her from, nuh?" she saying. "Outta some whorehouse?"

Miss Wiggins feel me staring at her and turn to me with a smile. "The old heart give out," she say before I can ask her what happen.

Same time, a man come in the room. "Dear Aunt, you can fix this?" He trying to stick his head back on his neck.

"Boy, what wrong with you? First you frighten the life out of me, now you want me to patch you up?"

All this time, the missionary and his wife staring at one another like two cocks getting ready to fight. Only thing is, one of the cocks en got the heart for it.

I looking at Miss Wiggins nephew trying keep his head on top his neck, and it occur to me that if somebody don't say something, he might spend all his time in the spirit world wrestling with that head. So I say, "Look, boy. You en bound to have that head, you know."

He turn to his aunt. "Who he?"

"What you mean 'Who he?' Where your manners? I *know* my brother en raise you so." She suck her teeth. "This young generation," she saying.

When I turn to leave she say, "Where you going? Help the boy with his head."

"Tell him use it for a football," I say.

Miss Wiggins looking at me like I en got no feelings.

But I going to see what damage the storm doing.

I left the two of them there in the room with the missionary and his wife.

Outside, the wind lashing the place.

IT IS MIDMORNING WHEN THE STORM PASS. People walking around like they in a daze, like they can't believe what they seeing. Housetops blow off clean clean, leaving the bare sides standing up; the four sides of Cephus house lying down on top one another flat like a matchbox somebody fold up; dead animals all over the place. A crowd gather down by Miss Wiggins house.

". . . and when I en hear she answer, I open the gate door and went in the yard." Miss Scantlebury voice coming from in the middle of the crowd. "When I open the back door and went in . . . Oh Lord Jesus." A loud honking. Miss Scantlebury blowing her nose and lifting up her apron to wipe it. She sniffle. "Just like she sleeping . . . with she shoes on and everything . . . like she was sitting down at the edge of the bed and fall back and drop to sleep."

"Look shut up, do," Miss Wiggins say. She sitting in a chair in the corner, hovering a couple inches over it with her legs folded like a Buddha, watching the people looking at her body on the bed. She look at me. "The way they getting on, you would think it is the end of the world."

A little boy peeping from behind his mother skirt. His eye-balls staring from Miss Wiggins body on the bed, to Miss Wiggins floating over the chair in the corner. Back and forth his eyes staring. He start one big tugging on his mother skirt. "Look, Ma." He pointing. "Look. She sitting down over there."

The mother look down. "Who?"

"She." He point at the body on the bed.

"Where?"

"Over there." He pointing. "In the corner. Pon the chair."

The mother box the boy on his head and hiss, "Look hush up your mouth, boy," she say, "What stupidness you talking?"

But her eyes going back to the empty chair in the corner every few seconds. Then she grab the boy hand and drag him away. "Come. I got work to do. This en nothing for a little child like you to see."

And the little boy looking over his shoulder at Miss Wiggins floating with her legs folded and fanning her face with her head cloth.

Down at the end of the gap, another crowd. A man body lay out in the middle of the road; the head in the ditch; blood all over the place. People eyes wide open, gawking at the head and the body. One of the fellas that does work at the joiner shop holding a sheet of galvanize with blood on it.

"This is what do it," he saying. He looking important, like he just win a prize or something.

The head in the gutter look familiar to people; but the man en belong to the Hill. He look surprise, with his mouth open in a 'O' and his eyes staring.

"Wonder where he from?" somebody ask.

"That is Miss Wiggins brother first boy," a old woman say.

"Oh Lord," a woman moan.

"What he doing out in a hurricane?" a man ask. "He en got no more sense than that?"

And Miss Wiggins nephew push the man in his back so that the man stumbling forward and flailing his arms like a windmill and twisting his body to keep from stumbling over the headless corpse. "Wah!" he bawling, and teetering, looking down, eyes wide open.

"What happen to you, boy?" an older woman scolding him.

The man back away in a hurry and standing at the back of the crowd biting his fingernails.

All sorts of things scatter all about. The ground soft and you can see the watermarks where the water reach up to the sides of houses—those that still standing up. But the water drain off. That is one good thing about living on the Hill.

The village look like if a giant trample through it mashing up everything out of spite.

Houses blow down and collapse into heaps of lumber, with a few little things scatter through the pile of break-up board: mattresses, enamel chamber pots (some with shit and piss still in them), clothes, furniture. People rummaging through, trying to collect the few things that en mash up altogether.

Some places where a house used to be is only the ground-sill stones and a few things scatter around.

Stocks roaming all over the place: sheep bleating, pigs rooting around, fowls scratching. And big arguments breaking out when people claiming things that en belong to them.

Two women standing up, pushing their fingers in one another face, quarreling. A big black pig between them, with its snout down in the ground, snuffling.

"This is *my* pig, you thiefing bitch," the taller woman say.

"What? What you call me?" The short woman fly up in the tall woman face, on tiptoes.

"A thiefing bitch." And the tall woman turning away real dignified and saying, "But g'long. Take it. It look just like you. It could be your brother. Take it." Her voice calm.

Meanwhile the pig chomping on something it just discovered on the ground and ignoring both of the women.

I can't help chuckling to myself. But I move on.

Trees lying flat with their roots showing naked, like women that fall down with bad feels and their dresses hoist up, exposing themselves; tree branches litter all over the place.

Down the main road, houses scatter about like dominoes on a table that God fly in a rage and upset because he was losing.

Out in Boysie ground, Boysie canes flatten. The breadfruit tree split in two; one half lying down flat, the next half still standing up but leaning sideways. And breadfruit scatter on the ground like green footballs.

The mountain got a brown bald spot on it, remind me of the time Leroy get in a fight in town and the badjohn slice out piece of his arm like it was a piece of ham.

But a lot of the houses look like the storm en even touch them.

Down on the beach, Boysie fishing boat tear loose from its anchor and washed up on the sand, lying on its sides. And his en the only one.

The sea puke up all sorts of things onto the beach— planks, tree branches, rocks, clothes, a bloated dead man with flies buzzing around the body and crawling into the open mouth and eyes.

Every time I see something like this, my heart does hurt me (That is only a expression. Who ever hear about a spirit with a heart?).

Before the sun get halfway up in the sky, Hutson the headmaster come up riding a bicycle (the road block up; no cars can't pass).

I mean, imagine this: the storm just run through the place; trees blow down; houses mash up; people wearing whatever they could get their hands on. And here come the headmaster, riding up the hill on this old black bicycle, dressed in a gray flannel suit—a gray flannel suit!— a white shirt and a black tie. He lean up the bicycle against the schoolhouse, take out his watch out his fob pocket, look at it, take out his bunch of keys out his pants pocket and, looking real important, he open the school door. He look round. A few people standing up in the road watching him.

"Good morning, Mr. Hutson," the couple people that standing up near him say. Their voices soft with respect.

He nod, with a little smile, like he doing them a favor by speaking back. "Morning."

He stick one hand in his waistcoat pocket, the next hand he fling out: "Tell people they can stay in the schoolhouse if they lost their house," he say. He walk inside.

News get round and people start moving in with what little things they scramble up. Before you know what happening, the place like a fish market: packed with people scatter all over the place. And nuff noise. Before he left, the headmaster get up on the platform, telling everybody to be careful with the kerosene oil stoves. He don't mind them cooking, but be careful they don't burn down the place.

But too much noise in the schoolhouse; nobody en hearing him: babies bawling; little children running all over the place like it is a big picnic and mothers bawling out their names, trying to control them, but finally giving up.

Is bacchanal, I tell you. Pure bacchanal. And the place smell like a cook shop: corn beef frying, frizzle saltfish, curry. My mouth watering like it forget I don't eat food.

Boysie boarding up the windows in his house that the wind blow out, and look down the gap to see Hammer-Head walking towards him with his carpenter tools.

Boysie start hammering faster, trying to finish nailing on the last board before Hammer reach him.

But he en fast enough. Hammer stop right in front Boysie house and start talking, like he talking to himself, saying he don't know why some people so follow fashion, taking out good jalousie windows to put in glass. Now look what happen soon as the first storm come along, nuh. Look what happen.

Boysie en saying a word.

By afternoon, the fellas working on Cephus house.

Cephus was lucky. The roof blow off but still intact; the sides just collapse whole. So all Cephus had to do was round up all the men he could get to help him bring the roof from couple houses down, in Estelle yard.

Old Miss Wiggins looking down at the hammering and nailing and saying, *I never see nothing so in all me born days. Not a shingle in fall off; not a board en break.*

Miss Wiggins floating in the air. New spirits does act like that. Excited. They enjoy doing things they couldn't do as humans.

Boysie father standing beside me, looking up at her real stern. Both of us hoping she don't decide to appear to Cephus and them, frighten the piss out of them. Some new spirits like to do that, to show off.

Some of the fellas that help bring the roof from Estelle yard left to tend to their own business. Cephus closest friends stay on: Boysie, Claude, Denzil, Hammer-Head. Even Leroy, and a couple young fellas that live up on the mountain.

A couple bottles of rum, some glasses, and a pitcher of water on a box in the yard. Every once in a way, somebody going over and firing a shot. Fellas working and making jokes and laughing.

Hammer-Head standing back giving orders.

"Heave! . . . Heave!" And the fellas pushing the side upright.

And when they got the siding upright, he hollering, "All right, take couple of them loose joists and prop it up."

And when the second side up, he bawling, "Claude, take a couple eightpenny nails and tack on the joist to the upright."

Bam! Bam! Bam!

"All right, now. Nail on the sideboards to the upright."

Somebody, breathing heavy, say, "Look, shut up your mouth and give we a hand!"

Hammer-Head standing back, looking up, wanting to know what hand they want. If they can't drive in couple nails. Somebody got to see they do the man house right.

He corking back the stopper on the rum bottle, screwing up his face and shaking his shoulders.

"Ease up, man. Lef some of the liquor for we," Denzil voice quiet as usual.

But Claude pointing out in that rumbling voice of his that it en so often anybody does get a chance to drink out Cephus, cheap as Cephus is, oui.

Fellas bust out laughing.

Leroy talking around the nails he got clench in his mouth. "Unna better leave Hammer lone, fore he drop a butt in somebody ass."

The fellas still laughing, but eyes glancing at Hammer to see how Hammer taking the rough jokes.

The last fella Hammer get in a fight with end up in the hospital unconscious for three days. Hammer nearly bust open the poor man head with that big forehead he got.

That night after the storm, the village quiet. People too tired to be stirring about.

When the wind blow down Cephus house, what en blow away get soaking wet, so he and Doreen sleeping over at Boysie.

Boysie lying down in the bed next to Inez, can scarcely sleep, knowing that Doreen sleeping on the other side of the partition.

Some time in the middle of the night, Boysie wake up hearing Cephus moaning like a bull cow on the other side of the partition, and Doreen voice whispering, "Wake up! Wake up, Cephus!"

"Uh? Uh?"

"You was bawling in your sleep." Doreen still whispering.

"Uh?"

"Is like duppy was riding you."

And Boysie straining his ears to hear Cephus murmuring, telling Doreen how he see his grandfather in his sleep, standing on the Hill, pointing toward the bay. And all around, the whole Hill was scorched—no trees, no people, nothing. And down in the bay, a giant creature rising up out of the water, looking straight at Cephus, heading toward the Hill. When Cephus look back around to where I was standing, I en there no more. (Of course not. I got out of his dream. No sense sticking around. Is up to him to figure out the dream.) In the dream, Cephus trying to run, but he en moving; he trying to holler, but no sound en coming out. "Th-that is wh-when you w-wake me up," Cephus murmuring.

Boysie lying in the bedroom listening.

Next morning, Boysie get up bright and early. And as he step out the bedroom door to go outside in the yard to fire a piss, his eyes rest on Doreen sleeping next to Cephus on the bedding on the floor. Her nightie hoist up, showing thick mahogany thighs. And as he turn away to open the back door, he got a strong feeling she looking at him, even though her eyes look closed.

Later, he, Cephus, and Kwame walking going down to the river. Cephus carrying a galvanized tub, Boysie got two buckets in his hands, Kwame swinging his little skillet as he hopping along.

Over by the hills in the distance, the sky is a golden glow
where the sun getting ready to rise; dew sparkling on the grass;
the air smell cool and fresh; the sounds of children shrieking,
splashing, voices, reaching Boysie and Cephus from down by
the river half a mile away.

Women, boys, girls, a few men, coming back from the
river with all kinds of containers filled with water on their
heads, slopping over the brim, splashing onto the dirt road.

In between the "G'morning" greetings they exchanging
with people, Cephus and Boysie deep in their own thoughts.

Cephus wondering how much crops he lost. He en had
time yesterday to check, what with trying to get the house put
back up. He wondering what the dream last night mean.

Boysie can't get his mind off Doreen. Here or late, it is like
she is a drug or something. He know he shouldn't be thinking
about his second-man woman like that. But he can't help it.

He shake his head, like a boxer trying to clear his head.
Then, Cephus voice:

"F-funny what h-happen, uh?" Cephus saying.

"What?" Boysie feeling guilty, as though Cephus was reading his thoughts.

"Th-the hurricane and the m-missionary c-coming the
same day."

"*Coin*-cidence." That is how Boysie pronounce it. "That is
all it is—bare *coin*-cidence."

A little frown crease Cephus brow. He hate it when Boysie
use big words like that, stressing them like he want to make
sure people hear them.

"Poppycock." The word pop out of Cephus mouth—
brap!—like a involuntary fart; sharp, not even a stutter.

Boysie head snap around. His mouth open. He staring at
Cephus. "What you say?"

Cephus clamp his mouth shut. It is like somebody in his
head using his mouth as a microphone. Talk about putting words
in somebody mouth! He en even know what the word mean.

Meanwhile, I holding my belly and killing myself with laughter to see the puzzled look on Boysie face.

Of course, Boysie father frowning. "What is the joke, uh?" he want to know.

"Take it easy, Dolphus," I say. "You en got no sense of humor."

Dolphus vex to see me laughing at Boysie. Dolphus more protective of Boysie now he dead than when he was alive.

I'm not like that, but I hate to see people laughing at Cephus, thinking he stupid because he does stutter. Dolphus vex because I let Boysie know that Boysie en the only body know big words.

"Da! Unca Cephus!" Kwame pulling on his father pants leg. "Who that?" He pointing at me and Dolphus.

Boysie looking down at him. "Who?"

"Them."

But of course Kwame pointing at bare space. "Two men."

Boysie and Cephus looking around, and when they en seeing nobody, Boysie thumping Kwame light across his head. "How many times I tell you stop making up stories?"

"But Da . . ."

But Boysie watching Cephus slow jerk-waist walk in front of him. Easy Boy. Never walk fast a day in his life. Boysie waiting to hear if Cephus going pop out with another big word.

But Cephus heart pounding in his chest.

They walking in silence. Kwame in front of them, skipping along, swinging his skillet.

At last Cephus say, "The spirits w-warning we."

And he telling Boysie about how I appear to him last night in a dream, how the word pop out of his mouth just now. "N-now K-Kwame s-seeing spirits too."

"Kwame got too much imagination," Boysie saying. "He always does things like that."

But Cephus feel different. He wondering why I dream him

last night, what the dream really mean. And even though the missionary wasn't in the dream, something tell him that the dream had something to do with the missionary and things that going happen in the village. But what? This en the first preacher that come to the country. Here or late, every crop season, soon as people got money to spend, evangelists coming from Away and setting up tents, or holding meetings at the race pasture in town. So what is the difference with this one? Cephus wondering.

Besides, what harm one preacher can do? Suppose what Leroy say is true—that the missionary going build a school and everything? That would be a good thing. Wouldn't it? Look how old the school building is.

But who is the two men Kwame just saw?

Later, as Cephus sitting on a boulder on the river bank and the voices of children playing in the river filling the morning air, a little girl walk right up to him.

Cephus jump back and bellow out, "Yah!"

Where the little girl's eyes were is just empty, bloody sockets. She standing right in front of Cephus, staring at him with her sockets.

Then the little girl turn and walk toward the children in the river.

And candy raining down; the children looking up, holding out their hands, catching the candy. Kwame looking toward Cephus with candy in his hands and saying, "Unca Cephus! Look!"

Then, out of nowhere, a big white eagle plummeting straight down and picking out the children's eyes. Kwame bawling, dropping his sweeties on the ground and clapping his hands to his face, but the blood streaming between his fingers, running down his face, dropping onto the ground and turning into wiggling maggots, and big black ants scurrying over and eating the maggots, but the maggots busting out of the ants bodies, but each time the maggots bust out, the ants eating them again, and it is like a circle—eating and busting out; eating and busting out.

Cephus spring up off the boulder, hollering, "Kwame! Kwame!"

Boysie and Kwame run up to him.

"What happen, mate?" Boysie asking him.

In the river, the children splashing one another and playing. People standing waist-high in the river, bathing, looking toward Cephus, Boysie, and Kwame.

"N-nothing."

"You sure?" Boysie ask him.

When Boysie and Kwame back in the river, Cephus sitting for a long time with his elbows resting on his knees. His chin cupped in his hands.

After a while, he watching Kwame splashing and kicking, trying to swim. All of a sudden it hitting him that it is soon time for Kwame to start school. Next September. But look how fast these pickney does grow, nuh?

It is hard for him to believe that it is five years already since he hold Kwame as a little baby, with Inez watching and laughing and saying, "Unna men does look so awkward holding babies. What happen, Cephus? You think he going break? He en a egg; he's your nephew. Hold him. What happen? You frighten you drop him?" And she smiling that big-sister, know-the-most half-smile.

Cephus looking at Boysie and Kwame and shaking his head. It is time for he to get a little pickney now. The fellas beginning to fatigue him already, saying that he firing blanks. He en firing no blanks. Things does happen in their own time. But he is a hard-back man; is time he had a little Cephus.

Coming back from the river with their containers full—

Cephus with his tub on his head; Boysie carrying a bucket in each hand—the sky turning silver gray in the east and the missionary and his wife standing in their upstairs balcony as Boysie and Cephus passing by.

The missionary smile and wave.

Boysie glare at the two backras on the balcony.

And Inez watching Boysie, Cephus, and Kwame coming up the gap. She smiling to see the water sloshing from Kwame little pail. By the time he get home, nothing en going be in the pail.

But as quick as the smile appear on her face, it wipe right off. She feel like scratching out Boysie eyes and kicking him in his seeds, because before he and Cephus left to go to the river, she stand in the kitchen and see Boysie and Doreen eyeing one another across the fence in the yard.

Cephus still in the house putting on his pants. Kwame tugging at her skirt saying, "I can go mommy? I can go down by the river with Daddy and Unca Cephus?" Boysie firing a piss by the hibiscus fence; Doreen coming back from her yard with the tub for Cephus to bring water in and glancing at Boysie in that sly way she got. And Boysie shaking his tommy, then stuffing it back in his pants, buttoning up his fly and looking over his shoulder at Doreen. The way Doreen eyes flicking at Boysie and then lowering, flicking and lowering, making Inez blood get hot. And she wondering how long the two of them got their eyes pon one another.

Later, when the sun begin to rise past the rooftops, the village like an ants nest—busy.

The missionary and his wife walking around.

The wife got on jean pants, sneakers, and a blouse with no sleeves; her ponytail reaching halfway down her back. The missionary wearing suspenders and a long-sleeve plaid shirt. And they waving and going, "Hi."

Some people just staring and then going back to what they were doing; some smiling and saying, "Morning"; one or two of the women say, "Morning, missis."

Inez looking on from her verandah, looking at the woman fade-out jeans and thinking, you can't tell which one is the man.

Around forenoon, the fellas take a break and gather at Thorne rumshop.

After the libation pour and the first shots burning in fellas bellies, Boysie turn to Mr. Thorne.

"Thorne, you is the party man up here. Where Roachford?"

Mr. Thorne rinsing a glass and shrugging his shoulders. "This is the second day after the storm, Boysie. What you expect? This not the only place the storm hit, you know." The gold tooth peeping through when he talk.

The fellas staring at him, not saying a word.

"Politicians." Claude leaning back against the side of the shop, holding his glass in one hand. He turn and spit through the shop window, as though the word foul up his mouth when he say it.

Just then, Estelle poke her head in the shop door. "The missionary taking in some of the people."

Estelle head in cornrows as usual, but they look like she just finish putting them in; the hair at her temples tight, pulling at the roots. Looking at her sideways, her forehead sloping like the women in them Egyptian paintings. A trace of grease shining near her hair. Her eyes big and slope up at the outside corners. Her big, cartwheel earrings swinging.

The way Denzil leaning against the shop counter and looking at her, you can see he proud she's his woman. He make a step toward her. He look even stockier than he is, standing next to Claude. "What you mean . . . taking in people?"

"What I just say." She look at Mr. Thorne. "I going come in tomorrow. After I get things straighten up."

Mr. Thorne wave his hand. "Take your time. I can manage."

"T-taking in p-people?" Cephus looking at Estelle. His shirttail open, showing his jooking-board belly; his underwear top showing over his pants waist.

Estelle look over at Cephus. "I was down by the school-house when he and his wife come down there. They say the people with children, that en got no place to go, they can stay with them for a few days till they make other arrangements to ease the crowding in the schoolhouse."

"Where he putting them?" Mr. Thorne looking at her over his shoulder.

"He put up a tarpaulin in the yard," Estelle saying. "And he take out the car from the garage. He say they can use the garage too." She look at everybody in the shop. "People moving in already."

Nobody en saying a word.

"Well." She pat the door post. "I got to go put on the pot. Cook something for them pickney." She look at Denzil. "You hungry?"

Denzil shake his head. Corn beef and biscuits on the counter. That and the rum can hold him till evening. But he got to see this for himself—a backra man giving black people something? He got to see this. "Wait for me," he say to Estelle.

And the two of them walking up the road toward the missionary house.

After Denzil and Estelle left, Mr. Thorne break the silence. "Ain't that something?" he say.

The fellas quiet.

But Boysie voice angry. "Yes, it's something!" he saying. "It's charity, that's what it is. Bare fucking charity! Who ask him?"

THAT NIGHT, THE STARS TWINKLING like silver jewels and the mountain looming dark over the village.

Quietness covering the Hill like a black blanket.

Even Mr. Thorne rumshop empty. Mr. Thorne sitting on a stool in the doorway, with the dim glow of a kerosene lamp spilling past his dark outline and casting a feeble pool of light onto the road in front the shop. His wife sewing machine going *rickety, rickety* in the house next to the shop.

With all the pieces of lumber and rusty nails all over the place, nobody en risking getting a nail-jook, or their foot slice open; plus, the electric pole in front of Roachford bungalow, where the missionary and his wife staying, fall down and the wire snaking all over the place. A pig get shock on it already earlier in the day, with people watching as the wire sparking and the pig squealing and quivering like it got epileptic fits before it gave one last grunt and died.

Cephus and Boysie sitting on Cephus front step, and the night is just different shades of darkness with dim spots of light coming from windows here and there in the village.

And the breeze cool, kissing the skin.

The words Cephus just finish saying hanging in the air between he and Boysie: "I j-joining back the Brethren." Out of nowhere, surprising Boysie. And when Boysie asking Cephus why, all he getting from Cephus is, "I c-can't explain. Is a fuh-feeling."

Cephus noticing a dead silence enveloping the place all of a sudden. Frogs stop croaking. Crickets silent. No rustling in the bushes. Even the breeze stop blowing.

And Boysie nudging him in his ribs.

"What that?" Boysie asking.

Cephus turn. A ball of fire hurtling toward them from down the gap, then stop a few yards away from where they sitting, hanging in the air, quiet. Same time, the smell of dead flowers entering Cephus nose.

Cephus hair prickling on his head and his testicles tightening up.

A deep chill settling around him, rattling his teeth, causing him to shiver.

Then, *whoosh.* The ball of light zooming a few feet straight up in the air and coming down toward them again.

And fear is a cold hand squeezing Cephus heart as he watching the ball of light, which he know is a hag—the obeah woman that live up the hill by herself and who does leave her skin and travel around the village at night sometimes like this.

Cephus can't move. His balls-bag still contracting.

A breeze fan Cephus. He turn to see what caused it, just in time to see Boysie tearing open his gate door and rushing in his yard. The gate banging shut behind him.

Cephus look back around. The ball of fire hovering close enough that he can reach out and touch it.

Cephus can't remember moving from where he was sitting, but he find himself busting through Boysie gate door and bamming on the back door. The door shut.

And panic invading Cephus head like a swarm of bees, filling his head with ringing noises and colliding thoughts, and he banging on the door and bawling, "OPEN! O-OPEN THE D-DOOR!" His eyes fastened on the corner of the house, looking for the hag to come around the corner any minute. His fists bamming the door; his heart pounding in his ears and kicking in his chest like it going burst.

The door open out. Inez in the doorway.

Cephus feel himself bounce into Inez. He turn and grab the door and pulling it in.

"What the *France* wrong with you?" Inez trying to get back her balance, and she looking from Cephus standing in front of her with his chest heaving, to Boysie over by the china cabinet pouring rum into a glass. The top of the bottle knocking against the glass. Boysie hand trembling.

"What wrong with the two of you?"

"Nothing," Cephus say. By now he sitting at the dining table with one hand resting on the table top.

"What you mean nothing?" The anger she was feeling after Cephus knock her out of the door almost gone. Now she worried.

But Boysie and Cephus en answering her.

Whatever frighten them out there and run them inside, they en going come right out and tell her, a woman. No sense even asking.

She peep through a crack between the boards that Boysie nailed up to replace the blown-out front window. Nothing out there. Just darkness.

Boysie and Cephus sitting at the dining table, quiet.

Her fingers touching and clinking the two silver bangles around her wrist that her Gran-Gran had left for her.

And Clemmie resting her hand on Inez forehead, soothing her, and looking at me with an accusing expression as if to say, why you make me have to come here to do this? She's your granddaughter too, you know.

Clemmie don't like moving around in the land of the living.

But it is a woman's job to comfort her granddaughter. I will take care of the boys.

And Clemmie casting a look between Cephus and Boysie sitting at the table, and me, a look that saying, I don't see you doing nothing right now.

But I don't feel like arguing tonight.

Meanwhile, Inez wrapping her head with her head wrap, checking her face one last time in the mirror. Whatever it is out there, it en going stop her from going to the Brethren meeting tonight.

When she start toward the front door, Cephus voice stop her dead. "W-wait for me. I c-coming."

Inez jaw drop open. She turn around slow. "What you say?"

"I c-coming t-to meeting. W-wait f-for me."

Inez speechless.

"Me too," Boysie say.

Inez staring at Boysie. "You?" is all she can say. She looking from Boysie to Cephus, back and forth. All these years the two of them stop going to the Brethren meetings, now *pow!* this sudden announcement, like a big rock dropping out of the sky.

But nothing don't overwhelm Inez for long. She get back her voice and say, "Look, if all you making jokes, I en have no time for that." She start heading for the door.

Cephus peeping outside before he and Boysie ease out the front door to join Inez.

As the three of them walking along, with Inez in the middle holding the smut lamp, the flambeau flame flickering from the wick in the neck of the bottle that Inez holding, casting light on dead animals, fowls, broken furniture, galvanize sheets. The shadows around them dancing. And Cephus and Boysie looking around them all the time. This getting on Inez nerves. She stop.

"Look, what happen to all you tonight?" she ask. "All you making me nervous."

"Woman, you going to meeting or not?" Boysie say.

She en going get no answer from them. They continue walking.

And all the way to the gully, all kinds of obstacles in the way. Once they had to clamber over a big tree trunk that fall across the path to the gully.

Cephus deep in thought.

The way the storm hit the same day the missionary come; the way Grandpappy (that is me) dream him the night after the storm; the hag that just run he and Boysie inside; the shadow that settle over Roachford house the night the missionary and his wife move in, when he and Boysie was passing, going to the shop. Somebody trying to say something. But what?

When Inez, Boysie, and Cephus walk in the clearing down in the gully, Brother Joseph sitting on a stool in his white robe.

Cephus feel like a little boy, with Brother Joseph red eyes boring into him. Brother Joseph eyebrows arch down in a frown. But they always like that, making him look vex even when he ent.

He en saying a word, just looking at Cephus and Boysie.

Boysie father sitting on a bench sharpening his cutlass. He nod at Boysie.

Boysie eyes open wide. His heart going *whubup* in his chest. He shake his head to clear it, and close his eyes. When he open them, his father en there no more. This is about, what? About ten years? Ten years that his father dead.

Cephus and Inez walking toward their parents.

Boysie look at the place where his father was just sitting down, and chilly bumps on his skin. He sit down on a rock, resting his head in his hands, trying to catch himself. He feeling giddy.

Inez reach where Granville and Violet sitting down together on a long, flat rock that look like it put there to serve as a bench for the Brethren meeting. Cephus behind her.

Inez bend down and kiss her mother. "How you keeping?" She touch her father shoulder.

"I keeping." Violet push out her chin at Cephus standing up behind Inez. "What bring *he* here?"

Cephus shuffling his feet. "Mamuh . . ."

"Leave the boy, Violet." Granville sitting down with his back straight. His empty sandals on the ground in front him; he rubbing his feet together, massaging them. "When you going come and help me put back up the pigpen?" he looking at Cephus.

Cephus got his hands in his pocket. "Tomorrow, Pa."

Cephus and Inez sit down near their parents.

Violet lean sideways toward Inez. "What happen with Boysie? Why he sitting down off there by heself? He shame showing he face at meeting? After all this time?"

Inez shrug "I en know, Mamuh." She looking at Boysie, still sitting down little ways off with his elbows on his knees, staring down at the ground in front him. She wondering the same thing as Mamuh. What bring Boysie to meeting tonight? Why he getting on so funny? Sitting down there by himself?

Cephus looking around, watching the people coming in the clearing. Mostly the old people. All of the young people there is women. Like Estelle, coming from the track in the bush now with her cornrows and with her big bangles shining from the light from the gas lamps that hanging from tree branches at the edge of the clearing.

Granville cleaning out his pipe with a piece of stick. He can't smoke at meeting, but he cleaning the pipe to occupy his mind.

Brother Joseph stand up with his staff, a long stick as thick as his wrist and reaching him to his shoulder, with a snake body carved on it, coiling round the staff from bottom to top.

But the snake got two heads. And the top of the staff is the two heads of the snake, with the two tongues lashing out.

People voices quiet down.

"Brothers. Sisters." Brother Joseph holding his arm straight up with his palm open. His beard reaching nearly to his collar-bone, covering his jaw and framing his cheekbones. His eyebrows knitting lines above his nosebridge; his eyes boring into everybody as he turning his head to look at all the people there. A tall, fierce looking man in his white robe and tall hat and holding his snake staff. His tall hat remind you of a lighthouse, the way it shape, and it is a deep blue, almost black, with silver stars stitched onto it.

Cephus looking at Brother Joseph and fidgeting when Brother Joseph eyes rest on his. Is like he can see through you and tell what you thinking.

"Greetings." Brother Joseph voice strong and firm. You wouldn't think that he older than everybody there, but he is.

"Tonight is the first meeting night after the storm." Brother Joseph tap his snake staff once on the ground. "This," he raise his other arm and sweep it around the clearing, following it with his fierce-eyed glare, "was only a warning!" His eyes come back to rest on the congregation.

"The spirits . . ." Brother Joseph pause. And in the silence, a pigeon cooing soft in his sleep, not even taking on the people, the light and noise below. "The spirits . . . Listen to the spirits. They're speaking."

Everybody eyes fasten on Brother Joseph. They serious with concentration. But they en hearing no spirits.

"In the middle of the storm," Brother Joseph saying, "A warning come to me."

His voice coming out of his mouth like it coming from deep inside a cave, rolling on rocks before it reach the opening, then thundering out. When Cephus was little, he thought Brother Joseph was God.

Somebody cough soft.

Brother Joseph eyes sweep the gathering again. "But. First things first. Right now, in the name of the ancestors, in the name of the spirits, let the meeting begin."

Brother Joseph always doing that: building them up and then making them wait.

His arm drop.

The drums start up. First, the big bass drum. Thumping. Booming. Now the smaller drums rolling, pattering, a *whubup-bap! whubup-bap!* that filling the gully with sound, rising into the branches of the trees.

The men hands blurring, beating the drum skins; their elbows working, their bodies beginning to sweat. The bass man standing up behind the drum that reaching him nearly to his chest; his eyes closed and his face cocked to a side.

The drummers starting up a deep-voice chant. Granville and the other elders taking it up. And the women coming in with a high response.

Chant and response. Men calling, deep like a underground stream; women answering, high, clear, reaching up into the tree branches. Once, twice, three times. And Cephus find himself joining in with the men, emptying his lungs, feeling like he purging himself each time his voice join the men voices—old rum fumes, cigarette smoke, curse words, everything flowing out into the night air—and a wind, a sweet, soothing breeze flowing in, clean, filling his whole body every time the women chorus enter his ears.

Is funny. He en know what the words mean. When he asked his father as a little boy, his father say, "We telling the ancestors that we know we like bad-behaved children sometimes. Like children, we en got the wisdom to know better. But we asking them to make we strong. Give we wisdom, and accept the little offering that we making." So he know what they singing now. But he couldn't tell you which word mean what, not even if you had his balls squeeze in a vice and asked him to tell you.

And Brother Joseph pouring a libation on the ground, and the liquor Brother Joseph pouring from the calabash look like a silver thread connecting the calabash to the dry earth.

Cephus noticing this and rocking from side to side, breathing deep, feeling good. He realizing how much he miss the Brethren.

The more the drumming going on, the more he getting into it, the more his surroundings becoming bare sound—coming in, going out; coming in, going out; filling his head. And motion—people rocking, and jerking.

His father voice joining his on one side. On the other side, it is Inez and his mother with the rest of women. And his head is a pottery jar, taking in everything, soaking it in.

The tempo pick up and he on his feet, jerking his body. His hands straight down at his side and is like something draining out his body, down through his arms, his hands, his fingertips. He shaking his fingers like he shaking off water. His feet shuffling at first; his toes sifting the sand, sand that the children bring from the beach every Saturday morning and spread out, till over the years the clearing is a light, sandy carpet.

And he joining the men's chorus. His voice feel deep, clean.

Now tambourines joining the drums. Jingling, bupping. The women. The women voices cutting into him like a needle lancing a boil. And the feeling he getting is the relief you feel when the puss oozing out, emptying the boil, easing the pain, healing. He stamping, and his stamping feet got a thudding beat all its own, a beat that joining the drumbeats in his head.

The drums start to soften, to slow; the tambourines jingling softer. And he know to soften his voice with the rest. Cause they coming to a end. The end. For now.

And Cephus sitting down in a daze. The night air hitting his face and arms like menthol. His arms got a little shine, with sweat.

The perfume of lady-in-the-night flowers easing into his nostrils, filling the gully like a fragrant fog.

And over on a rock underneath a flamboyant tree, Dolphus Blackman sitting down, still sharpening his cutlass, when all of a sudden Clementina standing in front of him telling him a piece of her mind. That surprise me. This is the second time tonight that Clemmie come back to the Hill. Like I said earlier, Clemmie don't like moving around in the land of the living too much. For some reason, she like resting in her grave. And I always asking her, Why you drawing up in a grave all the time? Get out and stretch your legs. The world en stop just because you dead, you know.

But she always saying, "Too many bad memories on the Hill."

So why you don't go to the spirit world, then? I always feel like asking her. But you can't argue with women. I dead and come back several times and they *still* is a puzzle to me.

Anyway, here she is in Boysie father face now saying, "Dolphus Blackman, why you don't leave the boy alone?"

But Dolphus only sharpening the cutlass and en taking her on. This going only make Clemmie vexer. I know *this* much about my wife.

So, as man, I got to go over and make peace between my wife and Dolphus. That woman got a real temper when she ready.

Well, I en got to tell you that Cephus en even notice when Brother Joseph get up off his stool and start talking. Because his head spinning seeing me and his grandmother in a big argument over in the shadows on the far side of the clearing, and Boysie father, Mr. Blackman, sitting down cool as ice, sharpening his cutlass.

The next thing Cephus hearing is Brother Joseph saying, "This missionary is a *curse* on this Hill. Mark my words!"

Cephus take his eyes off we over in the shadows to see Brother Joseph stamping his snake staff with each word. His voice raise. "Beware backra-men bringing gifts! Beware!"

And it is like the word "beware" explode in Cephus head and tear open a curtain. And Cephus seeing part of the same vision that I put in Brother Joseph a week before the storm hit.

A big, yellow bulldozer scooping out the hillside. But as the bulldozer bucket raise, it en dirt that Cephus seeing in the bucket. Instead, arms and legs dangling; blood dripping; voices screaming. And off near the edge of the pasture, this white man—Cephus can't make out his face—sitting on a rock feeding buzzards. He flinging out scraps and the buzzards swooping down, till the ground all around the rock where the white man sitting down black with buzzards.

The vision stop. Cephus come back to himself and Brother Joseph still talking, but Cephus en hearing the words. The vision was so clear, it was like he was looking through a window and seeing it plain as day.

Cephus shake his head to clear it. When he look back over to where me and Clemmie and Dolphus was, nothing. Only shadows.

All through the meeting, Cephus hearing Brother Joseph voice; he hearing the drumming and chanting; he dancing and chanting with everybody else when the time come, but it is like everything flowing through his head without stopping, including the sight of me, Clemmie, and Dolphus right there in the gully!

And months later, when the dynamite explode in the middle of the naming ceremony for his child, the vision he had there in the clearing that night would come right back to him. And the day the missionary died, he would remember Boysie father sharpening his cutlass the night he and Boysie join back the Brethren.

But now the *whap! whap! whap!* of the lead drum beating in his brain like a heartbeat; the rest of the drums joining in; the women voices clear like bells. And he remembering the last night the police raid the Brethren meeting—his fingers hitting the drum skins; people dancing. His hands moving so fast they is a blur. Boysie drum going *whabap! pap!* next to him. He closing his eyes and only feeling the drum skins, smooth. Voices wailing; sweat pouring down his face, trickling from under his armpits and down his sides.

And then the police sergeant, Big Joe, busting in the front door and tramping down the aisle.

And Cephus eyes opening. He moving, going "Ahumph! . . . ahumph!" to the rhythm. Is like he in two places at the same time. But he looking round and realizing he in the clearing in the gully.

His head full and spinning with everything that happening tonight.

He looking down at the ground and his feet moving like they belong to somebody else and he looking down at them from on top a mountain.

He en even realize when he stand up, when he start dancing.

The drums and the voices and the sound of his own breathing fill up his head, and pieces of the memory of that Saturday night long ago splicing in: him playing the drum; Estelle in the power; the police dragging away Grandpappy; a police club whacking his head.

And in front his eyes now, Inez and his mother swaying with their eyes shut, bupping their tambourines. His father jerking up and down, dancing. And the whole clearing full of sound.

"Ahumph! Humph! . . . Ahumph!" The visions he had earlier gone now, and the only thing in his head is the pounding of the drums, and under that a rushing sound, like a big river after a flood. "Ahumph!" His body jerking. Every "Ahumph!" feel like a heavy cough after Gran-Gran rub down his chest and wrap his body in pieces of hot flannel and cover him over with a blanket and tell him to go sleep and sweat out the cold and he waking up in the morning and the cold coming out his chest thick and yellow but he feeling good cause he can breathe clear again.

"Ahumph!" He moving now. He in the center of the clearing. The drums beating; the voices singing, chanting. The Brethren is only shapes rocking. Tambourines jingling. The men low voices and the women high singing bring a image of days when the rain falling, rain clouds in the sky, but the sun still shining through a space in the clouds, glistening the raindrops, and his mother saying to him as a little boy that the devil and his wife fighting.

And underneath all the sound there in the clearing, soft at first, so that he barely hearing it, *"Ssss,"* like a snake. And it getting louder, *"Sssssssss."*

And one of the brothers start up with a flute, so it is the drums and the voices and the snake sound and the flute rolling up in one in his head, like his head is a mixing bowl. And he feeling the sweat rolling down his sides from underneath his armpits; and his brain feeling like he just drink the best liquor in the world and it working on him. "A-humph! . . . A-humph!"

And he feeling like the Brethren closing in on him in the center of the ring. The women clapping; the men stamping their feet, dancing in place. And a thought jump in his head: "I wish Doreen was here." But quick so, the thought gone and he feeling Brother Joseph hand resting on his head, and he trembling like he got a fever.

The snake sound loud now, *"SSSSSSSSSS,"* and a ringing in his ears like somebody box him in them, *pheeeeng;* and the drumming and voices and flute fade like they in the distance. All of a sudden thunder roll, the loudest, longest rumbling clap of thunder he ever hear, like it coming from inside his body and vibrating him like a drum skin. He shaking. His arms moving like a rag doll. "A-humph!"

And he floating, flying, looking down at grassland and animals he never see in his life before, but he recognize them. The elephant and lion he recognize by name, from seeing them in that picture at the Royale Theater, the movie picture with that black man with his eyes open wide and saying "Bwana" every five minutes, a black man that en getting on like no other man Cephus ever knew, not like his father or any of the men on the Hill, a man that en getting on like a man at all.

But now Cephus floating, and in between the trees he can see housetops, and people moving around; children running and playing.

He want to go down and join the people down there: the women that walking with their backs straight and with the fanciest looking cornrows he ever see—"Like art," I whisper in his head. Yeah, like art, he agreeing to himself; slim men with straight legs; little pickneys like Kwame running around playing.

He floating there and looking sideways at me and the thought, "Lewwe go down, Grandpappy," reaching me through his eyes.

It is then that Cephus come to realize that time is a house with many rooms.

Because one moment it is daylight down below, then the next thing he know he standing in the middle of a village at nighttime in the midst of noise and panic caused by men with guns and torches, and it is like he watching somebody pushing their hand in a fowl run to pull out one of the pullets to kill—women, some with babies in their arms, running and screaming; old people hastening in the torchlight and shadows as fast as their feet can carry them; young girls and boys darting and dodging the hands of the men with rifles and pistols. A boy not much older than Cephus little nephew Kwame running straight toward Cephus with his eyes wide open with fright, but before Cephus can step aside or hold out his hands to catch him, the boy run straight through Cephus.

Cephus mouth drop open; he look down to see if his body still there; his head snap around and he look over his shoulder just in time to see a white man grab the boy and hold him under one armpit. The boy legs kicking; he bawling and pummeling the man with his little fists.

The man laughing. "Fiery little bastard, ain't ya," he saying.

Cephus looking around the clearing and his eyes making out a few more white men carrying pistols and holding some of the torches that lighting up the darkness. But most of the men with guns (the men with their hands in the fowl run, so to speak) en look no different from the people who scampering in panic.

Cephus notice that some of the village men putting up a good fight, though. A man with a cutlass, who look so much like Dolphus Blackman, Boysie father, that Cephus find himself blinking and staring, rush out from beside a hut and with one swing of his cutlass chop off the head of one of the men who could have been a villager except for the gun that the man holding to his chest even as his headless body fall to the ground.

Just then I say to Cephus, "Look," and Cephus eyes coming to rest on the doorway of a hut where a man rushing out with a spear in his hand. Something in the man's features look familiar to Cephus—maybe it is the way his lips look as if a carver chisel them; maybe it is the high cheekbones that make the man look like a younger version of Granville or me. But Cephus en had time to dwell on that, because coming around the corner of the hut is a young man with a long gun that look like a rifle.

A boy, couldn't have been no more than fifteen or sixteen, rushing out of the same doorway the older man just came out of, but before he can get out of the door the young man with the rifle fire one shot and the boy collapse right inside his doorway.

As soon as the woman's scream from inside the hut hit my and Cephus ears and before the boy in the doorway exhale his last breath I say, "Come," and right away Cephus back in the gully with the Brethren, sitting down on a stool with his elbows resting on his knees and his head hanging down. He look up; Boysie and Inez standing over him.

Boysie staring off into the darkness of the woods. Inez got a big smile on her face.

Brother Joseph hand resting on Cephus shoulder and he saying, "Welcome back, Brother Cephus." That is all he say; then he turn and walk away with his snake staff, long robe, tall hat, and knotted-together Masai braids halfway down his back.

Cephus looking round the clearing, and the flickering shadows cast by the torches in the trees reminding him of the vision he just had, because that is what he think it was—a vision that is already beginning to sink into the back of his memory.

Meanwhile, the men packing up their drums, Granville and Violet walking towards the track in the bushes, and it seem to Cephus that his coming back to the Brethren en no more than his parents expect, so they en making no fuss about it. It is almost like he is a little boy that run away from home and come back expecting everybody to be crying and glad to see him back but instead they getting on like he was only outside playing.

Cephus, Boysie, and Inez walking through the track, going up to the top of the gully.

The full moon shining now, lighting the way, looking like somebody shave a little bit off it.

Cephus noticing that Boysie still quiet. Whole night Boysie quiet. But he en really concerned with Boysie now. His mind more taken up with what happen to him tonight.

IT IS SUNDAY, A COUPLE DAYS AFTER the storm, and Cephus pelting things on a fire in the middle of his yard. Old pieces of lumber, tree branches that blow in the yard, a smash-up rocking chair, all blazing fire-red in the wind then crumbling to ash.

The fire crackling and roaring. Smoke mixing with the smell of roasting flesh, scorching feathers, and burning hair. A dead cat at the top of the pile grinning and staring, its fur singeing, exposing pink skin that soon roasting red, blistering and blackening.

A monkey lying back with its arms flung out, looking like a sleeping baby engulfed in flames.

Boysie coming from his yard next door holding a panty between his thumb and forefinger, a dead rabbit in his other hand, and pieces of wood under his arm.

All of a sudden, a voice booming, bellowing, singing through a loudspeaker, coming from the direction of Roachford house where the missionary staying.

And along with the loudspeaker voice floating on the breeze, voices singing,

Whaaaat a friend we have in Jeeeesus

All our sins and grief to bear
Whaaaaat a privilege to caaarry
Ehhhhhhhvery thing to God in praaayer.
Boysie and Cephus looking at one another.

Boysie pelt his rubbish into the fire. The rabbit drop right in the monkey arms, making the monkey look so much like a baby holding a toy in its sleep that Boysie got to shake his head to clear it. He glance at Cephus. Good thing Cephus en notice it, because Cephus would swear blind it is a sign.

"Doreen!" Cephus hollering.

"Yes." Doreen come to the kitchen door.

"K-keep a eye p-pon this fire for me."

"What I look like? Your servant?"

Blood rush to Cephus head; his chest tighten up. His hands getting ready to slap the words back in Doreen mouth, but he clenching his fists at his side.

One time his hands would've moved as if by themselves, Doreen would've been staggering back holding her face, then she would've been all over him like a windmill, hands slapping and scratching, screeching, and he would've been hitting her and wishing she would back off and don't fight back so he wouldn't have to hit her anymore.

But he find that the more he cuss and slap Doreen, the more helpless he feeling. It is like trying to hold water in your hands—the tighter you grasp, the more the water trickling through your fingers.

And here of late Doreen back-talking him, en showing no respect, and it is like nothing he do make any difference anymore. Doreen got this don't-carish attitude. He losing her, but he don't know why.

So now he just flinging off his hand, sucking his teeth, letting go one long steups, and saying to Boysie, "C-come, man."

And Boysie can't help noticing the tension between Cephus and Doreen.

As Cephus and Boysie leaving the yard, Doreen inside the kitchen kneading dough to make dumplings, and she cuffing the dough like it is a man. *What he think it is, nuh? What I look like to he? A slave?*

Here of late, she feeling trapped: getting up every morning, taking care of the stocks—feeding them, cleaning out the pens and coops, staking out the sheep on the pasture when Cephus busy doing something else—working like a brute beast long-side Cephus, planting, hoeing; going to the market in town every Friday and Saturday with a big basket full of provisions.

It is always: Do this. Do that. "D-doreen you feed the fowls? D-doreen you give the sheep their mash?" Like she en know what to do and he always got to be telling her.

And what she getting for it, nuh? What she getting?

Cephus so blinking cheap, wouldn't even let her buy a pair of stockings. "What you want stockings for?" he asking. "That foolishness is for town women that got money to waste."

When she saving up money to buy a decent frock, he vex. "What you want a new dress for? Trust some cloth from the coolie man. You got a sewing machine. Make your own dress."

But Cephus don't understand. Making a dress for yourself and buying a nice new dress from in town ent the same thing. What wrong with making yourself look presentable instead of looking like some country buck with clothes you make your-self and with your two foot grease down with coconut oil instead of wearing stockings like everybody else, uh? What wrong with that?

Buff! Buff! She cuffing the dough.

But I en got time to listen to Doreen complaining. Some people en know where their next meal going come from and she complaining because she got to work, because Cephus don't let her spend money foolish.

So I left to see what happening down in the missionary yard.

Cephus and Boysie just reaching the gate door to the missionary yard, which is enclosed with a tall galvanize fence like every other yard in the village, except that this one got a big tarpaulin stretch from one side to the other, covering it like a tent.

The preacher standing in front of a handful of women, holding a microphone. He wearing a light blue suit, holding a black book in his other hand and singing. His voice coming out of a little box hanging on a pole behind him.

I can't help sucking my teeth long and hard. *Look at this, eh? Look at this. Two things they does turn we people foolish with: booklearning killing the young generation common sense; the Bible turning them stupid as ram goats. Look at them.*

I get so carried away, I en realize I talking aloud till all of a sudden I feel Cephus eyes on me, staring at me over his shoulder; his mouth gaping open.

Sybil who does sell sweeties in the schoolyard staring like she seeing a duppy.

"Two duppies," Dolphus saying next to me. Dolphus standing behind Boysie with his cutlass in his hand.

Sybil resting her hand on her big bosom and closing her eyes like she going faint.

Poor Sybil. Sybil see Dolphus Blackman buried with her own two eyes. Couple years before that, she see them put *me* six feet down. Now there we is, both of we, in the gate door. And Dolphus looking like he ready to use his cutlass on somebody.

She gulping, fanning her face fast with her hand and elbowing the woman beside her.

Before you know what happening, everybody eyes fasten on the four of we in the gate door.

The singing drag to a stop.

But the missionary voice still booming from the box; he waving his hands like the old white man that does conduct the police band on bank holidays.

"WASH ME AND I SHALL BE WHITER THAN SNOW."

"Hear that shit? Uh? Hear that?" Boysie father bawling. He slapping the cutlass against his leg—*Blap!*

Everybody in the yard jump, everybody except Boysie.

Because Boysie glaring at the missionary like nobody else en in the yard except he and the missionary.

I say to myself, let me see how the missionary seeing this. I en know if you notice, but up to now I en had much business with the missionary or his wife. I en feel like polluting myself by going in their heads. But now I curious to see what he think of Cephus and Boysie.

The preacher staring through his thick glasses at the two men at the gate—one tall, bearded, and with a mop of hair on his head (Boysie); the other just as tall, but clean-shaven and wiry (Cephus).

The missionary stop singing, wondering why the people in the yard keep staring at these two guys with so much fear.

The bearded guy looks like a damned bulldog on a leash—all beard and eyes—two eyes glaring. But the other guy looks more peaceful.

The bearded guy says, "Let's go."

Boysie striding back up the gap, mad as hell. Cephus lagging behind because Cephus don't walk fast for nothing.

When they get back in Cephus yard Cephus say, "Y-you see my grandfather and your father?"

"Where?"

"B-behind we. B-back there. At the gate. You en see?"

And that is when Cephus find out about Boysie seeing his father in the clearing the night before.

And back in the missionary yard, the meeting break up. People make a rush from the yard as soon as me and Dolphus disappear from the gate. The whole congregation outside in the road, and everybody talking at the same time.

Sybil sitting on a boulder at the side of the road, fanning her face with her hat.

The missionary shouting through the microphone, wanting to know what's the matter, telling them to "let's get back to our service, please," and his wife looking through the back window wondering what going on, giggling at first to see her husband lose control of his service, but as she move to the front window and she seeing the fear on people faces, she feeling uneasy and puzzled.

As soon as people figure that me and Dolphus gone, they easing back in the yard and lugging their few belongings with them. All over the village, everybody that was lodging in the missionary yard after the storm begging a lodging with neighbors "for the time being, till I catch my hand."

Only one man stubborn. His arms fold across his chest.

His woman saying, "But Carlisle . . ."

But his face determined. "You fraid duppy? Uh? Duppy dead. Dead! What they can do you? I en going nowhere," he saying.

Right then Miss Wiggins nephew walk in through the gate door holding his head under his armpit and making faces with it—rolling his eyes, hanging out his tongue, and grinning. And his stump of a neck wagging and rotating on his shoulder.

And the same Carlisle that just wasn't afraid of no duppy stumbling back and gulping.

And when Miss Wiggins nephew toss his head in the air like he playing with a ball, Carlisle snatch up the bundle his woman fold up earlier and nearly knocking the gate door off its hinges backing through the gate and keeping his eyes on Miss Wiggins headless nephew.

"What happen, Carlisle?" Bewilderment stamped on Carlisle woman face.

But Carlisle feet pounding the earth, racing him along the side of the house.

When the woman get outside, Carlisle way down the road. The bottoms of Carlisle feet flashing; his arms pumping.

"Carlisle!" she bawl.

But Carlisle running so fast that the wind rushing past his ears preventing him from hearing.

And Boysie father laughing and slapping Miss Wiggins nephew on his back, man to man.

The missionary and his wife looking through the window, puzzled.

Next day, the news all over the village.

—"*. . . Dolphus Blackman and old Dada Cudgoe was watching the preacher service yesterday.*"

—"*You was there?*"

—"*No. Because the missionary give me a lodging don't mean I got to listen to Jesus talk. Patsy tell me.*"

A girl that shit herself with fright right there in the yard feel so ashamed when people looking at her and laughing that she take her bundle, the few things that left after the hurricane, and left the Hill. Nobody en see her since then.

But the missionary stubborn. The next Sunday he holding meeting in the road in front his house like nothing en happen.

A bunch of little children standing in the road watching him. Nobody else en show up.

But gradually, as the Sundays pass, a handful of people coming back—nothing like the crowd he had that first Sunday when me and Dolphus appeared, when the yard was full with people who had moved into the yard right after the storm; now it is five or ten at the most, standing in front the bungalow listening to the missionary preach.

But all of that changed from the day the lorry draw up in front the missionary house and unload big wooden crates, and the missionary start giving away food and clothes from Away.

THE DAY THE LORRY COME DRIVING UP the gap, Mr. Thorne shop look barren and "just plain pitiful," as Miss Wiggins saying. Miss Wiggins was a quiet woman when she was alive. Now you can't stop her from talking. She got an opinion about everything.

A couple bottles of hot sauce standing by themselves on one shelf; a tin of condensed milk so dented nobody won't buy it; the line of rum bottles down to four.

School start back, but the schoolhouse half-empty. More children running around the village than in school.

A few fowls scratching in the dust.

Shanty shacks all over the place where houses used to be—patched together with pieces of wood, tin, anything.

The lorry driving toward the missionary house, and Cephus, Inez, Doreen, Violet, and Granville working together out in the ground, working on Violet and Granville plot—chopping, clearing, hauling, trying to get things back to normal. The sun beating down, the sweat pouring down their faces like lard oil.

Evenings they going home, bathing off the sweat and dust but not the tiredness in their bones. Every night they sleeping heavy and waking up stiff in the morning facing more work.

Cephus fowls gone. Same thing with Inez. The hurricane blow the door off Granville pigpen.

Boysie fishing boat still lying on its side down on the beach.

And when Boysie tried to buy a new propeller the week after the storm, the white clerk in the store saying Boysie got to wait till the next shipment come in. "We out of stock," the clerk saying, a country redleg in a blue short-sleeve shirt and black tie, with his hair slicked back and greased down, who forget that his foreparents come to the country as prisoners and indentured servants. Had not for the little job in the store, he would be running around barefoot up in the country like the rest of redlegs in Redman Village.

And Boysie balling up his fist, trying to control himself because the clerk just tell him, "I not a fortuneteller" when Boysie ask him when the next shipment coming in.

When the lorry stop in front the missionary house, not a pig, goat, or sheep en in sight like they were a few weeks after the storm, roaming, scratching, and rooting for food. For weeks now, the smell of meat cooking is scarce as a new dollar bill.

Mr. Thorne leaning against the doorpost of his shop, looking down the road at the two men unloading cardboard barrels off the lorry and carrying them in at the missionary.

Later in the afternoon, the missionary walking from house to house.

"How y'all doing?" he asking.

And as he going through the village, the word spreading that people from Away send clothes for the victims of the hurricane.

Miss Scantlebury looking at the missionary and saying, "Victims?" Then she shaking her head and telling him, "No, thanks. I all right." This is the first time she ever hear that she was a victim.

As the old people always say, trouble don't set up like rain, and when it rain it does pour bucket a drop.

Next day, Boysie, Claude, and finny-foot Harold down at the harbor taking a break from off-loading the big Japanese container boat that towering over them like a big black sea monster and shading them from the afternoon sun. The mooring rope stretching and creaking; a cool wind blowing across the wharf.

Finny-foot Harold asking Boysie when the container boats going start coming regular.

"Next month." This one is just for trial, to see how things going work.

Harold want to know what going to happen to him then. All he hearing from the union is, some containers will be coming with mixed shipments—for different merchants; so they will still need men to work in the warehouse. But he asking Boysie, "How many men they keeping on?"

And Boysie getting irritable. He can't answer Harold question. He would like to know himself. But it is like the supervisors and the union keeping him locked out from information.

Harold forklift idling; Harold sitting cater-corner on the forklift seat, with his finny foot dangling. Claude leaning against the side of the building.

"I wish I could tell you, mate," Boysie saying.

"I don't know what use you is, eh?" Harold saying. "What use it is belonging to a union, eh?"

There was a time when Boysie would start talking about how the union fighting for the workers' rights; how, if it wasn't for the union, people would still be working for a shilling a day with no benefits, no job security.

But these words sticking in his craw. Since he become a shop steward, since this whole thing about the container boats start, he realizing that the union is just an extension of the Lawyers Party. Branker is general secretary of the union, he is a member of the Lawyers Party, he is a member of the House of Assembly. All of it is politics. And people like Boysie getting squeezed in the middle.

While all this turning over in Boysie head, the foreman come out the warehouse. A stocky, big-guts, round-face man that always wearing a sweaty felt hat. "Hey! Unna getting pay for idling? Uh? All you want me to fire your ass? Uh? Well get back out there and do some work!"

Finny-foot Harold crush out his cigarette. Claude and Boysie hear him say, "Yassuh, boss," under his breath, before he turn to face forward in the forklift seat and drive off.

Them is the last words they hear him say.

Boysie and Claude walking toward the gangplank to go back up on the boat when all of a sudden a voice high above them on the deck holler, "Look out!"

Boysie and Claude look up.

A container dangling from the ship's crane at a angle; one of the cables holding it dangling loose; and the container sliding from the other cable in slow motion, easing away from the cable, falling.

A forklift motor whining.

Boysie look over to see Harold gazing up at the big container above him with his mouth open, his eyes staring.

"Harold!"

Two voices holler out together as one. Boysie and Claude.

But before they could move, before they could say another word, the container crash down on the forklift, squashing it and rolling over on its side.

And the forklift look like a yellow beetle oozing red and black, oil and blood. Where the cab was, where Harold was sitting, is just flat, twisted metal with a black arm dangling out. The hand trembling. Harold fingers clench, then open slow. And stop.

The sun beating down on Boysie back. The whole place silent except for waves lapping against the wharf.

And the foreman trotting from the warehouse door. He stop in front the crushed forklift and pushing his old felt hat back on his head. "Where he is? Where he is?" he saying over and over.

And something in Boysie head explode. Next thing he know, his knuckles hurting and the foreman sprawl on the ground, scrambling to reach his hat.

And Boysie find himself walking up the harbor road. The hawkers that line the road calling out to him, asking him to buy this, that, and the other.

"Buy the lovely mangoes," one saying.

"Coconuts. Quench your thirst with the water coconuts."

Lorries rumbling past him, blowing dust in his eyes.

And the only thing going over and over in his mind as he walking home in the hot sun is the container falling and Harold face just staring up at it. Corbin. That fucking foreman. If not for him, Harold would be alive. And the anger bottling up in Boysie chest; his heart pounding; his temples throbbing.

But after a while, walking along the coast road, hearing the waves licking against the rocks, hearing the *clop-clop* of a donkey cart approaching and watching the driver sitting cater-corner at the front near the shaft with his head bowed like he dozing off, Boysie sigh. Corbin is just a slave driver doing his job.

Corbin en even belong to the union. The government say supervisors is management. They can't belong to the union. Not that it make any difference, Boysie reminding himself.

Corbin coming to work every morning with his sandwiches in a greasy paper bag his woman pack for him, yet he keeping himself apart from the men.

Feelings mixed up inside Boysie. Remembering Harold in his forklift crushed under the container, he feeling as if a hole in the pit of his stomach; he feel good for cuffing Corbin, but he feeling sorry at the same time, realizing how Corbin must have felt realizing that if it wasn't for him Harold would still be alive.

As Boysie step off the main road and walking up the hill toward home, Harold face in front him—Harold in his dungaree overalls and khaki short-sleeve shirt, sitting on the forklift, looking in Boysie face as if Boysie keeping news from him.

"What use it is belonging to a union, eh?" Harold had asked him. And Boysie asking himself the same thing. And it is at that moment that Boysie realize he made up his mind. He en going back to work at the harbor. Fuck it.

Inez watching Boysie from the side window, and the minute she see his face, the way he walking with his hands in his pants pockets and his head hang down, she know something wrong.

Same time, Doreen pulling her gate door shut next door and going in the house with a bundle under her armpit. A blue bundle.

And Inez wondering why Doreen was walking so fast, coming from down by the missionary house with a bundle under her arm.

But now Boysie stepping in the back door like he in a trance, filling the whole door and blocking out the light in the kitchen.

All thoughts of Doreen fly out of Inez and she hurrying over to Boysie. "What happen, Boysie? How come you home so early? You get lay off?"

A few minutes later, Inez down at Mr. Thorne shop watching Estelle weigh the flour in the scale. She notice that Estelle had to scoop deep inside the barrel to get the flour, and the scoop raking the bottom. But her mind on Boysie.

Boysie come home so early and en say a word since he get in the house. All he do is sit down in the back door and staring out in the yard.

Estelle voice interrupt Inez thoughts. "You get any of the freeness, Inez?"

"Uh?" Inez mind snap back to Estelle dispatching the flour on the other side of the counter.

"The freeness," Estelle say. "You get any of the things the missionary giving away?"

"What things?"

"Doreen en tell you?"

"Tell me what?"

And Estelle start telling Inez about how Patsy stop off in the shop to buy some sugar to make lemonade for Leroy, but all the sugar gone. So Estelle and Patsy stand up talking about how hard things getting. And that is when Patsy tell her how the missionary get clothes from Away and he giving them away. And not long after that, Doreen passing the shop with something blue under her arm not too long ago. Inez en see it? It look like a dress.

And Boysie out in the ground telling Cephus he left the job down at the harbor.

Cephus raising and chopping with the hoe, raising and chopping. "St-stop making sport, man," he saying.

But Boysie serious. "It's no joke, mate."

And the seriousness of it hitting Boysie for the first time. In a way, he feeling relieved. He en have to worry about if he going get let go when the container ships start coming, which is in a few weeks, they say.

But he out of a job. What Inez going to say?

"I got to find something to do," he saying, half to himself, half to Cephus.

Same time, Harold nodding to me, very polite. "Howdy do," he saying.

"Good afternoon," I answering. "You the fella just got killed?" I asking him.

He nodding.

Harold appearance act like a switch, turning on Boysie memories, and Boysie reminiscing to Cephus, telling him about how nice a fella Harold was. "With all the hard jokes we used to make about his finny-foot, Harold never lost his temper. Always pleasant."

And Harold saying, "See that? He never say none of that when I was alive. Why people like that?" he asking me.

I ignore Harold, because I noticing that while Boysie talking, Cephus busy thinking that now Boysie en working at the harbor, perhaps they can work together.

Doreen getting more and more unwilling, and it reach the point where he almost afraid to ask her to do something in the ground because she liable to bite off his head asking him if she is a slave. That is her favorite expression.

Maybe he and Boysie could put together and buy a second-hand pickup. They could sell things from the pickup, maybe even sell vegetables to the hotels. That way, Doreen and Inez wouldn't have to sell in the market.

It getting worse and worse each time Doreen come back from the market. Last week she singing a song about how she soon going find a man to treat her right, a town man, a good man, a man that does buy nice things for a woman.

The song en even rhyming.

Cephus know it en a song she heard on the radio—she made it up. But the last time she threw words at him in a made-up song and he say, "What you s-saying? Uh? Wh-what you s-saying?" she open her eyes wide at him saying, "I singing a song, Cephus. I can't sing a song now?"

When he ask Inez if Doreen got a man in town and Inez say no, he was relieved. But he still suspicious.

Harold squatting and throwing back his head and laughing hard. "Who this tie-tongue idiot is?" He slapping his knees.

I answer short. "My grandson."

"Oh," Harold say.

Boysie talking: about the harbor, the union, the container boats, politicians, Corbin the foreman. His words is like a river that overflow after a heavy rain. Cephus wrap up in his own thoughts, but Boysie en even noticing.

My eyes taking in Boysie black suede shoes, his wool-blend pants low on his waist and with the seams sharp like a knife, the gold watch glistening on his wrist, and I got to admit that Cephus dreaming if he think Boysie going pitch in with him and do farm work. He better find another way to keep Doreen.

Later, Cephus and Boysie sitting in Boysie verandah cooling out when Inez come out and ask Cephus how he like the dress Doreen get from the missionary.

Cephus sit up straight. "What dress?" Straight like that. Not a stutter.

Inez face blank.

Cephus get up without another word and head straight for his house.

And Boysie and Inez in their verandah can hear Cephus voice raise next door.

"C-carry it right back!" The first words out of Cephus mouth.

"Carry back what? What you talking bout?" Doreen voice soft.

Tramping and rummaging coming from inside Cephus house; Cephus searching for the dress Doreen bring home from the missionary.

"Wh-where it is?"

"Where what is? I en know what you talking bout, Cephus."

More rummaging coming from the bedroom. Silence. Then Cephus voice, calm now. "Wh-what is this?"

Silence.

"WHAT IS TH-THIS? . . . UH? WHAT IS TH-THIS?"

Doreen voice shrieking, "Gimme that out your hand! Cephus, leggo!"

Then, *paks!* A slap.

The house gone quiet.

Inez and Boysie looking over at the open bedroom window of Cephus house.

All of a sudden, Doreen holler out, "You hit me? Cephus Cudgoe, you hit me?"

And one big tumbling going on inside the house now. Things going *brug-a-dung!* like furniture tumbling over.

Inez raising herself out of her chair. "Sound like they killing one another in there."

Boysie voice stop her. "Where you going?"

Inez sit back down.

"That is man-woman thing. Why you going push your mouth in that?" Boysie sipping his drink, cool.

But after a couple more blows sound in the house, Inez say, "I can't let this go on."

She run down the steps and over in Cephus yard, open the back door, and stop inside the doorway.

Doreen hands like a windmill, scratching at Cephus face, cuffing. Cephus grabbing at her hands to hold them. Doreen raising her knee, trying to runch Cephus in his seeds. What tell her to do that?

Cephus face turn bloated with the blood rushing to his head. He step back, and give Doreen one hard backhand slap in her face.

That unfreeze Inez. She rush in between them.

Doreen holding her face. Then she try to reach around Inez, grabbing at Cephus. Inez grab Doreen hand.

"Stop this fighting!" Inez about a head taller than Doreen, and huskier, so she holding Doreen hand with ease.

"I going kill he! Lemme go! I going kill he, so help me God!"

"No you ent." Inez grabbing Doreen shoulder now and pushing her back.

Cephus watching them.

Doreen tiptoeing and hollering over Inez shoulder, "You's a cheap bitch! You don't want me buying nothing to make myself presentable, and when somebody give me something, you vex! This is *my* dress! Mistress Wright give me this dress and I *keeping* it! And if you put your hand on me again, so help me God I going kill you dead! Stone cold!" She kiss the back of her hand. "If I lie I die!"

Cephus looking down at the blue dress that cause all the trouble, crumpled on the floor.

And when Inez get back home she telling Boysie, "That woman en got no pride."

And all Boysie saying is, "That is the way she raised. You forget?"

How Inez can forget? The biggest fight she had with Doreen was when they were little girls playing. Inez had broken the head off the doll that Doreen said her granny had brought home from the white people she was doing servant work with—a white dolly with blue eyes and a few strands of yellow hair and pin holes in the head where somebody had pulled out the rest of hair.

Remembering it now, Inez telling herself that it was

because she couldn't stand the white dolly. But I know better. Always remember this: you can fool yourself but you can't fool the spirits.

Inez was vexed because *she* didn't have a dolly like Doreen second-hand dolly. She was jealous because of all the attention Doreen was paying to the dolly, plaiting the few strands of hair on its head.

The Sunday after Doreen get the dress, she get up bright and early, bathe and put on the same blue dress.

Cephus watch her powdering and admiring herself in the dressing table mirror, turning to watch her ass, squaring her shoulders and pushing out her bubbies. "W-where you going?"

"What you want to know for?"

"W-wherever it is you g-going, you m-must not be coming back here, eh?"

After a while, she sigh and say, "To church. I going to church, all right?"

And with that she walk out of the house.

And Cephus watching her walking down the gap. He feel like killing her, squeezing her neck till she fall limp. But what good that would do? It is just like the man down the main road that come home and find his woman with a man. He take his cutlass and chop up she and the man right there in the house. Now he walking about the place half naked, hair uncombed, muttering to himself, calling the woman name, "Marcia, Marcia."

So Cephus saying soft to himself, "All right. I g-going play it cool. Give her sufficient rope, she bound to h-hang sheself."

But his decision feel like ashes in his mouth. He feel like it is Doreen who controlling the situation.

When Doreen come back from church, Cephus left Boysie verandah where he and Boysie were cooling out. When he get in the house and swagger in the bedroom, Doreen in panty and brassiere.

Cephus en say a word. He grab her round her waist and fling her on the bed. He and Doreen wrestling, silent. Only the sound of their breathing rasping in the small bedroom.

Doreen face determined; her lips clamped tight. She kicking, trying to knee Cephus in his seeds. Her hands scratching at his face till he grab them. He straddling her, pinning her hands to the bed with his knees and unbuttoning his pants.

Doreen bucking again, fierce. Still no sounds between them.

But finally, Doreen panting, out of wind. Cephus knee her legs apart and enter her so fast, even *he* surprised that he succeed.

He pumping, grunting.

The cock outside the house crowing. Inez and Boysie talking in the house next door.

When Cephus fire, Doreen face sideways on the pillow, staring blank at the side of the house.

Cephus buttoning his pants, feeling like a man, thinking Doreen going say something, anything.

But all day it is nothing but silence between them. She cooking, feeding the fowls, cleaning up the kitchen, en saying a word.

Every Sunday morning from then, Cephus watching Doreen walk out the front door and he feeling powerless.

At Brethren meetings, nearly everybody looking at him funny, and the question in the air that nobody en asking is: Why you let your woman join the missionary church?

Inez acting cold towards Doreen, barely speaking, but Doreen behaving as though everything is normal. And in spite of everything, Inez feel herself admiring Doreen. Doreen en care if people vexed or pleased. She getting up every Sunday morning and walking down the gap to join the four or five people that standing in the morning sun in front of the missionary house.

Everybody eyes fastened on the missionary—Doreen; old Mr. Oxley that live up on the hill in his little house by himself; Gabriel, tottering and stink of rum from the night before; and two women that was living together from when Doreen was a little girl—wickers: neither one of them never had a man.

The missionary preaching from his verandah with his hair slicked back, the sun glinting on his wire-framed glasses, his hands gripping the parapet, and his knuckles white.

Gabriel rocking and saying, "Yes, suh!" loud, even when there en nothing to say "yes, suh" about.

Doreen in her blue dress that she get from the missionary wife. Sybil sweating and fanning in a heavy, short-sleeve purple dress with a white bib. Her arms filling the sleeves of the dress. The white bib is like a tablecloth on her big chest.

Mr. Oxley shoes look new. Feet that accustom to hitting bare ground all week scrunched up in hard leather shoes.

The drony singing of the missionary and his church people is a big amusement for the Hill—Pastor Wright starting the singing slow, and the church people trying to speed it up, but Pastor Wright singing right into his loudspeaker, forcing his voice, slow, reining in the congregation from galloping away with the song.

Sandra Wright sitting in a wrought iron chair fanning her face and looking bored.

This is the way it was for about a month, till Cedric Brown join the church.

Cedric, walking up the gap in his white short-sleeve shirt and black tie. The vaseline shining on his ears; his head up in the air as usual, en speaking to nobody.

Doreen looking at Cedric coming toward them and she feeling glad and puzzled at the same time. Glad because somebody else joining, somebody the same age group as she. But she puzzled because Cedric is the last person you would think would join anything in the village. Especially now he in the civil service.

But wait. Let me tell you about Cedric.

Cedric finish secondary school without one single certificate. Not one. It is like exams owe the boy a spite.

Although his mother see it different. She telling the neighbors, "Cedric pass. He tell me he pass. But some grudgeful-minded body work obeah on my son to make them people in Away mark his papers wrong and fail him."

Of course that start bad feelings among the people she telling this to—they think she accusing them.

And Cedric father, who don't talk much, only saying to Cedric mother, "Look Ida, the boy head hard."

When Cedric fail his GCE certificates, people in the village thought the boy would come to his senses and stop passing them with his head up in the air. But no, he start acting worse after he get a job in town—a messenger job with a jewelry store in town; but nobody on the Hill en know that.

Every weekday morning, he walking out of his mother house dress in suit and tie and carrying a briefcase.

Until one morning not long ago, the little boy that drown at the beach open Cedric briefcase just as soon as Cedric start walking down the gap to catch the minibus.

The women waiting to catch water at the standpipe see when Cedric briefcase fall open. They staring for a long time at what tumble out of Cedric briefcase: a greasy paper bag, suspended a little off the ground and shaking in mid-air (the little boy shaking it to let the fish sandwich fall out), and a quart bottle of lemonade that rolling in the road.

Cedric snatch up the sandwich and bottle of lemonade and clamp the briefcase shut.

The little boy and his sister holding their belly, bending over and laughing.

For days the joke all over the village is the "papers" in Cedric briefcase.

But last week, people start looking at Cedric different. News spreading that Cedric get a civil service job.

—*"I hear the missionary get it for him, and it is a good job too. In the prime minister office."*

The morning after Sybil hear the news, Cedric walking down the gap as usual, heading for the main road to catch the bus.

"Good morning, Cedric." It is strange even to me to hear Sybil sound so polite.

But Cedric passing her like he en notice her.

And Sybil hollering behind his back, "G'long! G'long, you poor-great jackass!"

Now Cedric standing at the back of the little crowd in front the missionary bungalow.

The missionary saying, "Come forward, brother. Welcome. Praise Jesus."

The following week, Miss Scantlebury join the little congregation in the road in front the missionary house, but only after a long struggle. She was a Brethren all her life.

But Darcy out of school now, knocking around the place with the other youths. Some days he does farm the ground with her—mostly when she pester him to stop idling with his friends and help her. Most days, though, the only time she does see him after he leave the house in the morning is when he come home at forenoon for his food and when he come in at night.

And last night she smell cigarette on him as soon as he step in the door. Plus he smelling-up behind that little wild girl from down the main road. It en long before he get she with child.

Miss Scantlebury wish she can get Darcy away from here—a seaman job; the farm labor scheme in Away—before he fall in with bad company and get in trouble.

If the missionary get a job for Cedric, maybe he can do something for she and Darcy.

So the Sunday after Cedric walk up the gap in his shirt and tie, Miss Scantlebury put on her good white dress and step out her front door.

Patsy sitting down every night looking at Darnley doing his homework near the kerosene lamp. Darnley getting near time where he can sit the eleven-plus exam to get into secondary school. All of the teachers saying how bright he is.

Leroy en paying him as much attention as he should. It is like if Leroy would be satisfied if Darnley grow up to be a tinsmith like him. Like father like son.

But Patsy don't want that. She want Darnley to get his education. Be a doctor or lawyer. But it going be hard. Perhaps the missionary can put in a word to get a scholarship for Darnley. You have to have a godfather to get anything in this country—you have to know some big shot or other.

So Patsy join.

And the congregation start to grow from there.

THINGS STILL EN BACK TO NORMAL when the missionary get his second shipment from Away. This time it is mostly foodstuff.

Nobody en want to be the first to go for the free food, but that night as soon as darkness settle, figures coming and going to and from the missionary house.

Next day Mr. Thorne in his shop smelling the aroma of corned beef frying, and he grumbling, saying the missionary undermining his shop. "It is one thing to give away clothes," Mr. Thorne fuming, "but when it come to food, he spoiling my business."

Denzil glance at the empty shelves. His voice slow as usual. "What business?"

"The rice taste like gasoline, anyway," Leroy grumble.

In the silence that follow, Leroy begin fidgeting. First time I ever see Leroy looking embarrassed. Finally he add, "That is what Patsy say."

"So Patsy nyam all the rice, eh?" Claude saying. "En left none for you? No wonder she so big and fat, oui."

Fellas snickering.

Leroy playing vex. "Well, you expect we to go hungry?"

"I g-got food in my ground," Cephus say.

"Yams? I *tired* eating yam. The missionary got *real* food. From Away. Rice, corned beef, oat flakes. What we supposed to do when he offer? Refuse?" Leroy belligerent. "None of unna en offer me nothing. The missionary give we food from Away. *Away.*"

And Cephus asking, "S-since when s-somebody g-got to offer you s-something to c-cook, Leroy? W-we don't live so."

And Boysie saying, like he talking to himself, "We didn't *used* to live so."

Cephus start a meeting-turn soon after that day.

But it puzzle him that Boysie en agree that it is a good idea.

Boysie agree to throw in a turn, "to support the effort." But he saying, "A meeting turn is small potatoes, mate. Throwing in a dollar a week and collecting your money when it is your turn, that is small potatoes, mate. What we need is a revolution."

Cephus noticing that since Boysie left his job at the harbor, all he talking about is revolution this, revolution that.

But a few people in the village, mostly other Brethren, coming every Friday and giving Cephus their dollar. Cephus writing it down in a book.

"I en want nothing to do with that," Doreen say when he ask her to keep the people names in a notebook for him.

Cephus shrug. "All right."

And Doreen vex as hell. Nothing she do en getting Cephus vex anymore.

The day she join the missionary church and Cephus ravish her when she get back home, she knew she had him. She was in control.

But nowadays Cephus going to his Brethren meetings, managing his meeting-turn, going down by Brother Joseph shop every evening after work, and it is like she never join the missionary church. It is like she and Cephus is brother and sister.

So she trying to pick a noise with him, to get him *say* something, *do* something. She would rather he say something, hit her, anything. At least then she would know what on his mind.

It is like he doing it for spite, getting more and more involved with the Brethren since she join Pastor Wright church.

And she don't like that. Cephus is the kind of man that does hold things inside and then explode.

Boysie is a different story. The first couple weeks after he left his job at the harbor, he getting up in the morning and going in the ground with Inez.

Inez, Cephus, Violet, and Granville finally clear all the tangled vines, tree limbs, dead animals, and other debris off the land.

Corn stalks shooting up. Potato slips, pumpkin vines beginning to grow. And the weeds growing faster than everything else.

Boysie helping Inez weed the rows. But by the time the sun begin to climb above the housetops, Boysie stopping and sitting under a tree.

Finally one day he say he going out in the fishing boat with Denzil. But that en last long either. Boysie restless.

One morning he get up and catch the minibus to town. Inez en see him till dusk-time.

First couple evenings after he come back from town, Inez ask him what he doing in town all day. He only shrugging his shoulders. "Nothing."

And Sandra Wright taking a stroll every morning through the village, up to the hill overlooking the gully, admiring the view: the bay below—the water stretching to the horizon; ships at anchor; the village activity down the hill—women hanging out their clothes; men and women striding toward the fields with their hoes; Leroy hammering in his tinsmith shop; the bearded, slightly bowlegged man (Boysie) sauntering down toward the main road to wait for the minibus.

One morning Inez see the missionary wife passing and decide to follow her as she strolling up the hill. Inez watching her walking among the rocks and boulders overlooking the gully, poking around, examining rocks, taking pictures. Finally, the missionary wife sit on a boulder, looking down at the village, at the gully, out in the bay.

Inez ease away and head back home. That night she tell Boysie what she see the missionary wife doing. And Boysie nodding his head like he know already. But that's the way Boysie is: even if he didn't know he would pretend to know.

One morning me, Dolphus, Miss Wiggins, Miss Wiggins headless nephew, and the little boy and his sister that drown down at the beach the day before a hurricane a few years back, all of us sitting up there on the hill watching Sandra Wright picking up rocks and examining them as usual.

She paying special attention to one particular rock in her hand, frowning, turning it over and over. She looking around to see if anybody watching her, sticking the rock in her knap-sack, and scrambling down off the hill.

NOT LONG AFTER THAT, TALK START PASSING around the village.

—*"The government building back a church for the Brethren."*

—*"No. The missionary building a church."*

—*"Don't make me laugh. Where he get money already to build a church?"*

—*"What you talking? He from Away ent he? People from Away got money."*

—*"No. It is government houses. A housing scheme for people that loss their houses in the storm."*

—*"Where you hear that?"*

—*"Elections is next year."*

What start the talk is the public works lorries that unload cement and lumber on the open spot where the Brethren church used to be before the government raid them and tear down the building years ago.

That same night, the Brethren having Men's Night down in the gully. The men sitting cross-legged on the ground in a circle in the clearing, puffing on the pipe, passing it to the left.

The pipe smoke drifting upward. Mosquitoes buzzing off and taking out their spite on everybody else in the village.

In Roachford bungalow, the missionary and his wife at the dinner table smacking their skin and struggling to eat. The mosquitoes buzzing in their ears. Back in the clearing, the pipe reach back to Brother Joseph. His voice coming from behind a cloud of smoke. "Brother Boysie got something to say. Brother Boysie?" Boysie stand up. "The government building a church for the missionary." Silence. Then, "How d'you know that?" This is Mr. Holder. "Reliable sources." Boysie sitting calm, waiting for the words to sink in.

Because, back in the room upstairs the shop on Bay Street, the Student, with the light hitting his glasses and his hand playing with his goatee, had said to Boysie and the handful of other men sitting on the floor, "Revolution has to come from the *people.*"

One fella had pushed up his hand with a puzzled expression on his face.

"Yes, comrade?" The Student looked glad that somebody was asking him a question.

"I thought revolution had to come from the barrel of a gun?"

But now all that coming from the Brethren men in the clearing after Boysie make his announcement is words.

"So what if the government building a church for the preacher from Away? What that got to do with we?" one man asking.

Another man saying, "No disrespect, but how we know what Brother Boysie saying is true?"

Other voices saying, Yeah. Perhaps it is a housing scheme like people was saying earlier today.

Mr. Holder raising his hand and saying he make a motion

that they send a delegation to the prime minister to find out exactly what's going on and to state their position, by Jove.

Claude waving him down. And Mr. Holder giving Claude a spiteful look.

Cephus saying he th-think they should wait and see.

Brother Joseph just sitting back smoking, watching and listening.

It is late into the night when Brother Joseph finally raise his hand to stop the talk, and tell the men to go home and think about it some more.

Walking home after the meeting, Cephus want to know how Boysie know about the church.

But all Boysie saying is, "I got my sources."

Couple mornings later, people standing around watching the public works men unloading their tools off the lorry.

"All you really building a church?" big-mouth Sybil asking.

Another woman voice come from the crowd. "Is true it is a housing scheme all you building?"

Suddenly questions swarming around the men. Who going get the houses? They going to be free?

The men shrugging and pointing to the man in the felt hat and short-sleeve blue shirt that getting out of the little blue beetle car "Ask the boss-man."

But the only person the boss-man talking with all morning is the missionary. The missionary holding a big sheet of paper in one hand and pointing here and there with the other hand. The boss-man nodding. The wind blowing and ruffling the paper.

Hammer walk up to the boss-man when he by himself. "I is a carpenter," he say.

The boss-man stare at him. "So?"

"I was wondering if you could give me a little work here."

"This is guvment work."

"I know, boss. But . . ."

"You want a guvment job, apply in town." The boss-man walk away.

As the weeks going by, the church going up. Hammer en saying a word.

But every night when the village quiet and Hammer standing behind the tree watching a form ease up in the dark, knock at the side of the hut, and the watchman voice coming from inside—"Who that?" and the woman voice saying, "Is me," and couple minutes later Hammer hearing the bumping and moaning inside, Hammer tiptoeing past the hut and thiefing everything he can carry away—cement blocks, lumber, sand—and hiding it under his house.

One night Hammer heart nearly fly up through his mouth when he turn around with a bag of nails and come face to face with a fella and a little boy with a bucket.

The fella nod; the little boy start scooping sand into the bucket and when he finish, put the bucket on his head; the fella lift up a bag of cement, put it on his shoulder, and he and the little boy walk away without saying a word.

One night when Boysie and Inez lying in bed staring up in the rafters, Boysie voice startle Inez. "You know what really burning me up, Nez?"

Inez quiet.

"They building the church on the same spot the Brethren church used to be on before the government tear it down."

But Mr. Thorne couldn't care if they build the church on his mother's grave.

Every Friday afternoon he humming as soon as he see the

paymaster drive up in his small car and rest his suitcase on the bonnet of the car.

The workmen lined up, holding out their hands and stuffing the money in their pockets.

Mr. Thorne wiping the glasses, preparing for when the men going knock off, when the shop going be packed with men drinking and eating corned beef and biscuits.

The Friday they finish the church, Boysie stand up in the shop watching the men washing off under the standpipe and changing into their good clothes. He finish his malt, slap down the change on the counter and left the shop, heading for the beach.

Down on the beach, the sun hitting his bare back, the waves swishing and dying on the shore. He can see his boat coming in with Denzil at the tiller.

Boysie sitting on the jetty, watching the seagulls swooping and wheeling, remembering the talk he had with Brumley yesterday. The prime minister coming to the Hill to open the church.

He and Brumley were sitting in the shop on Bay Street as usual. Civil servants walking past, going back to their offices from lunch.

Brumley asked him, "When're you fellas going to make your move?"

Boysie still can't get accustom to how proper Brumley does talk. A short, baldheaded, middle-aged man, always clean and neat in his shirt, pants, and sandals. If Brumley had a chance he could've been a doctor or lawyer. Instead, he's a messenger for the lawyers on Broad Street.

Boysie watching Denzil drop anchor. The fishing boat rocking on the swell.

He couldn't answer Brumley yesterday.

Now he saying to himself, "When I'm going make my move? Patience, mate. Patience."

It is Sunday morning. The rich smell of the earth rising and filling the nostrils after the sharp shower that stopped just as quick as it started.

A white Mercy-Benz and a police jeep breaking the stillness coming up the Hill. Two motorcycle policemen in front, blasting their engines and making a lot of unnecessary noise. They stop in front of the church.

One of the policemen peeling off his white gloves, making a big show, while the other one adjusting his hat on his head; then they standing at attention next to the Mercy-Benz; the policeman driver opening the back door of the car.

Roachford step out.

Tall, brown-skin Anthony Roachford, the prime minister, smiling, looking around and breathing deep, like he inhaling a sea breeze. His curly hair plastered flat on his head and glistening in the sun. His moustache look like it greased down. His white shirt-jack suit and white shoes running competition with the sunlight.

A man in a rumpled-up suit with a bag weighing down his shoulder taking pictures.

Big-mouth Sybil run right up to Roachford with her fat self and throw one big hug around him.

The photographer on one knee squinting through his camera.

Roachford hugging Sybil and smiling into the camera.

As soon as the camera flash, the smile drop off Roachford face; his hand slide off Sybil shoulder. He straighten himself, tugging at the bottom of his shirt-jack and walking toward the church steps, pulling himself out of Sybil arms.

And Sybil by herself, still smiling, empty-handed, shame-faced, looking around to see who looking at her.

The missionary and his wife at the top of the church steps.

And at the bottom of the steps, Doreen, Miss Scantlebury, Leroy, Patsy, and the rest of the congregation standing in front of the church.

Roachford nodding, smiling, clapping Leroy on his shoulder, winking at Doreen, walking through the little group of church people. When he reach the top of the steps, he shaking the missionary hand and bowing to the missionary wife.

The missionary hand him a scissors and he cut the ribbon that stretch across the front door of the church. He grinning at the photographer. A flash from the camera casting a silver light on everybody for a second.

The missionary, his wife, and the church people clapping.

Roachford, the missionary, and his wife enter the church. The church people climb the steps. Sybil behind with her pocketbook in her hand.

Inside, everybody looking around at the mahogany pews, the red carpet down the center aisle, the black piano up on the platform at the front, the electric lights dangling overhead, the big picture hang up at the front of the church behind the pulpit—a beardy-face, long-hair white man in a white robe, with his heart exposed and bloody holes in his hands.

This is the first time the congregation see the inside of the church.

Pastor Wright clearing his throat and introducing "your beloved prime minister who's been gracious enough to take time out of his busy schedule to visit us on this auspicious occasion."

Roachford step up to the pulpit. "Brothers and sisters," he say. But before he can get any further, a deep man's voice coming through the open church windows from under the tree near the church. Boysie. "God blimmuh!"

"Take THAT!" Claude bawling.

Blap! Domino slamming.

Boysie, Cephus, Denzil, and Claude playing dominoes under the tree next to the church. They slamming the dominoes extra hard and swearing with the curse words to the top of their voice, with the "rass-hole" this and the "pussy cloth" that and,

"You think you can play dominoes? Lemme show you how to play dominoes." This is the hardest anybody ever hear Denzil talk.

Roachford pause, then keep on talking like nothing en happening.

His voice droning on, talking about this model of cooperation between the church and the state, and the PLP government's commitment toward feeding the spirit as well as the body.

The women in the church fanning; Leroy running his hand under his shirt collar and his eyes fixed on Roachford as if he trying to pretend that Boysie and them voices en coming through the open windows clear as a bell.

The congregation jumping whenever the dominoes slam like explosions. *Whaddacks!*

Sshhurr. Dominoes shuffling.

"Y-you think you good? Y-you think that is a RA-RA-RASSHOLE p-play? L-lemme show you how to play K-KISS-ME-ASS dominoes!" Cephus voice en as deep as Boysie and Claude own, but he hollering like the excitement of the game bursting from his lungs. And people in the church that accustom to laughing at Cephus when he stuttering, vex as hell now. They en see nothing to laugh at; they staring straight ahead, serious.

Doreen nearly smacking herself in her face with her fan; her face feel hot; sweat pouring down her forehead, but not from the heat of the sun. She never feel so shame in her life. Pastor Wright going blame her for what happening. He bound to recognize Cephus stuttering voice.

But the missionary en in no mood for blaming anybody. He sitting upright behind Roachford with his face red as a cherry.

His wife sitting in the chair next to him, biting her lip, trying to hold back the laugh.

But Miss Scantlebury thinking, No. The preacher wife wouldn't be laughing at what these hooligans doing.

Whaddacks! Blap! Blap! Is like Independence Day fireworks out there.

The missionary eyes flying to the window every time the dominoes slam.

Roachford turn to look over his shoulder at the missionary. "And anything you need . . . *anything* . . . my door is always open to you." He turn back to face the congregation. "God bless all of you." He cut his speech short.

And when he bending down to get in the car, he taking a hard look at the men under the tree.

Boysie, Cephus, Denzil, and Claude looking at the dominoes in their hands like they just minding their business playing a game of dominoes.

But Boysie watching Roachford out of the corner of his eye and saying to himself, "Phase one."

And after church done, the sisters coming out and dropping remarks about, "some people en got no respect for God nor man" and, "Imagine that. Carrying on like hooligans in front the big prime minister."

Words like "worthless" and "heathens" reaching the fellas ears under the tree.

The church brothers passing with their heads straight, en speaking.

Patsy got Leroy by his arm and dragging him along, with her face push up in the air. Leroy with his little self and Patsy, a big, strapping woman nearly twice as big as Leroy.

Cephus and them laughing, rocking back and slapping their legs.

"Brother Leeeroy," Claude saying. And Cephus and Claude bawling with laugh. Denzil eyes squinch up, his shoulders shaking, and he wheezing this little laugh that he got, "Whee, hee-hee."

Boysie just watching. His thick beard and moustache camouflaging his expression.

Miss Scantlebury stopping and saying, "You boys should be *shame* of yourself." She walking on, slim, tall, and upright, with her white hat cock to a side on her gray hair.

Sybil, fat, with her arms filling her sleeves, passing with her head straight and her face up in the air. But a little smile on the corner of her mouth.

Doreen passing with her head straight too.

But soon as Cephus get home, Doreen light into his tail.

"You make me shame today! You and that Boysie and the rest of your hooligan friends. I was never so shame in all my born days! If you en got no respect for the house of the Lord, then show some respect for the prime minister. Show some respeck for me!"

That is when Cephus leggo.

"R-respect?" Cephus voice nearly blowing off the roof. "Woman, you b-boldface. Standing up in here talking bout r-respect? L-look at you. W-where that dress come from? Uh? S-somebody old clothes that they done with. Y-you know who shuh-shitty b-backside was in th-that dress? Uh? You t-talking bout respect? Joining this man church. Th-this b-backra from Away. P-pon your knees. P-praying to a white man unna call Jesus and you t-talking bout respect? I got five minds to b-bust one cuff. . . ."

Doreen staring at Cephus. She never hear him talk so long yet. If you hear Cephus say two sentences at a time, that is a lot. Now he carrying on. But she recover herself.

"Yeah? You going beat me? Yeah? Try it. Try it, see if I don't *scald* you today." But she backing off. She back-back through the bedroom door and shut it.

"Y-you going scald me? You going sc-scald me?" Cephus standing up outside the bedroom door with his hands straight down by his sides, his fists clench, and his body leaning forward; his face nearly touching the door.

"Yes! So help me, I would scald you. Wait till you sleeping and put on a saucepan of water and scald your ass!"

You wouldn't think she just come out a church.

Cephus en say nothing.

Doreen voice come from in the bedroom, little softer now. "And if you don't watch yourself, I going leff you."

"Wha-what you say?"

Cephus feel like his heart drop through his belly. His mouth all of a sudden dry. She sound like she serious. But he keeping his voice firm.

As man, he can't back down. He square his shoulders. "Y-you g-going leff me? Uh? G-go long, nuh? Go long. Leff if you want to leff."

But Doreen can tell by the way his voice soften up that he en mean it. He frighten.

Next day Cephus come home starving hungry. It is midday, the time Cephus accustom eating. And the damn pot empty. He holler next door, "Inez, where Doreen?"

And Inez want to know if she is Doreen mother; she en nobody watchdog, and if Cephus want somebody to keep a eye on his woman he ought to . . .

And Cephus hollering, "A-all right! All right!" He forget that Inez and Doreen en speaking. He slap some butter on a piece of bread, make some swank with cane syrup, water, and a lime.

That evening when he come in from the ground, Doreen taking two plates from off the top of the larder and setting them on the table.

"W-where you went?" Cephus want to know.

"What you mean where I went?"

Cephus open the pot, staring at the split peas and rice. Salt fish and gravy simmering in the frying pan. "Th-this is what you cook? Suh-suh-salt fish?"

Doreen keeping her voice low. "Don't raise your voice so, Cephus. Everybody listening."

"T-TO HELL WITH EVERYBODY! I working hard all day, c-come home this forenoon and the pot empty? N-now you cooking suh-salt fish? *Salt fish?*" He practically screaming the last word.

Inez next door in the yard, scaling some fish that Boysie bring back from the boat, saying under her breath, "Beat the little slut."

Next thing you hearing is *palang!* Cephus take the pot of rice and fling it out in the yard.

And he bawling, "Uh-I c-come home this forenoon starving hungry! Nothing to eat! Next t-time that h-happen, you going *taste* my hand!"

Inez look up to see him stamping out the house with his face set up, walking out in the ground.

He and Boysie together under the breadfruit tree.

One time, she would step next door and find out what wrong between Doreen and Cephus.

But now Inez scaling her fish and minding her own business, thinking that Cephus shoulda bust Doreen ass from the day she join the missionary church.

But let me tell you what really eating out Inez. It is remembering the day after the hurricane, when she stand in the kitchen and catch Boysie and Doreen in the yard eyeing one another. *That* is what eating her out.

And just then, Claude coming up the gap, tall, stoop-shoulder Claude, striding long, smacking a newspaper against his leg.

And Inez watching he, Boysie, and Cephus under the breadfruit tree.

I drift over by the fellas.

"Look at this," Claude saying.

And the three of them looking at the front page of the newspaper, at the headline—"PM Cuts Ribbon for New Church," and at the picture of Roachford hugging Sybil, with the caption underneath: "Man of the People. Warm Welcome for Local Son."

But a little ways off in the background of the picture, two ragged, barefoot children—a little girl in a loose smock and a little boy with no shirt and his big belly hanging over his short pants, both of them barefoot—standing next to what used to be a house but is only a pile of broken lumber.

The little girl sucking her finger and playing with her ear. Cephus heart racing because it is the same little girl that stand up in front him the day after the storm, down by the river, with bloody sockets where her eyes used to be. Now she look normal.

The little boy next to her got his arms fold across his chest; the two of them just staring into the camera.

Boysie, Claude, and Cephus just gawking at the picture.

The two little children is the same brother and sister that drown at the beach. A wave come in and tumble them up, and nobody never see them again.

The news all over the Hill— two dead children show up in the picture of Roachford and Sybil.

But in town, the picture causing a different kind of excitement.

The same time Cephus and them looking at the paper, the photographer that take the picture sitting in a rumshop on Bay Street, looking at the brown rum in his glass. He do everything the prime minister say. He make sure none of the hurricane damage show up in the pictures he take. He make sure he set the F-stop so that the camera only focusing short—the background blurry. Them children and the collapsed house wasn't in the picture when he develop his pictures last night.

But the prime minister en listening. All he do is stare at the photographer, then wave his hand and dismiss him from the office.

Now the shopkeeper looking at the photographer sitting by himself.

Later, when the shopkeeper hand the photographer back his change and say, "See you tomorrow," all the photographer do is give a sickly smile, pocket his change, and walk out of the shop.

That is the last anybody see of the photographer.

The next couple days, the opposition party driving around with loudspeakers, talking about what a shame it is, the prime minister cutting a ribbon for a new church for a missionary from Away—a foreigner—while children starving, houses still not repaired from the hurricane. "THIS IS A SHAME!" the loudspeakers blaring. "A BLOODY DISGRACE!"

And people shaking their head and saying: "That's true. Is a blooming shame."

The very next day after the opposition cars start driving around lambasting the prime minister and his party, bright and early, public works lorries show up on the Hill with workmen.

Quick so, before the morning sun reach halfway up in the sky, the workmen build a hut, more lorries coming with lumber and galvanize sheets, and a civil servant in shirt and tie going around talking to people at the standpipe, at Mr. Thorne shop, in the road, going from house to house telling people to come to the "office," which is what he calling the hut that en much bigger than a outdoor toilet, and sign up to get their house repair, or a new house if they lost their house altogether.

Boysie and some of the other fellas standing in the road watching the men unload the lorries.

Couple days later, little wood houses going up—one room, with a partition dividing it into a bedroom and a front room, and a kitchen attached at the back.

It is a dark night, and the Brethren sitting forming a half-moon around the edge of the clearing down in the gully.

A lantern hanging from a tree branch close to Brother Joseph and turning his face into a mask of light and shadow.

"Brethren, sistren." Words popping out of Brother Joseph mouth like shots from a rifle barrel—staccato. "Listen. I have something to say."

The flambeaus, pint bottles of kerosene with burning wicks, flickering in the center of the gathering. The flames looking as though they consuming the paper wicks.

The wind whispering through the tree leaves overhead. Up in the branches, a dove cooing soft in its sleep, settling in.

Tonight, instead of his usual white robe, Brother Joseph wearing a purple boubou with gold embroidery that Boysie bring back for him when he come back from at sea.

Brother Joseph hair falling down past his shoulders behind his back in long locks that used to be Masai braids. Years ago when his second wife come to undo them and plait them back as she accustom doing, he shake his head. "Don't bother." No explanation.

Now his eyes deep in their sockets, touching everybody. His beard dangling like tangled-up ropes, touching his chest.

At last he say, "High wind know where old house live."

Everybody quiet, waiting for him to explain.

"These last few years, I watch the Brethren come to almost nothing," he continuing. "Hadn't for the old people like myself and a few young sisters—Inez; Estelle," His words coming out quick and sharp. "Wouldn't be no more Brethren."

"Now. Sudden. Like a thief in the night. Two things hit the Hill." He looking around at every face. "The missionary . . . and a storm."

Cephus watching the way the shadows showing the sink in Brother Joseph cheeks; his eyes, big, red, and glaring under the eyebrows that arch down and pushing the skin at the top of his nose bridge together.

"I en as strong as I used to be," Brother Joseph continuing. "I getting down."

People murmuring.

"No, man . . ."

"Tchuh . . ."

Brother Joseph raise his hand to quiet down the Brethren. "My eyesight en what it used to be. . . ."

Cephus remembering when Brother Joseph used to be a powerful stick licker in his young days, traveling all over the country challenging other stick men.

Although he put down his stick years now ("I's a peaceful man," he tell his first wife), and his beard gray and his two cheekbones like they standing guard on his face, he's still a powerful man.

Cephus feeling Brother Joseph eyes on him. He pulling himself back to listen to what Brother Joseph saying, and Brother Joseph by his side saying, "Step forward." Brother Joseph raising Cephus hand in the air. "This is the man."

Cephus balls scrunched up. His belly feel like it drop out.

He wondering what he do now. He en thief nothing; he en kill nobody; he en sleep with nobody wife. What he do?

People looking at one another, puzzled.

Nobody en want to come straight out and ask Brother Joseph what he talking about, so silence stretching long in the clearing.

"From now on, this is my right hand," Brother Joseph saying at last.

Cephus feeling like a big rock drop down from the sky and stun him.

Looking back at it now, seeing everything that happen, I realize that I made a big mistake putting the idea in Brother Joseph head.

Why you so surprise? You think spirits don't make mistakes?

I shouldn't have mixed up myself too much in what was going on. Cephus is my only grandson and I wanted him to succeed Brother Joseph. But I realize now that people got to make their own destiny. You can lead a horse to the water, but you can't make it drink. But at the time I felt that I had to give them a little push start. Big mistake.

Back in the clearing, the Brethren whizzy-whizzying to one another.

Finally, Mr. Holder, Doreen father, stand up and clear his throat. "I say." Mr. Holder standing erect in his dark gray wool suit and holding his walking stick. "I say. D'you mean Cephus," and he glancing at Cephus and his lip curling like Cephus got lice, "is your *assistant?*"

"Yes."

Brother Joseph voice in Cephus ear. Boysie nodding his head at Cephus, serious. Inez smiling.

Mr. Holder saying, "Hmph," and sitting back down.

The meeting come to an end shortly after, and before they left the gully, Boysie, Denzil, and Claude clapping Cephus on his back. Estelle touching him light on his arm before she and Denzil walk off.

Granville, his father, come over, clap him on his shoulder and say, "Come by tomorrow."

That is Pa, Cephus thinking. Probably going give him a calf or something.

His mother tiptoe and kiss him on his cheek.

And Cephus stand up watching his parents go off through the track, with his mother holding on to his father arm.

"You ready?" Inez say.

Cephus turning toward Brother Joseph, but Brother Joseph saying, "We will talk tomorrow."

Inez hooking her arm in Cephus arm and she, Cephus, and Boysie starting off through the track. The three of them quiet.

Only thing Cephus can hear is their footsteps.

Brother Joseph in his hut watching Cephus, Boysie, and Inez leaving the clearing and walking up the track.

He hope he didn't hear wrong. Sometimes nowadays he can't tell the difference between his own thoughts and when the spirits talking to him. He hope he didn't make a mistake this time.

His sight en what it used to be; when he get up on mornings now, it taking longer and longer for the sun to warm the stiffness out of his old bones. But even though he can still lay with a woman and sow his seed—thank the Big Spirit for small favors—another two months and his twelfth pickney will be born—he know his time getting short. The Brethren need young blood. It is time to train somebody to take over.

He hope he made the right choice.

And he remembering the way the spirit hold Cephus the first night he came back. Cephus down on the ground moving like a snake; his tongue flicking out. Long time Brother Joseph en see the spirits possess somebody like that.

And for the first time that night, I began to have second thoughts. I really didn't think this thing through before I put the idea in Brother Joseph head. Leading the Brethren is a big responsibility . . .

"You damn right," a voice say.

I look around. Dolphus. With his cutlass. "That is nepotism, that's what it is."

All of a sudden, Dolphus using big words like "nepotism." It is like Dolphus the duppy picking up bad habits from his living son, Boysie.

"Who ask your opinion?" I say. "Mind your own business."

But snapping at Dolphus didn't make me feel any better.

Next day, Doreen pass near big-mouth Sybil new house, going to the shop, and hear Sybil voice inside coming through the glass venetian front window.

". . . Can't-talk, stuttering Cephus taking over the Brethren?" She letting go a big belly laugh.

Doreen stop to listen.

"Yeah. That is what I hear." The other voice in the house low. Doreen can't recognize who it is.

"Girl, what you expect from them people? Pounding drums, dancing and getting on like heathens down in that gully?" She lower her voice. "I hear they does sacrifice young babies down there, you know."

And a low voice saying, "You lie. . . . That is true?"

And Doreen can hear the sound of Sybil kissing the back of her hand. "God lick me down dead if I telling a lie. . . ."

Doreen walk on, thinking about what she just hear.

Cephus en tell her a word. He come in last night and went straight to sleep. This morning, he get up and drink the tea that she put for him, and went straight out in the ground. En say a word.

Lately, the church keeping Doreen busy—visiting old people with the missionary; helping make the church look presentable before church meetings—she feeling useful. Somebody beside Cephus depending on her.

But since the bassa-bassa they had after Cephus and Boysie and them start making a racket outside the church, Cephus en say another word about her joining Pastor Wright church.

Now Brother Joseph choose him to take over the Brethren? Cephus? She feel like laughing. Cephus leading the Brethren?

Same time Doreen passing Sybil house, a group of Brethren elders down by Brother Joseph shoemaker shop.

Mr. Holder is the spokesman.

Let me tell you about Doreen father: a tall, slim, gray-haired man with a thick moustache, always in a suit, white shirt with the collar fraying out, black shoes, standing upright with the cane that he does walk with ever since he come back from fighting in the war. Nothing en wrong with him, mind you. He just think he look good with a cane, a suit, and a top hat. Only he had to stop wearing the top hat after he fall down one day with bad feels: the hat was keeping his head too hot.

Before he join the regiment and went away to fight in the war, every Sunday morning as God send, he would walk all the way to the Cathedral in town. Them days, you had to walk; wasn't no buses running like nowadays.

But ever since he come back from the war, he join the Brethren; nobody en know why; he never say. One Saturday night, he just walk in the meeting with his suit and cane and sit down with his back straight and holding the cane upright between his knees, with his two hands resting on top the knob.

Between you and me, he smell so much hell over in Away,

with the other soldiers calling him names like Sambo and gol-liwog, it turn him into a different man.

The week after he come back from the war he walk in the cathedral one day. The place empty.

He walk right up to the front of the church and stand up looking at the gold plaques on the backs of the pews, plaques with the names of plantation owners and merchants inscribed on them.

Mr. Holder pull a hammer from under his jacket and start ripping off every plaque.

When he finished, he put the hammer back under his jacket and walk right up the aisle and out the door.

He never set foot in the cathedral again.

Now he standing up in Brother Joseph shoemaker shop. "I say. We think you taking this thing too far. My God, man. Cephus? . . . Indeed!"

That is how he does talk, I swear. Ever since he come back from the war.

The other men keeping quiet and Mr. Holder going on about Brother Joseph handing over the reins to this young whippersnapper (he does use words like that), "when we got perfectly good, faithful men in the Brethren, men who was here when these young runagates was in Thorne rumshop drinking rum and whore mongering."

And Brother Joseph sitting down on his stool, en picking his teeth to say a word.

When Mr. Holder done talking, all Brother Joseph do is look Mr. Holder straight in his face and say, "Which among you is perfect?"

Mr. Holder stick his face in the air, say, "Hmph," and stride right out of Brother Joseph shoemaker shop.

That afternoon, he come round by Cephus house. When Doreen hear the knocking and go and look out through the front window, she nearly faint.

See, I en tell you this before, but Doreen father never like Cephus. When Doreen come and say she going to live with Cephus, he start raising his voice and saying how he going tar her behind if she so mad as to leave his house to live with a vagabond like Cephus.

But his mother, who raise Doreen from when she was a baby after Doreen mother dead in childbirth say, "Cephus en no vagabond. Cephus is a decent boy. Besides, it is time for the girl to be moving out. You expect her to draw up under you all her life?" And that was that. Old as Mr. Holder was, Doreen grandmother was the boss in the house.

But ever since Doreen move in with Cephus, Mr. Holder stop speaking to her, and he acting like Cephus en living.

So now Doreen staring at her father with her mouth open.

"I can come in?" he say.

Doreen rush and open the door. "Yes. Yes. Come in, Da."

But he en stay long. Cause it turn out that he come to tell Doreen to tell Cephus not to take over from Brother Joseph. "Tell Cephus to step aside," is what he say.

"I can't do that, Da." Doreen voice soft. She hope that she and her father can make up. But she can't do what she father asking. "Cephus is he own man, Da," she say.

And Mr. Holder stamp his cane on the floor. Doreen jump. And he turn without saying another word and walk straight out the house.

Doreen watching her father walk down the gap—his straight back, his long legs, the cane, the gray hair on his head—and she thinking that they never going get back together like father and daughter.

She turn toward the newspaper parcel on the mahogany center table. Crywater at the back of her eyes.

But by the time she try on the clothes and looking at herself in the dressing table mirror, her father is a memory in the background.

The white blouse against her dark skin; the puffed-out sleeves and little ruffles round the collar. She turning around looking at her behind, admiring herself. She looking at herself and seeing a new person. Her heart beating like she just done loving up. The clothes even *smell* different.

My heart beating (in a manner of speaking), and I thinking how frustrating it is being a spirit. At times like this, I does wish I was still alive. Time for me to leave.

THE YEAR COMING TO AN END. A few Sundays ago, Pastor Wright come up with this idea to hold a harvest Sunday near the end of the year, "to thank the Lord for his bountiful blessings." Never mind a hurricane hit the place not long ago and people catching hell.

And every Sunday at the beginning of the service, while people still rustling in their seats, getting settled, he reminding the congregation to remember to keep the best of their crop to bring for the harvest service. "The Lord deserves our very best," he telling them.

This Sunday in particular, Doreen sitting in the front pew waiting for service to begin.

She hear a whizzy-whizzying behind her. People talking low. She look over her shoulder.

Lionel, the young fella that does make furniture at the joiner shop walking down the aisle. His pants a little too tight and the legs reaching above his ankles; his green-and-black striped socks showing.

A big smile on his face; he nodding to right and left, saying, "Morning."

But everybody eyes fasten on the big drum under his arm.

The drum glistening with varnish. All kinds of fancy designs carved into the side: a snake winding around from the bottom to the top, winding through a set of dancing people—men, women, and little children.

Lionel walk right up to the front pew, across the aisle from Doreen, sit down, and rest the drum between his legs. He nod at Pastor Wright, still smiling.

He make this drum himself. He *know* the pastor going like it.

"The service need livelying up," he tell his father before he left home.

"You sure you know what you doing, boy?" His father looking skeptical. "That man don't look like he like no drums," Lionel father saying.

"Yes, Da. Pastor Wright different."

"If you say so." His father voice en sound too convinced.

But Lionel walk out the house proud.

Now he sitting looking at the missionary wife.

With Mistress Wright on the piano and he on the drums, he thinking, people *bound* to get in the power.

But Pastor Wright staring at Lionel serious.

Sandra Wright sitting on the piano stool and looking over her shoulder at Lionel with a little smile on her face.

This make Doreen start wondering again why Mistress Wright married Pastor Wright, a man old enough to be her father. She and Mistress Wright could be the same age, Doreen thinking.

Sybil lean and touch her shoulder next to Doreen and whispering, "But what that boy doing with that big foolish drum, eh?"

But Doreen en answering, although Sybil whispering loud enough that the whole church can hear.

"Grinning like a lizard," Sybil saying. "Look at him." She indignant. "But look at him."

When the missionary get up to start the service, first thing he say is, "Young man, I'm going to have to ask you to take that . . . that *tom-tom* out of my church."

Lionel looking cafuffle at first. *His* church? Lionel asking himself. From the way the pastor always talking—especially when he passing around the collection plate or asking for volunteers to clean the yard and things like that—Lionel thought the church belonged to all of them, a place fit "for the honor and glory of God." So why the Pastor telling him to take the drum outside *his* church? Besides, what wrong with livelying up the service a little bit?

The pastor continuing, "The house of the Lord is no place for heathen instruments."

Well, who tell him to say that?

When Lionel hear "heathen instruments," his skin get hot; his face is a serious mask. What Pastor Wright talking bout? This is the best drum he ever make—taking the time to search for just the right tree trunk, then on evenings after work when everybody left the joiner shop, carving the design on the drum, staining it, varnishing it.

"Did you hear me young man?" he hear the missionary say.

Yes, I hear you, Lionel saying to himself. But he still en moving. He can feel the drum between his legs. His eyes and the missionary making four.

All of a sudden, something in the missionary face make the blood fly to Lionel head.

He in *his* village, with *his* drum, and this white man from Away telling him what to do with it.

"Frig you!" His voice rush out before he even think about it. "Frig you!" He stand up. "Take your church and stick it up your ass!" He start ripping off his tie. "And see this?" He tearing open his shirt. "Take this!" He ball up the shirt and tie that the missionary give him and fling it at the pulpit.

People mouth and eyes open wide.

The light glistening on the pastor glasses. His jaw slack; his eyes, big behind the glasses, got him looking like a fish out of water.

With that, Lionel bend down, pick up his drum and walk right outside, en even noticing the people in the church looking at him.

The top of his underwear showing above his pants waist.

He was mad to take off the pants and fling *them* back at the old backra, but he catch himself just in time. His underwear got a hole.

If I didn't remind him about his holey underwear, the boy woulda expose himself right there in front everybody and spoil the whole thing. The shirt and tie is enough. Everybody get the point.

Boysie and them outside under the tree hear when Lionel bawl out, "Frig you!" They sitting down, holding the dominoes in their hands, watching him stamp out the church door, bare-back, with the drum under his arm.

After Lionel left with his drum, the missionary looking around the congregation.

Everybody speechless.

Then a murmuring break out.

The pastor raise his voice. "People." The whizzy-whizzying bate down. "It's time for me to straighten some things out."

"Bringing drums into the house of the Lord is an *iniquity.* An *iniquity!*" He pause. Then he continue saying about how he don't want to see *any* of his flock playing those heathen drums; he was lenient with them and allowed them to bring their tambourines—"against my better judgement, mind you. Against my better judgement"—but from now on, no more tambourines, no more of those rags on their heads.

Rags! some of the women thinking. What he talking bout rags!

He polishing his glasses with his kerchief. "Hats are more fitting for the house of the Lord. More dignified."

No more dancing, no more getting in the power. "You've got to be civilized in the house of the Lord."

"C-civilize!" Cephus holler. "C-civilize!"

His spoon suspended in midair; the steam rising from the bowl of coucou in front of him; he look like he going choke, sitting there at the table in his bare BVD's. Doreen always getting vex and saying, "You think you look good walking bout the house in only your bibadees?" But this time she en saying nothing.

"Wha-why he think he can c-come here and t-tell we bout 'civilize'?"

Doreen looking at Cephus and saying, "I think he right. It is more decent. This beating drums and dancing like unna does do, that is for savages, not respectable people."

Cephus voice get quiet. "Y-you calling me a savage, Doreen?" He put down the spoon in the bowl.

Something in Cephus voice warning Doreen.

"All these years you l-living w-with a s-savage?"

Doreen sigh. "Look Cephus, I en want no fight." Her voice soft.

And a few nights later, her voice just as soft—at first.

After prayer meeting, Doreen standing in front of the church saying goodnight to the rest of the sisters. Nobody else en going her way. The village quiet; people houses shut down. She didn't realize it was so late.

She turn and start walking up the gap. Even the rumshop back down the hill quiet. Cephus must be home already.

Boysie walking up the gap from Mr. Thorne shop. He hear footsteps on the track on his right. A group of women. One of them look tall, like Miss Scantlebury. Up ahead, the missionary crossing the road, going home.

Boysie look around. Nobody else but he and the mission-ary in the road. But he can still hear the church women voices on the track leading from the main road. Another time, Boysie thinking. Another time.

This playing dominoes outside the church on Sunday mornings getting stale. The church people get accustom to it. Remind him of the demonstrations he used to see sometimes when the boat docked in Away: policemen looking bored, like they know what to expect—it is just another duty they accus-tom doing. And Boysie always would stand on the sidewalk and look on and think, this en make no sense. Because even the *demonstrators* marching with their placards in the air, chanting, always had the same serious expressions but they never looked determined. It was like they was only going through the motions, performing some kind of mock ritual.

Just then, Boysie hear footsteps in front him in the dark and make out a shape he didn't notice before. A woman.

When he get a little closer, he notice it is Doreen. He make longer steps.

"What you doing out so late?" Boysie say when he get alongside Doreen.

"Prayer meeting," Doreen say. "I didn't know it was so late." She look at him. "Where Cephus?"

"Home."

They walking fast together in silence.

Then Boysie grab Doreen elbow. "Slow down, girl. Why you in so much hurry?"

Doreen slow down with Boysie. "Cephus en going like me coming home so late."

"You late already," Boysie say, and pull her off the road, behind a tree. Next thing you know, they kissing. Boysie hands hoisting Doreen skirt and Doreen whispering, "No. No, Boysie." But she en pulling away.

Boysie dragging her panties down to her knees; Doreen

stepping out of them. They breathing heavy. Doreen leaning back against the tree; her head back; her legs apart. And Boysie taking his penis out his pants.

When Boysie put it in, Doreen let out a breath, "Aaaahh," like somebody letting air out a inner tube. And they humping there against the tree. Boysie puffing, Doreen moaning and groaning.

And the birds up in the branches shifting, taking their heads from under their wings and looking down at the two people under the tree, one with her head back and moving from side to side and groaning like she in pain and hollering every once in a while, "Oh God, Boysie. Oh God." And the other person with his back hunch and his knees bend, humping away, with his two hands brace against the tree. The birds looking down, muttering and shifting on the branches, vex because these two people wake them up.

And Inez lying down in bed wondering what keeping Boysie so long. She hear when Cephus come in earlier from over at Brother Joseph.

And next door, Cephus getting up from the dining table and looking through the front window. Not a soul en on the road. He wondering what Doreen could be doing so late at the church. He turn back inside.

When Boysie and Doreen done, Doreen pulling up her panties; Boysie buttoning up his fly. They en talking.

When they step back in the road, Boysie say, "You go along. I will wait."

And he watching Doreen walk up the gap. He feel like calling her back for a second round, but another mind tell him, No. Another time.

His knees trembling, and he know he smell like salt fish. He turn toward the track that lead to the river. He got to rinse off himself and give his knees chance to settle down.

And Cephus looking through the window again, watching

Doreen coming up the gap. A movement catch his eye, like somebody walking down the track to the river. But is only a new moon; he can't make out who it is.

His heart beating fast. That is what Doreen was doing all this time? In the bushes with some man?

But when he look back at the spot where he see the man, he en see nobody.

And Doreen look so innocent when she come in the house, all he ask her is, "What unna doing down at the church so long?"

EVERY EVENING AFTER CEPHUS BRING in the cow and flock of sheep off the pasture, he sitting in tepid water in the tub in the yard, soaking some of the tiredness out of his body before going down at Brother Joseph shoemaker shop to reason well into the night.

People passing the shop at night seeing the door closed and hearing Brother Joseph voice inside as low and mellow as the lamplight that coming through the shop window.

Brother Joseph is like a walking library. And Cephus brain like a sponge, soaking up knowledge about rituals, herbs, things Brother Joseph learn over the years about dealing with people. And patience. Brother Joseph stressing this to Cephus nearly every evening. "Before you do anything, always reason first. The spirits will guide you."

This particular evening, Cephus following behind the cow, trudging home with his head down, tired.

Finally he beginning to see his way after all the cleaning up and starting over after the storm. The land looking like a farm again, not the mess of twisted up vines and storm rubbish the whole family—he, his parents, his sister, and his woman—clean up together. Now he doing most of the work by himself, because Doreen spending nearly all her time down at the church and at the missionary house. She is secretary, she say. "I got responsibilities," she tell Cephus when Cephus ask her why she down at the church every day.

But what she en tell Cephus, and Cephus come to find out, is that she is the one taking care of the yard full of fowls, the couple goats (one with kid), and the black-belly sheep that the church members give the pastor—every week somebody bringing something.

Plus, she and other church women keeping the church clean and visiting the "shut-ins"—which is really only two elderly members (Miss Cobham, with diabetes and high blood pressure; and Miss Grimes, "suffering from the heart," as she always say).

It look like to Cephus, and to me too, that the church people, especially the women, doing most of the church work while the pastor wife walking around up on the hill picking up rocks ("collecting samples," Doreen say), and the pastor driving into town in his big, brown car two, three times a week.

Lionel say he was smelling of liquor one day when he come back from town. But some people saying Lionel only saying that out of spite because the pastor throw him and his drum out of the church.

These last couple days, Doreen down at the church helping prepare for the harvest, spending nearly the whole day arranging the produce in front the altar.

Meanwhile Cephus crops beginning to peep up from the ground again, but Doreen have less and less to do with them. The pumpkin vine, that live through the storm without a scratch, flourishing. Two of the sheep walking in front of him now have their bellies swell with young.

Kwame come running up to Cephus, puffing and blowing. "Unca Cephus. Unca Cephus."

Cephus bend down and swing Kwame over his shoulders.

Kwame sitting down on his shoulders. "Unca Cephus," he say again.

"Wha happening, Palooka?"

"Aunt Reen carry you pounkin at the church."

Cephus stop. "What?"

"Aunt Reen carry you pounkin at the church. You know you pounkin? That you say you en want nobody touch?"

Cephus swing Kwame back down and squat down to look in his face. "When?"

"This forenoon." Kwame eyes open wide. He talking like he out of breath.

Cephus walk in the yard, pick up his bicycle leaning against the house and hop on it.

And Kwame running behind Cephus down the gap, his little hands pumping, his heels nearly touching his behind.

Cephus fling down the bicycle against the front steps of the church, open the front door, march right down the aisle, grab up his pumpkin—his lovely pumpkin that he looking forward to eat in some soup—he grab it from the pile of fruits and ground provisions that stack up in front the pulpit, march right back down the aisle, pick up his bicycle from where he fling it down, and start walking back home holding the bicycle handle with one hand and with the pumpkin under his other arm.

Kwame walking next to him, looking up at his Unca Cephus every now and then but en saying a word. Because he can tell by the look on Unca Cephus face that Unca Cephus real vex.

When Cephus walk in the back door, Doreen at the stove with a spoon to her mouth, blowing the gravy to cool it, and tasting it.

The smell of the food making the water spring up in Cephus mouth; his belly growling.

"T-take your blasted things and g-get out this house." Cephus en raising his voice.

Cephus voice so calm that Doreen en know if she hear right. "What?" She staring at him with her mouth open. Her hand down at her side holding the spoon.

"I say I w-want you out my house right now." His voice still calm.

Doreen heart bupping in her chest. "What I do, Cephus?" But she looking at the pumpkin under Cephus arm and she know.

She draw up a chair and sit down at the kitchen table. All sorts of thoughts running through her head. What she going do? Where she going go? What get in her head to make her carry Cephus lovely pumpkin down at the church for the harvest service? Why this happen now she with child?

"Cephus. I with child." She looking down at the kitchen floor. Is over a week now that she puking every morning.

"What?"

"I expecting," Doreen say.

A long silence in the house.

Finally, "W-what it is? A b-boy or girl?"

Doreen look up at Cephus. "It en *born* yet, Cephus." She en smiling or nothing; she just looking at him with this tired look on her face.

Cephus put back the pumpkin under the bed. A child. Jesus Christ, a child.

He forget all about the pumpkin and how vex he was. You can imagine that?

How you en know Doreen making up the whole thing? I ask him.

When the thought enter his head, he look at Doreen. But seeing her sitting down there with the ladle still in her hand, staring at the floor in front her, his heart soften.

"I going down by the shop," he say when he finish eating.

"G-guess what?" he tell the fellas as soon as he get in the shop.

"What?"

"Doreen expecting."

"Expecting what?" Claude always making joke like that.

Cephus playing he vex. "With child, man."

Boysie en saying a word; he only looking at Cephus. Because, after that first night behind the tree, Doreen telling Cephus she going to church meeting, but she and Boysie meeting in the canefield.

That is the first night since Brother Joseph announce Cephus as his second man that Cephus en go down by Brother Joseph shop and sit till late listening to Brother Joseph.

First chance Boysie get, he step next door to ask Doreen about the child—if she think it is his. Inez gone with Kwame to visit her cousin up in the country. Cephus gone down on the main road to sell a sheep to a fella. The coast clear.

Boysie sitting in Cephus back door sharpening his cutlass and looking at Doreen hanging out clothes on the line. Every time Doreen stretch up to pin a piece of clothes on the line, Boysie heart pounding. He hitting the sharpening stone against the cutlass, keeping more racket than is necessary, he clearing his throat, trying to get Doreen attention.

And Doreen smiling over her shoulder, saying, "Wait," soft, when they hear this knocking at the front door.

Doreen step up on the step to pass him, and Boysie running his hand up her dress and feeling her thigh. She stop and smiling down at him. "Let me go and see who it is, nuh."

Doreen talking to somebody at the front door, then heavy footsteps coming through the house.

Boysie turn around.

Who you think he see? The preacher.

The preacher thin lips stretch in a smile that look false to Boysie. He holding out his hand for a handshake.

"Ah. The man of the house," the preacher say. Imagine that. As different as Cephus and Boysie look, the missionary think Boysie is Doreen man. And it is like he think Boysie hard-o'-hearing, his voice so loud.

Boysie staring over his shoulder and up at the preacher, en saying a word.

"I've been wanting to talk to you. Man to man? To share the word of the Lord?" He end like if he asking a question.

Boysie still sitting in the doorway, en saying a word.

"I know you are a busy man, but . . . Ah, may I have a moment of your time . . . to pass on to you the word of our Lord and saviour Jesus Christ?"

The preacher gray eyes magnify behind his dark-rim glasses. A black Bible in his hand.

Boysie stand up.

When Boysie turn to come in the house, with the cutlass in his hand, the missionary eyes pop open behind his glasses. He step backward and butt up against the dining table.

He panic. His eyes looking wild. He swallow; his goggle bobbing up and down in his neck.

"Ah, I see you're a busy man, Mr. Cudgoe. Some other time?"

Boysie walking toward the missionary, slow.

"Boysie."

Doreen standing next to the china cabinet holding her hands.

And the missionary stepping through the front door.

Boysie rush for the front door; the missionary look over his shoulder, see Boysie, and pick up his step.

When Boysie turn around, the smile drain off his face.

His father standing in front of him.

Dolphus vex. "You let him get away," he telling Boysie.

"What was I supposed to do, Daduh?" he ask his father. "Chop him up in Cephus house?"

"Stop chasing pussy and get serious," his father say, and turn and walk through the side of the house without saying another word.

"Who you talking to, Boysie?" Doreen asking.

"Nobody," Boysie answering. "Nobody."

MANY FULL MOONS PASS. Kwame growing taller and just start elementary school. But not for long.

Not long after Kwame start school, Inez pass the schoolhouse one day and see his class sitting in a circle under the flamboyant tree in the yard. The teacher, a young fella that live down on the main road, sitting in the middle saying, "Little Miss Muffet."

And the class of little pickneys sing-songing to the top of their voices, "LITTLE MISS MUFFET."

"Sat on a tuffet."

"SAT ON A TUFFET."

"Eating her curds and whey."

"EATING HER CURDS AND WHEY."

Inez wondering what foolishness they teaching the children. She is a big woman and up to now she don't know who this Miss Muffet is, and what is curds and whey. She thought they stop teaching the children this stupidness since independence.

Next day she can stay all the way at home and hear the children bawling,

"LONDON BRIDGE IS FALLING DOWN, FALLING DOWN,
FALLING DOWN
LONDON BRIDGE IS FALLING DOWN, MY FAIR LADY."

When she and Boysie and Kwame sitting at the dining table eating their dinner that evening, Inez say to Boysie, "I don't like what they teaching them children down at the school."

"What they teaching them?" Boysie ask.

And when Inez explain, Boysie say, "Take him out."

"And do what?"

"I can teach him."

Inez take a hard look at Boysie and figure she will give the school another chance.

But a few afternoons later, Denzil come through the gate door with his fishing net sling over his shoulder and a bucket of snapper on his head and tell Inez, "You better go down by the schoolhouse and see what they doing with your pickney."

Inez untie her apron and stride right down to the school house to see what Denzil talking about.

When she get in the schoolyard, first thing she see is Kwame class sitting in a circle around the young woman teacher under the evergreen tree.

Kwame and a little girl in some kind of play. The little girl wearing a long yellowish wig made out of fiber. She standing up, looking down at Kwame who kneeling in front of her and clasping his hands and saying, "Rapunzel, Rapunzel, let down your hair."

The teacher in her long dark skirt and white bodice looking at Kwame and the girl, smiling. She raise her finger to her lips for silence when she see Inez walk into the schoolyard.

Inez stop, her hands on her kimbo.

Kwame beaming at his mother because he remember all the words. The teacher en had to tell him this time.

Inez sweep across the yard like a hurricane, grab Kwame by his arm, yank him up, and before anybody in the yard know what happening, they seeing her back, the back of her head, her legs striding, her hand gripping Kwame and dragging him, Kwame stumbling at first but then running to keep up, looking over his shoulder.

The teacher speechless. The little girl with the long wig staring with her eyes open like marbles.

That afternoon after school let out, Mr. Hutson come riding up the road, park his bicycle at the side of Inez house and rap at the front door.

Inez invite him in, ask him if he want a glass of lemonade, and while Mr. Hutson sitting at the table sipping the lemonade, Inez wipe her hand on her apron and start talking.

"Mr. Hutson," she say, "I had this on my mind for a long time. What kinda jackass you is, eh?"

Mr. Hutson nearly choke on the lemonade.

And Inez start right in, asking him how he could take people children and turn them into blasted little fools like himself. This is a new day, she saying, and if Mr. Hutson think she going let a blooming . . . a blooming (she can't find the right word) *thing* like himself turn her child stupid, well, well . . . he sadly mistaken.

"Well, I never," Mr. Hutson say, and plop the lemonade glass on Inez table and march out of the house. "You will regret this." He wagging his finger at Inez before getting on his bicycle and riding off.

When Kwame teacher ask the headmaster what Miss Blackman say, the headmaster say, "That woman is a blasted cunt."

The teacher nearly faint with surprise at the words that come out of Mr. Hutson mouth.

It is not long after this that the police arrest Boysie, and the same schoolteacher overhear Mr. Hutson saying, "Let me see how she's going to manage now, stupid cunt."

Meanwhile, Doreen baby showing.

Inside the church on Sunday mornings, the church singing remind you of a funeral.

Rock of aaaaaay-ges . . .

Droning.

The preaching drifting through the open windows of the church—a foreign, nasal voice. Flat. Not like Brother Joseph with his voice rising and falling, his long pauses, some words popping at you like bullets, making the Brethren shake, shout, stand up and spin around. No. Pastor Wright voice making some of the congregation drowsy.

Heads nodding. Sybil fanning, as much to keep awake as to keep cool. Doreen staring as though her eyeballs prop open with matchsticks.

And outside, Boysie and them shuffling and slamming the dominoes, cursing half-hearted. And it is just another background noise to the church people now.

"This isn't working," Boysie say this particular Sunday when they sitting in the breezy shade after the church empty and the church people gone home.

"What about the plan?" Claude asking Boysie.

"Wha-what plan?" Cephus want to know.

Denzil and Hammer-Head looking at Boysie with the same question on their faces.

But Boysie just looking at the dominoes in his hand, thinking.

He still catching the minibus to town every morning and climbing the steps up to the room above the shop on Bay Street.

Every morning the room still full of men like himself, unemployed, waiting for the Student. And every day the Student coming in, books under his arm; thick glasses; light complexion with freckles; a mop of brown hair on his head, wild; beard; long-sleeve dungaree jacket and no shirt underneath; muscular.

Every day it is the same words: neocolonialism; dialectics; the masses; socialism; capitalism.

And Boysie asking him every day after political study, "What about the plan? You don't think it is time?"

And the Student placing his hand on Boysie shoulder, looking full in his face and saying, "Patience, brother. The time isn't ripe."

So now all Boysie saying in answer to Claude is, "The time isn't ripe."

Cephus, Denzil, and Hammer-Head looking cafuffled at this talk about a plan. Claude got a what-you-mean-the-time-en-ripe expression on his face.

But Boysie beginning to doubt whether the Student really has a plan.

The next week, the government call elections.

Saturday morning, and a van with a loudspeaker on top of it stop in front Mr. Thorne shop. Who you think get out? Erskine Skinner, a fella who used to live down by the main road, running around the place in short pants and barefoot like all the other boys even after he start going to secondary school.

But Erskine is a doctor now, running for a seat with the opposition party, the PDP—the People's Democratic Party; or as most people call it, the People's Doctors Party.

Skinner teeth glistening like pearls in his shining black face. He wearing a long-sleeved white shirt and jeans, and moccasins with no socks.

Sybil staring at him and her fat round face look like if she salivating. "Five minutes, that is all I want. Five minutes," she saying under her breath.

And the woman next to her asking, "What you talking about, Sybil?"

"If I can get he inside my house for five minutes."

And the woman shaking her head with disdain for the slackness Sybil talking, although she thinking the same thing herself.

Erskine is that kind of man.

Before you know it, people flocking to the shop like flies to a carcass. Mr. Thorne shop full.

Rum flowing. The smell of frying corned beef and onion coming from the back of the shop. People eating and drinking.

Skinner in the middle of the crowd with his shirt sleeve rolled up to his elbow, talking and laughing loud.

"Make sure you vote for me when the time comes," he saying. He tossing back a shot of rum to show he is one of the fellas.

A few nights later, the Lawyers Party hold a meeting on the pasture.

The whole village turn out.

The master of ceremonies up on the platform cracking jokes, holding up a jooking-board and saying, "All you women. Same way all you does wash the dirt out of your men nasty underwears, we go wash the rest of the Doctors Party yard fowls out the House of Assembly!"

A man voice in the back of the crowd hollering, "Last time it was 'SWEEP THEM OUT.' Now it is 'WASH THEM OUT.' What it going be next, 'BURN THEM OUT'?"

It is funny how people have a way of inventing history. To this day, people on the Hill tell the story of the heckler that night as if he was some kind of prophet.

But that night the crowd reacted the same way people always react to hecklers, depending on which side they on. Some people chuckling; some turning around and glaring at the heckler nasty; some hollering at him,

"Oh, shut your mouth!"

"Shut your damn beak!"

When the first politician get up to talk, people start clapping.

Decourcey Craig is a favorite with the crowd even though he en running in the district. And it en hard to see why.

Craig is a short, brown-skin man with hair slick down with grease, and a moustache like the Mexican bandits in the cowboy pictures that they does show every Saturday at the Royale. The suspenders and ties he always wearing so pretty you would think it is carnival. This time his suspenders got his pants so high, his privates print out in front for everybody to see. It is worse than if he was naked.

A couple boys up front pointing at the front of his pants and sniggering.

Right away, Craig start talking about who in the Doctors Party living with who; who thiefing what; who always getting pissing drunk upstairs Mason rumshop in town.

And the crowd bawling with laugh, pushing him on. "Talk yuh talk, man."

And Craig really warming up. "And that Dr. Bostick? Calling himself leader of the opposition? His wife going to waste. Good-looking woman like that. Going to waste. You see them in the papers, all about the place. Mr. and Mrs. Bostick. All of that is for show." And Craig stopping and looking out at the crowd. He lowering his voice. "The man like boys."

Although I know he was planning it, I never really expected he would really come out and say it. But he is a politician. It is like politicians is a whole different kind of human altogether.

So now the pasture in a uproar. Voices saying,
"Wha?"
"You making sport!"
"He is a cock or a hen?" a man voice bawling.
And people laughing at this last remark.
But Cephus shifting from one bare foot to the next, saying

he en c-come to no meeting to hear people t-talk people business. That sorta lick-mouth talk is for women.

Craig raise his hand to quiet down the crowd.

And Boysie hollering: "What about the *issues,* mate! Discuss the *issues!*"

But people shushing Boysie; some looking round with their face setup and sucking their teeth and telling Boysie to shut his damn mouth.

"If you don't want to hear, why you don't go home and let people hear what the man saying?" a man voice asking Boysie.

And Cephus chiming in and saying, "Hear what? Hear g-greasy-head C-craig t-talking g-gossip? Unna come here to hear a p-political meeting or to hear p-people business?" And he going on and on, talking about how every elections, that is all the politicians does do. Talk foolish talk and crack jokes.

And I listening to him and noticing how talkative Cephus getting here of late.

But people around him busy trying to hear what Craig saying.

One man barking, "Look, shut up your tie-tongue mouth! Or let me come over there and shut it for you!"

While all this going on, the crowd break out in a uproar. Some people laughing; some staring at one another with their eyes wide; one woman close to Cephus and Boysie saying, "You lie," and chuckling.

Meanwhile, Craig walking off the platform and another politician coming on.

Roachford is the last politician to talk that night. And the crowd clapping and bawling at everything he say.

"This term," he say, "if you all put us back in power, we're going to make some *fundamental* changes in this country." He looking around, grabbing the mike like he going wring off its neck. "We don't want to see another cane blade in this country! Those days are done! *Slavery days done!*"

People bawling, raising their hands, jumping up and down.

"Let the massas cut their own canes!" he shouting.

More bawling; more hand-waving.

"This is a new day!" He pause. "An *industrial* day! With your help, I'm going to turn this country into an industrial *giant!*"

The whole pasture bawling, "Yeah! Yeah!"

"Industry! Tourism! *That's* the name of the game!"

And the crowd gone mad.

Even *Cephus* clapping.

When the noise bate down little bit, Boysie deep voice boom out, "And what about we farmers?"

Roachford peering in the crowd to see who talking.

Voices in the crowd saying,

"Oh shut up! You en no fucking farmer!"

"You want to be backward all your life?"

And Roachford just standing there, letting the crowd answer for him.

The next day, Boysie in the room above the shop on Bay Street telling the Student and the fifteen or so men in the room about Roachford cane blade speech last night.

"Typical neocolonial, petit bourgeois bullshit," the Student saying.

"Yeah. But the people liked what he was saying. You should've seen them," Boysie saying.

"Them is lumpen proletariat," Cyril saying. Cyril is a short, stocky fella that always walking with an armful of books and repeating all the words he hear the Student say.

Up on the Hill, though, it en Roachford cane blade speech that people talking about.

Craig finish his warm-up speech last night with a piece of gossip that got the whole Hill in a uproar.

According to Craig, somebody see Bostick, the leader of

the opposition party, in the back seat of his car with somebody from the Hill.

While Cephus was stuttering on and on about he en want to hear no gossip, the crowd break out in a uproar.

"What he say?" somebody close to Cephus asking. "Who he say it is?"

Craig telling the crowd how somebody catch Lionel, the fella the missionary put out of the church with his drum, in the back seat of Bostick car down by Sunrise Beach.

Next day the news spreading.

Denzil, passing by the standpipe going to the beach to take out Boysie fishing boat, hear the talk.

"How all you know what Craig say is true?" he ask.

Everybody look at him, cut their eye, and continue talking like they en hear him.

When Lionel overhear Sybil when he pass by the pipe saying, ". . . nasty wretch. In the back of Bostick car . . ." he look around and see all the women by the standpipe looking at him, but it is hard for him to believe they talking about him, even though he heard Craig with his own ears last night.

Then, the people around him in the crowd just stared at him, and it seemed as if a space opened between him and everybody else, like they backing off from him.

But he wake up this morning feeling like it was a bad dream. That feeling en last long.

When he get to the joiner shop to start work, the only body speak to him when he say "Good morning" is Branker, who own the shop, although Branker's greeting is only a short "Morning" and not the regular, "What happening young fella?" The three other fellas in the shop en speaking to him at all.

All morning Lionel caning a set of mahogany chairs, people passing the open shed. Some stopping and looking in, whizzy-whizzying, looking at him. The other fellas working in the shop talking among themselves, looking at him and laughing. And he threading the cane on the chairs, making patterns with his toes in the sawdust on the floor, wondering why a big politician like Craig come up on the Hill and tell such a big stinking lie. And why people that know him all his life believe it so easy?

He don't even *know* Bostick much less to get in his car.

And I can vouch for that. But I going tell you how this whole rumor started . . . later.

Lunchtime, when Lionel go to walk out from under the shed with the fellas to go to Thorne shop for lunch, the fellas walking together, ignoring him.

All of this happening and it en feel real to Lionel. Yesterday he was one of the fellas, today he feeling like a leper. It is like he in a dream. He believing that by tomorrow, everything going come back to normal. After all, it en true. And what stunning him is how the rumor start in the first place.

What Lionel en realize is that the fella that say "This is a small world" hit on the truth without realizing it. I know. I was there when he said it.

You see, when the missionary put Lionel out of the church with his drum, Lionel walk home fuming. He *know* why the pastor make him shame. It is because he think Lionel screwing his wife.

The first time Lionel went to the missionary house, he standing up in the yard waiting for the missionary to bring out the chairs Lionel promise to repair.

The missionary wife come out in the yard wearing skimpy little white shorts, and when she going back in the house, Lionel can see where the bottom of her ass begin. Lionel can't keep his eyes off her; he en accustom to seeing women half-naked so.

The missionary had to say, "Lionel. Lionel," before Lionel could take off his eyes and take the two mahogany chairs from the missionary. The missionary wife waving at him from the back door and smiling when he leaving the yard.

When Lionel carry back the chairs, the missionary wife standing up real close to him, examining the chairs. "That's so neat!" She pointing at the cane.

Lionel smelling her perfume; their arms almost touching. Lionel got to put his hand in his pants pocket—he en wearing no underwear.

"Good job, Lionel." Pastor Wright watching him from the back door.

Next Sunday, the pastor wife smiling at him when he come in the church.

Lionel offer to make two high-back chairs for the church. Free.

And it is when Lionel was carrying the high-back chairs to the missionary house that the missionary come in and catch Lionel and his wife in the yard.

The missionary wife rubbing one hand on the smooth mahogany and on Lionel arm. "You're so talented," she saying.

And Lionel en even hear when the gate door open. The blood rushing in his head; he short of breath.

When he hear somebody clearing their throat behind him, he jump. His head whip around. "That you reverend?" He swallow.

When Lionel left, the missionary rubbing his glasses with his handkerchief and glancing at his wife. "Nice guy, huh?"

"Pul-leaze," his wife say, and walk off.

The next time the missionary in town, he stop off at Roachford office for a visit as usual.

When Roachford ask him how things going, the talk get around to Lionel.

"The guy's a troublemaker," he say to Roachford. "A subversive." And he telling Roachford how Lionel walking around the village, stirring up people against the government.

Roachford leaning back in his chair, with his hands formed in a steeple. He know that the missionary lying. He knows what's really happening—he has his spies in the village. Something's going on between Lionel and the missionary's wife. Roachford holding back a smile. A young boy dipping his spoon in the missionary's bowl.

But when the missionary say, "I think he knows what's going on," Roachford suddenly getting serious, even though he en sure if this is another lie.

But it is true that Lionel had come in the yard one day when the missionary was saying, "Are you sure?"

And his wife say, "I'll know for sure when I get the lab results on the rock samples."

"It's amazing," Pastor Wright saying. "You mean to say we're sitting on top of this stuff?"

Lionel saw when the missionary wife frowned slightly at her husband and gave a little shake of her head. But Lionel gone to his grave not knowing what he was hearing that afternoon.

Later when the missionary left Roachford office and Roachford and Craig discussing what the missionary said, Craig say, "Say the boy is a faggot, man."

"What? . . . A what?" Roachford looking at Craig like he gone mad. "Wha . . . what's the connection?"

"Tell people that somebody caught this Lionel and Bostick together. That way, you turn this Lionel into such an outcast, it is a good chance the pressure will drive him from the village. And if he say anything about what he heard Wright and his wife talking about, nobody'll pay him any mind. That way, you do Wright a favor, you safeguard the project, *plus* you start a rumor against Bostick."

And Roachford looking at Craig amazed. He got to admit that when it come to dirty politics, Craig is a genius.

So that is how the rumor about Lionel and Bostick got started.

And that is also how Cynthia Gittens got her ass killed.

Cynthia sitting at her desk outside Roachford office overhearing Roachford and Craig.

A week later, two little boys going home from school through a cart road in a cane field find a woman body in the middle of the cart road. The woman hair neat, still in place, except for a little blood that cake on it. Her skirt hoist up and showing some nice, round legs. One of the fellas bend down and see white panties; the other fella only staring at her face. The woman mouth open; a fly buzzing around it. Her eyes staring. He never see a duppy looking surprise before. He never see nobody that get kill before.

The little boys didn't know who it is: Gittens don't live near there.

But when people that know Gittens get the news, they gossiping:

— "What she doing up in a cart road in some man car?"

— "How you know she was in a car?"

— "What else, then?"

— "She with she little poor-great self. Look how she end up."

And Mistress Gittens friends trying to cheer her up to her face, although they talking behind her back.

But how you can cheer up somebody that lost her only girl-child? All Mistress Gittens saying is, "Cynthia. What kinda brute would do that to Cynthia?"

In the church at the funeral service, other people sobbing, but Cynthia mother there in her black dress and black hat only dabbing her eyes.

In her heart she telling Cynthia, you too stubborn. From the time you lost that job for talking back to that white man, I tell you, you got to be like bamboo. Bend when the wind blow, if not it go break you. But no. You saying you en bowing and scraping. Then you come home last week saying how you disillusioned. You thought Roachford had principles, was different from the rest.

And Cynthia voice coming to her plain in the church, "But Mama, I couldn't sit there and pretend I didn't hear anything. I had to tackle him about it."

"Well look where it get you, nuh?" Mistress Gittens saying behind her kerchief. "Look where it get you. Six feet down."

When they lowering the coffin in the grave, Cynthia mother start this moaning that sound like it coming from deep down in her guts. And when the mould start bupping on the coffin, she bawling and trying to jump down in the grave and her brother, short, stocky, gray-haired, holding her, struggling with her. Other men coming over and helping him with her, while the crowd droning,

Aaaaabide with me
Faaaaast fall the evening tide
Thuuuuh darkness deeeeepens
Loooord with me aabaaaaaide

And Inez by the graveside remembering when the manager fire Gittens from Wilkins store for doing her job, for asking for ID when the white man take out his checkbook. Inez remembering Cynthia walking out the store with her back straight, her white blouse tuck in her skirt waist, neat.

Couple nights after the funeral, Inez in the house. Kwame sleeping; Boysie down at the shop. Cynthia come right in the bedroom and tell her, "Blackman." That is what she always used to call Inez: by her last name. "Blackman," she saying. "Roachford is no use. One day he'll get what's coming to him." And she start telling Inez what she overheard in the office, and how Roachford offer to let his chauffeur take her home after she work late, and how the chauffeur turn the car down a cart road between some canes.

Inez tell Boysie when he come in that night.

WHEN ROACHFORD COME TO THORNE rumshop a couple days before the elections, Boysie position himself at the counter close to where Roachford standing up.

The shop jampacked.

Fellas reaching over one another shoulder, trying to reach the rum bottles and the plates with the corned beef and biscuits on the counter.

Women and children on the step and at the doors with their eyes wide open and their hands stretch out for the dollar bills Roachford chauffeur handing the women and the loose change he tossing at the children.

A woman voice hollering out, "Stop shubbing, nuh? Stop shubbing! Unna greedy bitches going shub me and make me trample these little pickney? Unna en see children in front here?"

But nobody en paying her no mind.

Mr. Thorne short-sleeve shirt stiff-starch-and-iron and his moustache turning gray; his hair brushed back and vaseline on the back of his ears. Every once in a way, he taking off his glasses and wiping them.

Today he en sitting down behind the desk like he accustom doing; he standing close to Roachford, looking at Roachford and smiling, barking at Estelle to hurry up and serve the people, eh. Hurry up!

And Estelle running back and forth getting another bottle of rum, glasses, ice water, and between that she got to serve Sister Scantlebury who come in for a pint of lard oil and half-pound of meal.

Estelle big hoop earrings hitting against her neck every time she turn her head. And she cursing under her breath, calling Mr. Thorne every bad word she know, from a kiss-me-ass advantage-taker to a rass-hole slave driver, saying how she had five minds to tell him what to do with the little rass-hole job.

Roachford slapping fellas on their shoulders, saying how he got big plans for the Hill. After all, this is *home.* This is where he grew up, he saying.

That is when Boysie raise his voice and say, "Mr. Prime Minister!"

A space open in the noise.

"Mr. Prime Minister. What you know about the Gittens girl?"

The whole shop gone quiet.

Boysie noticing everybody eyes on him, and he leaning against the counter and hooking his thumb in his belt buckle, like the starboys in cowboy pictures.

"Talk yuh talk, Boysie!" a man voice holler out. But the words slurring. It is only drunken Gabriel. Gabriel only got to *smell* a rum bottle and he pissing drunk.

Hands pushing through the shop door, holding out for the money that Roachford driver handing out. But the driver staring over his shoulder at Roachford; his mouth open slight.

And Mr. Thorne behind the counter glaring at Boysie. If looks could kill, Boysie would be stone cold. Thorne is a Lawyers Party man.

"I beg your pardon?" Roachford staring at Boysie with a little frown on his face.

"Your secretary. The woman they found in a cart road." Boysie little smile exposing the gold split at the side of his mouth. His gold watch band glistening against his black wrist.

Roachford put a sad expression on his face, like somebody putting on a shirt. "Boysie, that is a tragic case," He shaking his head. "Sad. Very sad. The police're investigating, and my government will leave no stone unturned . . ."

"The rumor is she heard something she wasn't supposed to hear," Boysie saying.

Now, even the people that was squabbling for the freeness quiet now, waiting.

Roachford clear his throat. "Well, Boysie, I wouldn't know about that." He turn to the crowd. "This is my cousin, you know. Always giving me a hard time. Even as little boys, heh-heh." He chuckling.

"Boysie," Mr. Thorne saying behind his hand, "have some respect, man."

But Roachford raising his hand. "No. No. Let him speak."

"En *me* should be speaking, mate."

And people in the shop looking at Boysie like they can't believe what they hearing.

Roachford pulling himself upright, trying to look down at Boysie. "Now see here. . . ."

But he and Boysie is the same height. Besides, Boysie muscular; Roachford running to fat. His arms look like a woman's arms in his short-sleeve shirt; his face is a round brown ball with a moustache.

Roachford chauffeur lean close to him, whizzy-whizzying in his ear.

Roachford look at his wrist watch. "My driver just reminded me. I have an appointment." He look straight at Boysie. "But we must continue this conversation some time."

And with that, he shake Mr. Thorne hand; people open a way for him, and he and the chauffeur head for the door.

Next day, Boysie ass was in jail.

Tell the truth, he lucky he didn't end up like the Gittens girl—dead.

The only thing save him is his aunt.

Miss Roachford show up at her son big, fancy house that she wouldn't've been able to visit when she was alive. She and Cynthia Gittens walk right in Roachford bedroom while his wife taking a shower.

"If you do Boysie like you do this poor girl here," Miss Roachford say, "you'll regret the day you were born."

Roachford wife come out of the shower and see her husband staring, with beads of sweat on his forehead. When she asked him what happened, he speechless.

The Sunday morning start out cool and sweet. The rain had just stop falling. You could smell the warm dirt; the steam rising off the tin roofs; the air feel clean and clear.

Boysie, Cephus, Claude, and Denzil sitting under the tree next to the church. They decide that this is the last Sunday they going be doing this.

Hammer-Head leaning with his back against the tree, with his hands in his pockets, watching the other four men slamming dominoes. He thinking that what Boysie say is true. This domino game outside the church pon a Sunday mornings was a good idea when it start out, to make the church people miserable, but now it is a habit. It is time to do something different. But what?

I almost got to bite my tongue to keep myself from putting any idea in his head. Let them figure out things for theyself. That is what they got brains for.

Just then, a police jeep stop by the church.

Hammer-Head ease his back off the tree and back off little bit. "Fellas," he say easy.

When Cephus and them look at him, Hammer-Head nod toward the police jeep. Six policemen walking toward them with their clubs in their hands.

"Rass-hole," Hammer say under his breath, and he gone—like a jack rabbit, running through the grass, and the tall cuscus grass going *swishswishswish.*

Cephus and them can barely see Hammer from his chest up, scorching through the tall grass. And the grass waving furiously as though it moving out of the way to let Hammer pass.

Boysie, Cephus, Claude, and Denzil en got time to start running. By the time they jump up, knocking over the table, the six policemen all around them and another jeep full of policemen drawing up.

The police en say a word. Clubs raising and lowering. Boysie and them trying to cover their heads, and blows raining down, beating the four of them down to the ground.

The policemen hauling them up by the back of their pants and walking them on tiptoes with their pants up in the crease of their ass.

Boysie get the worst of it. Blood dripping down from his head to the front of his shirt.

By this time, people come out of their houses watching the policemen walking Boysie, Cephus, Claude, and Denzil to the police station down on the main road. The jeeps driving behind. It is like the police displaying the four men.

Big-mouth Sybil saying, "Serve them right, for disturbing the people church service."

"Look, shut up! I say behind her. "How come you en in church, anyway?"

She look around and stumble backward. She collapse to the ground in a faint.

About dusk time, people in their front yards cooling out.

187

"Unca Cephus!" Kwame holler out, and start running down the gap toward Cephus, Claude, and Denzil.

Cephus holding a piece of white rag, red with blood, to his forehead.

Claude, tall and hunchbacked, walking more bent over than usual, holding his side, walking bowlegged.

Denzil holding his belly and his waist and grimacing.

Miss Scantlebury walk up to the three of them. "What happen?" she ask.

Estelle running out the front door bawling, "Oh Lord Jesus! Lord have mercy! Wha happen, Denzil? Oh God!"

Inez hear when Kwame holler out for Cephus and *she* run out. "Where Boysie?" She looking at Cephus, Claude, and Denzil. Her eyes wild. She grab Cephus arm. "Where Boysie?"

Cephus en answer there, but later, when he sitting down in his front-house with Doreen and Inez looking in his face, that is when he tell them, "They k-kick me every place but on me tongue." He stop for a long time, en saying nothing, only looking in space. "You shoulda hear C-claude bawling, 'Muh balls! Oh God, muh balls!'"

Cephus face serious as a judge; what he say en nothing to laugh at, but Inez fighting back a giggle.

And at that same moment, Claude home lying down flat on his back on the bed, naked. Claude seeds swell till they shining. And Pearl dipping a washcloth in hot water and Epsom salts.

All of a sudden a sound like a cow in labor rolling through the whole village. It is Claude bawling when Pearl clap the hot washcloth on his balls.

"What is that?" Doreen asking.

But concern for Boysie got Inez deaf. She asking, "What happen to Boysie, Cephus?"

Cephus shrugging. "W-we was in d-different rooms."

And that is true. They separate the men soon as they got them in the station house. But Cephus en telling Inez how he hear the blows raining in the room where they carry Boysie, and a man voice saying, "You is Mr. Big-shot? Uh? No respect for the prime minister? Uh?" And in between the words, the blows hitting, *Buff!* . . . *buff!* And Boysie taking it like a man. Cephus en hear him holler once.

Next day Inez sitting in a courtroom dark with mahogany paneling, mahogany benches, mahogany everything. A judge in a black robe and with a curly white wig on his head glaring at Boysie and saying, "Nine months!" banging a mallet on his desk, collecting his papers and walking through a side door. Quick so.

Inez heart drop. Nine months! That is as long as it take to carry a baby! Voices all around her.

A man voice shouting, "This is justice?"

And voices shushing him. One woman's voice whispering, "You want to get lock up?"

And a policeman swaggering over with his club in his hand saying, "Who say that!"

Violet got her arm around Inez shoulders; Granville patting Inez light on her arm.

A policeman grabbing the back of Boysie pants and hustling him out of the courtroom and he twisting his body and looking back at Inez, Violet, and Granville.

One of his eyes puffed up and closed; his hair look like wild grass on his head, the pocket of his shirt torn and flapping down; one of the sleeves hanging, almost off; his shirttail hanging out his pants.

Just as he and the policeman reach the door, Boysie stop. "LONG LIVE THE REVOLUTION!" he bawl out.

The policeman give him one big tug and haul him through the door.

A whole set of buzzing start in the courtroom. Everybody talking same time.

"What he say?"

"Something about a revolution."

"What revolution?"

"What I know? Poor fella. All the licks they give him musta turn his head."

People looking at Inez with pity in their eyes.

And Inez just as stunned as everybody else. But at the same time, she proud of Boysie. Although she en know what revolution he talking about.

Tell the truth, I en know what he talking about either.

Because the other men that Boysie meeting with in the room above the shop on Bay Street for weeks now, the Student with his bushy hair and sandals who filling their ears every day with words like "neocolonialist lackeys" and "people's revolution" —not one of them en show up in the courtroom.

As a matter of fact, even as Boysie bawling "Long live the revolution," the Student sitting on a park bench with a small group around him. One of the men, a short man who does clean toilet pits and haul a night soil cart, asking the Student, "What about Comrade Blackman?" (That is what they does call Boysie.)

The Student gazing up in the sky like he really belong up there but somebody put him down here on the earth by mistake.

"Comrade Blackman is striking a blow for the revolution," the Student saying. "The lumpen will see there is no justice and they will rise up."

The night soil man persisting. "But ent we supposed to do something?"

The Student ignoring him, as though he got better things to do than argue with one of his followers.

And outside the courtroom, as they shoving him in the police van, emotion welling up in Boysie chest, ringing in his ears; his heart pumping. Yes. Long live the revolution!

He feel like he reach a turning point in his life.

Not long after the trial, Boysie overhear two of the warders in jail talking about the elections: Roachford and the People's Lawyers Party win again.

But Boysie mind en on the elections. People's Lawyers Party, People's Doctors Party, it is all the same thing, just different letters—PLP, PDP.

Boysie wondering how Inez getting along. And Doreen. How Doreen doing? He regretting now that he started acting cold toward her after she hit him with the news that she was pregnant. But he panicked. And Doreen never made a scene, never complained. Inez and Cephus still en suspect nothing.

Boysie feeling ashamed. Soon time for her to have the baby. He hope she all right.

DOREEN GOING TO THE SHOP WHEN a sudden slanting rain start pelting down, soaking her, raising up that earth smell from the dirt road. She dodge to the side of Pastor Wright bungalow to shelter.

Same time, Sandra Wright come running down the gap with her head down.

"Come in out of the rain," she say down to Doreen.

Doreen run around into the verandah.

Sandra Wright come back out of the house, drying her hair with a towel, and telling Doreen how she should've come in the verandah to shelter instead of huddling by the side of the house. "These tropical rains," she saying. "So sudden. I can't get over it."

Doreen agreeing that the rains really does come down sudden. Then she run out of anything else to say.

To break the silence, she burst out, "What you does be doing up in those rocks every morning? You en fraid you hurt yourself?"

Sandra Wright fixing Doreen with a stare; then she relaxing. "Geology is a hobby I've had since I was a little kid," she saying.

The rain down to a bare drizzle and the sun back out, and Sandra Wright still talking about different kinds of rocks, not seeing Doreen glancing all around and fidgeting.

Finally she catch herself and say, "Anyway, that's how I got started."

She look down at Doreen belly. "When is it due?"

"Oh, I still got a long time," Doreen say.

"How is your husband?"

Doreen thinking about Boysie. She jump, feeling guilty. "Who?"

"He's kinda cute." Sandra Wright nudge Doreen.

"Oh. Cephus?" Doreen looking bashful. "He en my husband. We living together."

And that is how the pastor come to find out that his flock "living in sin," as he put it.

Sunday morning and Doreen sitting in church thinking about how nice it will be to go to church service early Christmas morning just like Miss Straughn down on the main road who think she better than everybody else because she belong to the Anglican cathedral.

Doreen going over in her mind what she going wear Christmas morning, when suddenly Pastor Wright voice thundering,

"It GRIE-E-E-VES me today to hear that some of you are living in sin. Not living as man and wife before the eyes of God." He got this painful expression on his face. "FORNICATION . . ." and he pointing a finger straight up in the air, "is a *sin* and an abomination in the eyes of the Lord."

"Amen," a couple of the women saying. But they nodding their heads, fighting to keep awake.

The light glistening on the pastor glasses, but Doreen can feel his eyes on her. She shifting on the seat and feeling ashamed of her pregnant belly.

"It *grieves* me. Children of the Lord living in sin." His words running together. "Raise your hands, thoseofyoulivinginsin. Yes. *Raise* your hands. Con*fess* before theLordJesusChrist."

No hands en raise.

"I said . . . RA-A-A-ISE your hands, thoseofyoulivinginsin. C'mon." Pastor Wright eyes sweeping the congregation. "You can hide from the Lord's servant, but you can't hide from JESUS, praisethenameoftheLord."

Hide! Who hiding?

Excuse me for breaking in here, but let me explain something.

Except for the Brethren with their long elaborate ceremonies, nearly everybody else on the Hill living together. Who got money to go in town and pay the government for a license to live with somebody?

I remember when Leroy nearly had a fit when Patsy come out kinda timid and suggest they been living together all these years and that "I was thinking that maybe it would be a good idea to get married. What you think, Leroy?"

When Leroy en answering, Patsy taking it for a yes and saying how they should go down next week and get the license.

And that is when Leroy bawl out so hard Patsy nearly jump right through the roof. "A license?!" The veins standing out on Leroy neck. "A license?! . . . I's a blasted motorcar?"

Patsy had to hurry quick and say she was only making a little joke.

That is the way things are on the Hill.

So when Sandra Wright tell her husband, "You know Doreen isn't married?" he looking at her with a blank expression on his face.

"Sister Cudgoe," she explaining. And she going on, "I bet most of your congregation isn't married, either. Wanna bet? They call it 'living with' each other. Isn't that great? That's *great.*" And she letting out a whooping laugh.

And Pastor Wright saying, "Why do you test my faith so, Sandra?"

So now Doreen in church listening to Pastor Wright going on about "fornication" and "bastard seed."

And at the end of the sermon, he giving them a chance to "set things right in the sight of the Lord." He announce a mass wedding for the first Sunday of the next month—first Sunday in the new year—to "begin the new year right."

It is as though the words is an electric current running through the church.

Leroy balls shrivel up; his stomach feel like it dropping out. Of course, Patsy sitting beside him happy as hell. At last she going get married.

Doreen walking home after church not hearing or seeing anything around her. The pastor might as well have put her out of the church. It en even make sense *thinking* about getting Cephus to agree to let the missionary marry them.

That is the last Sunday Doreen step foot in the church. She en going let Pastor Wright make her shame in front everybody like he do to Lionel when Lionel bring his drum to church.

The morning of the mass wedding, the whole village standing in the road in front of the church watching the couples standing in the hot sun, and the missionary in a beige suit saying, "Do you," and he looking at the couples in front him, "take your partner to be your wedded spouse?" and so on.

Doreen home cooking. Cephus watching her out of the corner of his eye.

Ever since Cephus got arrested, he is a changed man.

Cephus stopped shaving. He staying home, keeping to himself, only going to Brethren meetings or down by Brother Joseph shop on evenings.

Sometimes at night, he and Doreen sitting in the house together; the kerosene lamp sputtering and the shadows dancing on the walls. Roaches scurrying in the larder, flying up in the shadows among the rafters. Rats squeaking and scratching in the kitchen.

And the silence between Cephus and Doreen heavier than the baby in Doreen's belly.

FRIDAY MORNING AND INEZ STANDING in front of her house with her two baskets on the ground waiting for the lorry to come down to carry her to town. The sky over the hills in the distance lightening up; the grass at the side of the road damp with dew.

Inez still can't believe Boysie in jail.

Just then, Cephus push open his gate door and come out with the basket of provisions that Doreen is to carry to the market.

"Morning, Cee." Inez can't help staring at the beard that growing on Cephus face, the first time in her life she know Cephus to stop shaving.

They standing up talking about how cold it is on mornings when Doreen come out pushing her big belly in front of her. The conversation stop. Inez and Doreen acting like they en see one another.

Every time Inez see Doreen her blood does boil; she cutting her eye at the little slut and the baby she carrying in her belly. Because Inez believe that it is Boysie child Doreen carrying. What make her think so? She en know. Just a strong feeling.

Ever since the morning after the hurricane when she catch Doreen and Boysie eyeing one another, she noticing other times when they en think nobody noticing. Boysie eyes resting on Doreen; Doreen glancing at Boysie sly.

Sometimes Inez come *that* close to packing her things and taking Kwame and moving back with her Pa and Mamuh. But as woman she got to stick it out. Can't run home to your parents house every time something happen.

One day she was standing in the kitchen watching Boysie sitting in the back door, and I had to hold her hand and prevent her from picking up the frying pan and busting Boysie head. She standing there with her hand paralyzed. And later when she telling her mother about it, her mother giving a wise nod of her head.

Now Boysie in jail and she thanking whatever it was that prevent her from crowning Boysie with the frying pan. Besides, most of the times it is Doreen she really feel like killing.

The lorry chugging down the road and stopping in front of Inez, Cephus, and Doreen, rumbling, stinking up the fresh morning air with gasoline fumes.

Cephus handing Doreen basket up to the fella that working on the lorry.

Inez looking on in disgust as Cephus holding Doreen hand and helping her up on the lorry.

Doreen trying to catch some sleep by the time the lorry get in town. But how you can sleep the way the driver driving? She bouncing up and down, bumping her behind on the hard bench, nearly hitting her head on the roof sometimes; everybody rocking from side to side, nearly falling over every time the lorry swing a corner. The way that madman driving, he enough to kill the baby in her belly. Boysie baby.

And Doreen heart beginning to bup in her chest, thinking about Boysie in prison: wondering what he doing; imagining him sitting down behind bars—the gold split in his front teeth; his gold watch and chain and rings that they must be take away from him; his beard that used to tickle her neck.

She clenching her fist and she can feel her face frowning, remembering the last time she and Boysie in the canes.

Boysie sliding his gold watch back on his hand, whistling low between his teeth. Doreen looking at the gold cross glistening against his chest, the chain draping around his neck.

"Boysie?"

"Uh?"

"What would happen if I get with child?"

Boysie glance at her, buttoning up his pants, buckling his belt with the two gold guns cross in a x on the buckle. "You're not pregnant," he say at last.

"Yes I is." Doreen voice soft. She looking down at her hands, so she en see Boysie expression.

When a long time pass and Boysie en say nothing she look up. He staring at her.

And that is the last time they meet.

Before Boysie get lock up, he passing her with his head straight, like he en know her no more.

The lorry engine humming. The women voices raise above the engine,

". . . Why you face look so sour? Your man en cutting the mustard?" This loud voice behind Doreen end off with a long cackle.

"Girl, that is the last thing we do before I left the house this morning. . . ."

And Doreen keeping her eyes shut, playing she sleeping. It is soon after that last time with Boysie that she start rousing Cephus once in a while on a morning before he go in the ground to start working.

She can tell that Cephus surprised. Long time now since she is the first to make a move. But Cephus en saying nothing. That is Cephus. You never know what he thinking.

Mornings is the best time. With the cocks crowing, the fowls clucking in the yard, the pigs grunting in the pen. Everything up and hungry and ready for the new day—including Cephus.

Sometimes she can swear Inez and Boysie next door can hear them—especially with the morning so quiet—because tell the truth, sometimes it so good she can't keep quiet. Besides, she wish Boysie would hear, see what he missing.

After she tell Cephus about her being with child, and before the arrest, Cephus walking with his shoulders fling back and telling people how he hope the child is a boy, even though he and she scarcely saying ten words to one another when they in the house together. As long as she was in the pastor church and Cephus in the Brethren, it was as if she and Cephus were strangers—except when they loving up.

Now that she stopped going to the church, he treating her as if she delicate—en want her to lift anything too heavy, telling her, "G-get s-somebody to help you with the baskets when y-you get in town."

But ever since the police arrested he and the other men, something eating him out.

The lorry rocketing around a corner and Doreen open her eyes to see Inez watching her.

Usually Inez would be jumping in, talking the worthless talk with the other women, but this morning she en saying a word. Doreen close back her eyes.

When they get in town, the streets nearly empty. The streetsweepers pushing their long-handled brooms, sweeping the mossy cement gutters at the sides of the road.

A man with a peg leg sitting cater-corner on his donkey cart with the reins dribbling through his fingers. The milk bottles clinking in the cart. The donkey plodding along—*clop, clop*—head drooping.

A few people on the road walking to work.

Open-sided buses driving into the bus stand and passengers spewing out like maggots out of a dead animal's guts; other lorries with rows of benches, minivans with the back doors off, stopping where Doreen and Inez lorry stop, next to the bus stand.

Doreen and Inez joining the throng of women with baskets on their heads, striding toward the market.

The sun now easing up over the buildings, but the market buzzing already—filling up with hawkers.

Those that have stalls laying out their things in their stalls. But Doreen and Inez and some of the other women hunting around to find a good spot to put down their baskets and lay out their provisions on the ground.

Doreen feel as if the basket pushing her neck down into her body. Soon she going have to stop coming to the market.

Later, after the hawkers settle down, the servant girls is the first to come shopping, buying things to cook for their missis.

They want the best things, but they want to pay next-kin-to-nothing for them. But you really can't blame *them*. At least they does buy; and they can only work with the money the missis give them.

The ones Doreen *really* don't like is the women that does come in their fancy cars, feeling up the things, wrinkling up their noses; then they don't even buy, or if they *does* buy, they think hard to spend the money.

Like this one standing in front of her now. Fairly tall, brown-skin, hair down to her shoulders, gold chain, gold bangles, gold rings; and the perfume!

"Do you expect me to pay a dollar for this tiny papaya?"

Papaya! Woman grow up like everybody else calling the thing a papaw. Now she talking bout *papaya*. "I just pick it fresh yesterday evening, mum. These papaws sweet."

"Yes, but in the States. . . ."

Why you don't put down my papaw out your hand, Doreen thinking, *and go back to the States, then. Where you can buy papaws as big as a hog for ten cents?*

Doreen tune out the woman voice. But the woman still fingering the papaw. And after all the talk and feeling up, she walk away without buying it.

But as unmannerly as the woman is, Doreen can't help admiring the way she look as she walking away—long, wavy hair glistening in the sun; and all that gold she wearing; and the dress, a plain, low-cut, blue dress that look expensive; and delicate looking slippers with heels, look like they make out of real leather.

Doreen feel like a real country buck in her corn rows (Cephus say he en want her pressing her hair and looking like no frizzle fowl), her maternity frock that she make herself (Cephus making a noise every time she say she going buy a dress from in town. "Every week you trusting cloth from the coolie man," he saying. "What dresses you want?"), her legs grease down with coconut oil ("St-stockings?" Cephus want to know. "Stockings to go in the market?").

Doreen looking at the back of the brown-skinned woman and sighing. Cephus don't understand. Why she can't be in fashion too?

Inez sitting, almost squatting on her little bench, looking at the way Doreen holding her back when she straightening up from bending over, the way she waddling with her belly push out in front her, the way she wiping the sweat from her face, sitting down, and fanning herself with her kerchief. Inez feeling sorry for Doreen.

She get up and walk over to Doreen. "You feel all right?"

Doreen jump and look up at Inez. The surprise stamped all

over her face. She take a long time before she answer, then: "Just a little bad feels. It en nothing."

"Here." Inez pull a little vial of smelling salts out of her apron pocket. "Use this."

"Thank yuh."

And that evening, for the first time in a long time, Inez and Doreen talking on the lorry going home.

The last thing Inez say before going in the house is, "Talk to him. Find out what bothering him. I know Cephus. He en going tell you first. Cephus does keep things bottled up."

But later that night, Inez lying with her hand resting on Kwame little back (Kwame sleeping in the bed with her now Boysie in jail), and thinking about Doreen telling her earlier about the missionary wife explanation for rooting around in the rocks up the hill. "She say she always like geology," Doreen say.

And Boysie in the jail cell, stretched out on the mattress on the floor with his hands clasped behind his head.

THE DAY BOYSIE COME HOME FROM JAIL, he walking up the hill after getting off the minibus and the place look strange. New. First place he passed is Leroy tinsmith shop. He raise his hand to say "Hi-ya."

Leroy look off and keep hammering.

Boysie brow knit up, wondering what wrong with Leroy, but he keep walking.

When he reach the standpipe, a bunch of women standing up with their bucket handles sling over their arms, waiting to catch water.

Boysie smiling bright, walking like springs in his heels, glad to be home. "Good morning," he say to the women.

A couple of them mumble back a grudgeful "Morning"; some stare him full in his face and en speak.

And as he walking away he hear big-mouth Sybil whizzy-whizzying, "The jailbird coming home. . . ."

Later, Boysie in his yard mentioning to Claude how people were acting when they saw him earlier.

Claude brush it off. "Leroy is a brother in the missionary

church. They think the police arrest we for disturbing the church service. Who side you think he go take, eh?"

"But Leroy always is a man that make up his own mind."

Claude shrug. "Leroy get baptize last Sunday. Don't worry bout him, oui."

"But what about the women them?"

"What happen to them?" Claude saying. "Is gossip they gossiping. You know what women give."

The aroma of food coming from the house into Boysie yard. Inez and women from the Brethren sweating in the kitchen, cooking. Children running around the yard, playing.

The fellas knocking back the liquor like it is water.

Soon as Brother Joseph left after clasping Boysie and saying how good it is to see him back home, the men bring out three gallon-bottles of rum and set them on the table in the yard.

Boysie noticing that nobody that belong to the missionary church en there, only his regular friends and a couple other fellas that show up for the freeness.

Denzil and little Kwame sitting off by themselves, playing drums. A serious look stamp on Kwame face; his hands pattering on the drum skin. It look to Boysie that Kwame grow twice as tall since he was in jail.

Hammer-Head standing over Denzil and Kwame, knocking a bottle and spoon and singing a calypso he just make up.

"They kill she in the cane piece
And nothing en go happen
They send in all the police
But none ah we en frighten
They put we in the jailhouse
And bust up we midsection
The last thing that they do
Is, they thief the whole election."

Cephus sitting on the ground in front Doreen, resting his head back against her belly.

"Look him." Claude jerking his chin at Cephus.

The fellas catching on to Hammer calypso and they joining in

"AND BUST UP WE MIDSECTION"

Boysie and Claude looking at Cephus and remembering hearing Cephus in the station house bawling out, "Waaaugh! D-d-do! Ah b-beg yuh!" Then a silence. Then, "WHA-WHA-WHAT YOU GOING D-DO WITH THAT?" Then a bupping, scraping sound like Cephus tie down in a chair and he trying to move it. "It en me! It en me! Do, I beg yuh! I en even know the girl! It is Boysie! It is Boysie, I tell you! I don't even know the girl! Do! I beg you!" The blows knock all the stuttering out of Cephus voice.

Now the fellas in the yard bawling, "THEY THIEF THE WHOLE ELECTION" and Boysie looking at Cephus sitting with his head resting against Doreen and thinking that if he can't trust somebody like Cephus who he grow up with almost from the time they born, who else he can trust? Friendship? Ha! Friendship is only another misused word.

Later in the night, when most of the people gone home, Claude, Denzil, and Hammer-Head sitting down around a table underneath the plum tree in the middle of the yard, listless, their heads hanging with the liquor.

Hammer crooning to himself, "They put we in the jailhouse," and Claude muttering about how Hammer-Head take off like a jack rabbit soon as he see the police and now singing bout "They put *we* in the jailhouse."

Boysie and Inez sitting on the back step, with Inez sitting between Boysie legs and resting her head on his chest when Cephus ease over to Boysie and Inez. "B-Boysie," he say.

Boysie look up.

Cephus clear his throat. "Uh-I . . ."

But Boysie wave his hand. "Forget it, mate," he say. "Forget it."

Cephus look like he going cry. "H-how you expect m-me to forget it?"

But Boysie only waving his hand in a dismissing way again.

Inez looking on, wondering what happening between the two of them.

And Boysie father sitting on a low branch of the plum tree in the middle of the yard, staring down at Cephus.

Kwame hands pause on the drum. He staring up in the plum tree at the man that looking down at Unca Cephus like he want to kill him.

Kwame never see this man before. He looking around and noticing that nobody en paying the man in the tree no mind. He turn to ask Mr. Denzil who the man is, but Mr. Denzil playing the drum with his eyes closed.

Next day cephus nearly drop dead when he see Boysie father. Cephus out in the ground hoeing when he feel somebody watching him. He look up and drop the hoe. His head feel big; his heart pounding; the sun blazing hot but the chilly bumps raise on his arms, making his skin look like a grater.

Dolphus Blackman standing in front of Cephus dressed in the same gray suit he buried in. He barefooted, bareheaded, and holding a cutlass in one hand. The cutlass glistening like a brand new knife.

Cephus looking into Boysie father eyes but seeing only darkness.

Cephus feel a ant bite on his foot. He look down. His whole foot cover with ants as big as cockroaches, and they advancing up his leg like a army.

Cephus stamp his foot; a mind tell him look up. Boysie father drifting toward him. Not walking, drifting. He standing upright about a foot off the ground and coming straight for Cephus with a grin on his face.

Cephus forget the ants on his foot and leggo one long bawl, turn around, and take off.

It is like his feet en even touching the ground. The wind whistling in his ears; his heart pounding in his chest; his arms pumping; he grunting.

When he reach the gate door, he tear it open and bound in the house, eyes wild, and panting.

Doreen standing in the middle of the front room.

"Hide me!" Cephus bawl. "Hide me!" And he run in the bedroom and bang the door shut.

Doreen bamming on the bedroom door. "Cephus! Cephus! What happen, Cephus!"

"Don't let him in!" Cephus bawling. And Doreen noticing he en stuttering.

"Don't let who in?"

"Boysie father!"

"Who?"

"MR. BLACKMAN! BOYSIE FATHER!"

Doreen feel like a stone drop in her belly. She look around, but the yard empty.

A cold sweat break out on her face and arms and a pain tearing at her belly.

By the time Cephus open the bedroom door and walk out after he en hearing no noise on the other side of the partition, after he en see Boysie father come in the bedroom, Doreen sitting down with one arm resting on the dining table and the other hand resting on her belly.

"Call Inez," she say.

Doreen baby born with Cephus peeping through the front window to see if Boysie father outside.

Inez in the bedroom telling Doreen, "Relax. Let it come out," and glancing over her shoulder and telling Kwame, "Look, go outside and play. This en no place for a little boy!"

And Doreen squatting and looking down at the baby head popping out.

The coast clear, so Cephus stepping out of the house and

trotting down to Brother Joseph shop to tell him about Boysie father.

"Meet me here tonight," Brother Joseph saying when Cephus finish talking.

That night the bedroom full of women looking at the baby. Inez in the kitchen boiling pap for Doreen, "to build back your strength." And Cephus leaving the house to meet Brother Joseph.

Brother Joseph draping a blanket over his shoulder (Cephus wondering why, because the night still warm). Brother Joseph taking his kerosene lamp off the shelf, picking up his snake staff and telling Cephus, "Come!"

When they get in the clearing down in the gully, the feeble light from the kerosene lamp barely fighting back the shadows.

Brother Joseph begin chanting and the night all of a sudden start to get cold.

It seem as if the shadows closing in on Cephus and Brother Joseph. Cephus wrapping his arms around his body and looking around, trying to see into the dark. But Brother Joseph standing with his hands in the air, chanting. His voice rising and falling.

When Boysie father appear, Cephus jump and Brother Joseph rest his hand on Cephus shoulder to keep him from running.

I step up next to Boysie father.

Cephus eyes like two marbles; he trembling. "Gr-grand-pappy," he say.

And a whole set of spirits show up, just standing around minding other people business—Miss Wiggins nephew, still holding his head under his armpit; Miss Wiggins; the little boy and girl that drown at the beach; Cynthia, with a sad look on her face; the photographer that take the pictures when Roachford open Pastor Wright church; plus others that I en recognize. It is like it is a jumbee party and everybody show up, even those that en invited.

But Brother Joseph acting as if they is just regular people. In fact, he start right in asking Boysie father what he think he doing, huh? What he think he doing? Why he frightening the boy?

But Dolphus start attacking *me,* saying I responsible.

"For what?" I want to know.

"If you'd raised him right he wouldn't start talking all over his face as soon as the licks get too hot for him down at the police station!" And he going on talking about, "Why nobody else en talk, uh? Tell me that! Why only your tie-tongue grandson blabbering Boysie name all over the police station?"

This getting me hot, although I know he got a point. I getting ready to defend Cephus, to say that Cephus en say nothing the police en know already. Everybody know it is Boysie who attacked Roachford in the rumshop, asking him about the Gittens girl.

But Brother Joseph jump in. "Wait. Wait. Cool your passion," he saying.

And to tell you the truth, standing there, I had to admire how cool Brother Joseph is in the midst of a bunch of duppies arguing.

But Cephus close to shitting his pants. He trembling; his mouth open; his eyes moving from one of us to the next.

He inhale deep, then manage to stammer out, "Uh-I en m-mean no d-disrespect." His voice pitched high and shaking. He continuing after taking another breath and licking his dry lips. "B-but I d-d-didn't mean to s-say nothing bout B-Boysie." He looking around.

The dead little boy and girl big eyes focused on him. The little girl clutching a dolly that is the spitting image of her, down to the sea moss tangled in her hair, then it turn into a Cephus doll. The little girl wringing its neck and leering at Cephus.

Cephus bladder release. Piss running down his legs. His voice and his face crying now, although his eyes dry. "Th-they ha-had p-pliers, g-getting ready to squeeze my balls."

Everybody staring at him. Dry sobs catching in his throat. He backing out of the clearing.

And Dolphus looking at me real scornful. "That is who you want to take over the Brethren?"

The bush swishing; twigs cracking. Once we hear a thud as Cephus slam into a tree trunk in the dark, running.

Brother Joseph sit down on a rock with his head down and his shoulders slumped. "We got to talk," he say.

We chased the little boy and his sister and the rest of us sat in the clearing with Brother Joseph, who start out by telling Dolphus that what he do, frightening Cephus like that, was irresponsible.

And Dolphus flabbergasted, can't utter a word, to see Brother Joseph, a human, chastizing he, a spirit.

I chuckling to see big, bad, cutlass-wielding Dolphus in this predicament, but Brother Joseph turning and pointing his finger at me. "And you?" he saying. "You give me wrong advice."

And it is *me* now who can't say a word to defend myself, because it is clear from Cephus behavior a few moments ago that he en got what it takes to be the leader of the Brethren. At least, not yet.

It is then that a quiet come over the gathering.

Because standing there in the middle of the clearing is my father, Papa, who, almost three hundred years ago came to this land that looked like his home but was not, this hill overlooking the sea, where he couldn't live like a slave so he died like a man.

Looking at him there in the clearing, a memory come back to me: of the old man that everybody called Baba planting a mahogany tree on my father's grave; the voices of men singing and women wailing drifting on the wind up to the plantation house; the kitchen woman who betrayed my father seeing him step through the wall of the kitchen. They find her lying flat on the kitchen floor, straight and stiff as a board, with her mouth and eyes staring open.

Since that day when they buried him right where Roachford yard is now (that whole property used to be a burying ground), my father remained a spirit, not coming back to the land of the living. So he is the most senior of us all there in the clearing.

Even Brother Joseph quiet now.

And my father starting right into me, cautioning me about meddling too much in human affairs. "People have to find their own destiny," he say. Then he telling me if I keep it up, I going end up back in the human world before my time.

It is then that I panicked. "And what about he?" I ask, pointing at Dolphus. "He does interfere too."

"Don't worry about him," my father said. "Worry about yourself."

His words were like cold water dousing me.

Next day Cephus in his hammock. In broad daylight, it feel as if what happened last night is a dream, until I swing the hammock and fling him flat on his ass on the ground.

Kwame up in the tamarind tree in his yard, looking at a gray-haired old man wearing a khaki pants rolled up nearly to his knees spinning Unca Cephus out of his hammock.

Doreen in the house watching Cephus get up from the ground and start talking to himself, flinging off his hands and saying, "Wh-why you do that for?" And she feeling worried. Cephus acting real funny here lately: keeping to himself; brooding about the place; growing a beard. Now he falling out of his hammock and talking to himself.

Meanwhile, I taking my time answering, trying to cool my temper. Finally I say, "You embarrassed me."

Boysie father there too, watching Cephus and shaking his

head from side to side. "What we going do with this boy, nuh?" he saying. "What we going do?"

"You stay out of this!" I say. "This is family. Go mind your own business." I don't trust Dolphus. Dolphus unstable.

I turn back to Cephus. "Boy, all the talking I do with you when I was alive, you mean none of it en stick in that hard, coconut head of yours? What wrong with you, uh boy? You mean I dead and gone and *still* got to be worrying about you?"

"Y-you worrying so much about me, h-how come B-Boysie f-father nearly kill me yesterday? Uh? Where you was?"

"Never mind that."

"N-never mi . . . !" Cephus gone speechless.

If he know Boysie father was right there watching him he woulda be *more* than speechless. He woulda drop dead.

I wait till he cool down, then I told him what I came to tell him. "We decided last night that you en fit to take over from Brother Joseph. That was a mistake."

Doreen stepping out of the back door, walking toward Cephus. "Cephus, who you talking to?"

"No-nobody." Cephus voice irritable.

Same time, Kwame climbing down from the tree and running in the house, pulling at Inez skirt. "Mamuh, Mamuh, a old man just pelt Unca Cephus out his hammock."

Inez staring down in his face.

"And they out there talking."

That same evening, soon as Inez finish her housework and before Boysie get back from in town, Inez grab Kwame by his hand and the two of them walking up the small path that snaking up the hill, through the bush to the obeah woman.

The obeah woman house deep in a clearing on the hill. Fowls pecking in the yard. A snake hanging from the fork of a tree, staring at Inez and Kwame approaching.

The obeah woman standing in the doorway in front of the thatch hut with her arms folded in front of her, dressed in a sleeveless flowered frock that fitting her snug right down to her hips, then flowing loose down to her calves. She barefooted. A young, copper-skinned woman that en look a day older now than she looked when Inez first saw her years ago as a little girl.

"Come in," the obeah woman say, and turned and lowered her head and stepped through the doorway.

Inez standing inside the doorway clasping Kwame little hand in hers, waiting till her eyes accustomed to the gloom.

The aroma of incense filling the hut, but underneath that is the musky smell of sweat and a young girl in heat, the rawness of the ocean, the dampness of rich earth.

"Sit down," the obeah woman husky voice telling Inez.

Inez sitting on the low stool with Kwame standing between her legs in front of her.

"There's nothing wrong with this boy," the obeah woman saying.

Inez jump. How she know what I come for? Inez asking herself.

"I know everything," the obeah woman husky voice telling Inez.

The snake that was outside in the fork of the tree slithering past Inez and Kwame, sliding up the obeah woman leg, coiling in her lap, and staring full at Inez.

Cold bumps rising on Inez skin. The hair at the back of her head prickling.

The snake tongue flicking in and out, and Inez heart pounding, her breath quickening.

The obeah woman holding her hand out and Kwame stepping toward her till he standing in front of her staring in her face.

"This boy has the gift," the obeah woman saying. Her hand resting on Kwame shoulder.

All this time, Kwame en utter a word since he reach the clearing in front of the hut.

Inez gasping, her head spinning, the moistness between her legs dampening her underwear, the muscles in her vagina contracting in spasms, a warmth centering in her womb and spreading to the tips of her fingers and toes, the snake eyes fastened on hers, holding her gaze like two magnets, and the smell of rumpled sheets, sweaty armpits and sex in the afternoon filling her nostrils.

The obeah woman glance down into her lap and scold the snake. "Behave yourself," she say. A trace of a smile softening her words.

Later, walking back down the track in silence with Kwame, Inez feel like she was doing something wrong, like she was off with a man in the bushes somewhere. She don't feel like talking to anybody right now. She en feel like going home to a quiet house either. Instead, she feeling a urge to go by the beach and wait till Boysie and Denzil come in with the fishing boat.

Since he come out of jail, Boysie stop going in town every morning like before. Instead, he going out in the fishing boat with Denzil. Only once in a while he going in town.

But Inez en really going to the beach to meet Boysie.

She and Kwame walking past the fish market where the hawkers waiting with their trays for the fishing boats. Inez scarcely hearing the talking and laughing of the women as she and Kwame heading for the pier where the police launches does tie up.

Inez sitting at the end of the jetty with her feet dangling over the water, watching the seagulls circling and swooping.

Out on the horizon, the sun is a orange ball and the fishing boats are dark dots coming to shore. A cool breeze massaging Inez arms; the shrieks of children playing and splashing in the waves drifting over the water.

"This boy has the gift," the obeah woman had said. But Inez looking at Kwame sitting quiet beside her swinging his legs and gazing at the sunlight sparkling on the water like twinkling stars, and she wondering how anybody could say that it is a gift for a little boy to be able to see spirits.

To Inez, it is a curse more than a gift.

FOR THE THIRD NIGHT IN A ROW, Doreen dreaming that she standing at the edge of a forest. Women screaming and holding their children. A boy, no more than about fourteen or fifteen, busting out of his house with a spear in his hand and running right into a tall young man pointing a long rifle; the rifle fire off; the boy fall back and collapse. The tall young man walking towards Doreen, holding the boy in his arms, and with an apologetic expression on his face.

"His name is Kojo," the young man saying to Doreen. "Raise him well."

Doreen waking up, lying flat on her back with her heart palpitating and her mouth dry.

And the obeah woman from up the hill standing over the bed.

But Doreen can't move. She trying to cry out, but the only sound coming from her is a groaning like a cow in labor.

Cephus shaking her shoulders. "You a-all right?"

And she coming back to normal and propping herself up on her elbow and saying, "Yes. Just a dream."

And the baby sleeping peaceful on the floor on the bedding next to the bed.

The next few days, Doreen trying to get Boysie attention every time she see him. But Boysie looking straight. She want to tell Boysie about the dream, to get his opinion about what to name the child. After all, it is *his* boychild.

Cephus is out of the question. The child en his, plus ever since the police arrest him, it is like he turn foolish, moping around the place and now, here of late, talking to himself.

After it look to Doreen like Boysie avoiding her, she decide on the baby name herself. Kojo. Just like the young man in the dream said.

Cephus just shrug when she tell him.

All the Brethren turn out for the naming ceremony. It was a clear morning with not a cloud in the sky. The air crisp, clear and fresh; the dew bathing people feet as they walking through the grass to the gully.

Boysie taking deep breaths as he walking along.

Cephus walking with his head down, en talking.

In front of the two men, Inez and Doreen talking low. Inez carrying the baby in her arms.

When they get to the gully, Doreen look out of place. All of the women wearing white robes; Doreen wearing the green dress with puff out sleeves that she get from the missionary.

And later when the baby passing around for everybody to hold, Brother Joseph scowling at Doreen and Cephus. Doreen standing there with her two long hands down at her sides and Cephus just looking down at the ground with his hands behind his back, scuffing his toes in the dirt.

Brother Joseph clear his throat hard, Cephus look up and grab hold of Doreen hand.

This is the part of the ceremony where the mother and father supposed to be holding hands.

Granville—Cephus father and the oldest living relative in the family—raise the baby above his head.

"Kojo . . ." Granville start to say, when all of a sudden, a loud explosion rolling over the hill and down into the gully. *Blooom!*

Granville stop with his mouth half-open. Everybody in the clearing looking up over the rim of the gully where the explosion come from.

The baby start kicking and hollering in Granville hands.

Doreen looking at the baby like she fraid Cephus father going drop it.

Cephus look up at the rim of the gully too, but his face en showing no concern.

"Kojo," Cephus father continue, "What is mine belong to your father. What belong to your father belong to you. Live long and strong." He pass the baby to Brother Joseph.

Up to now I been telling myself, it en Cephus baby but he happy. Why spoil it? Especially since all he been doing is firing blanks. But hearing Granville carrying on about what is his belong to Cephus and what belong to Cephus belong to the baby is the last straw, and I'm about to reveal the truth in a blinding flash of discovery when I hear my father voice saying, *The truth en always yours to reveal,* and the thoughts I was about to send out bouncing back and vibrating me like an electric current.

Brother Joseph turn towards where the sun rising, the direction where their ancestors come from, and raise the baby up in his two hands.

People looking in the direction where Brother Joseph facing, the same direction the explosion just come from. A puff of smoke drifting over the trees at the edge of the gully. And the sun is a silver ball glistening through the trees.

The first thing everybody see when they come up the track from the gully after the ceremony is the missionary and another white man on the hill overlooking the gully.

The other white man holding something in his hand; he and the missionary examining it. He say something to the missionary, and the missionary slapping his hat against his leg, holding back his head and bawling to the sky, "Yaa-Hoo!"

That was a sight. This is the same man that they nickname the Undertaker because he so long and bony, and his face always so serious.

Other people from the village coming and joining Brother Joseph and the Brethren, looking up at the two white men on the hill.

The same time the dynamite explode, when the Brethren was down in the gully, the missionary wife in the bushes down by the river letting go this piercing holler, like she in pain; she sobbing and moaning. Her back against a tree; her eyes closed and her head tossing from side to side.

Lionel hands braced against the tree next to her head, and he jooking with force, grunting and staring straight in her face. *You bawling? You en bawling yet,* he saying to himself.

Few minutes earlier, as he was walking on the track longside the river, going back home from bathing, who he see but the missionary wife walking slow, tossing pebbles in the river, wearing a dungaree skirt that reaching above her knees, a armhole blouse like a T-shirt, and slippers.

The water gurgling over the stones; farther up he can hear voices where people catching water and bathing.

His skin still wet; his short pants damp and cold.

He and the missionary wife glance at one another and look off. But as he getting ready to walk past her on the track, she touch his arm. "Lionel."

He stop.

"I'm sorry," she say.

"For what?"

Then she start telling Lionel how it was her husband who was responsible for the rumor that spread about Lionel. "I don't know *how* he did it, but . . ." She pause for a long time, then start talking about how her husband is a close friend of the prime minister, how her husband is a jealous man—if she even *look* at another man, he accusing her of sleeping with him. And, my God, it is worse, since Lionel is black.

Which is true. I was there the day he come and catch her touching Lionel arm. "My God, Sandra. He's a *nigra,* for God's sake!" he say to her after Lionel had left.

So now she saying again how sorry she is, and how she know how it is to be a outcast.

Yeah? Lionel thinking. Anybody ever call you a buller? Say they see you in a car with a man?

She talking but Lionel en hearing another word; he only looking at her mouth moving, thinking that because of she, people calling him a buller, saying he like men, ignoring him like he en living. Or when they *do* notice him, they dropping nasty remarks and laughing.

Before Lionel know what he doing, his hands on her shoulders and they kissing, and she breathing heavy, and he pulling her off the track into the bushes, hoisting up her dungaree skirt.

Now he pumping; he feel strong. Every time he give a hard jook, a "Hm!" forcing out of her throat and he wish they could see him now, see who is the buller.

And just as the pleasure in his body building up, driving him, his head going wild, his whole body feel like it ready to explode, he grunting, ramming, and she hollering, her eyes squeezed tight, her head tossing, just then a loud explosion boom, sounding like it coming from up on the hill near the gully, but it shaking the ground under Lionel feet, rippling up his legs, and Lionel gritting his teeth and releasing a long grunt from deep in his guts, and the missionary wife screaming, "Oh God! Oh God! Oh Jeee-sus!" And it is as if the very life sucking out of Lionel, draining him.

That is the last quiet morning the Hill had for a long time after that.

The rest of the morning pass as usual, quiet and peaceful as ever. Birds twittering; sheep bleating; mothers getting the children ready for school; Cephus going out in the ground to start work; fishermen swimming out to their boats that anchor little ways off from the river bank; clothes flapping on clotheslines; water gushing into galvanize buckets at the standpipe.

And Inez watching Boysie walking down the gap with his bowlegged sailor walk, going to catch the minibus for town, and she wondering what drawing Boysie into town. Even though he stop going as regular as before he went to jail, once or twice a week he still catching the minibus on mornings and en coming back till night.

Lionel swaggering home, weak in the knees from the session with Miss Wright, but with his manhood swelling out his chest. The morning breeze cool and sweet. Life good. His penis stirring, remembering what just happen . . . Miss Wright with her eyes lowered, pulling up her panties while he buttoning up his fly with his shoulders squared off, looking full in her face. He *got* she now. Maybe this evening, maybe tomorrow morning same place. . . .

Sandra Wright sitting on a big rock on the river bank, feeling the moistness in her panties, gazing at the ripples the water making as she toss in a pebble. God, that Lionel. So black, so strong. Billy would kill her if he found out.

She looking around. What if one of the villagers saw them earlier? A faint smile stretching her thin lips. Her heart racing with a mixture of pleasure and anxiety.

And down on the beach, around the standpipe, in Mr. Thorne shop, gossip floating already like a breeze.

—*"Since they catch Lionel in Mr. Bostick car the boy like he turning foolish. Always by himself. En working at the joiner shop no more. You see him this morning, smiling to himself?"*

—*"You think he foolish. A little bird tell me they see he and the missionary wife in the bushes down by the river this morning. . . ."*

—*"What? You lie. The missionary pelting dynamite up the hill and that she-she boy pelting it in the bushes?"*

—*"All you always gossiping, eh? . . . One of these days God going strike unna dumb. What I want to know is, who is that white man dynamiting up on the hill? What they dynamiting for?"*

—*"Girl, Sybil say . . ."*

—*"Sybil . . . Sybil. What big-mouth Sybil know?"*

And so it going.

The white man left in his jeep torrectly after he and the missionary come walking down from up on the hill. The smell of dynamite gone from the air, leaving it clean again. But only for a while.

Couple weeks later, the whole place turn upside down. Big yellow trucks come blatting up the hill, splitting the morning air like thunder.

By afternoon, dynamite exploding, *batoom!*

And the trucks stirring up dust, scattering chickens in the road, nearly running over a hog, hauling off stones and dirt.

Two civil servant fellas in Mr. Thorne shop. The tall one with the red bow tie telling the other short one, "It's amazing. The whole damn hill is made of the stuff."

And Mr. Thorne got his head cocked, listening, wanting to ask them what they talking about. But how would it look? He, Mr. Thorne, PLP man—it is *his* house they connect their electric wires to when they keeping political meetings on the Hill—how would it look, him having to find out what going on from two civil servants? How that would look?

He stocking the salt meat in the barrel under the counter and fuming.

For weeks the whole place full of noise. The big lorry

wheels leaving ruts in the dirt road. Dust everywhere—in people food, in their bed at night when they ready to go to sleep, dirtying up the clothes Doreen put on her line to dry.

The anger building up in Inez chest until one day she rush out in the road when one of the lorries passing and hollering, "YOU THINK THIS IS A THOROUGHFARE? YOU CAN'T SEE LITTLE CHILDREN RUNNING AROUND HERE?"

But the noise of the lorry engine drowning out her voice; the driver staring straight ahead, one hand on the steering wheel, the other arm on the window, en even turning to look at her.

And Inez turning and marching back into the yard where Kwame pitching marbles, making his own play.

At least if he was in school she wouldn't have to be worrying where he is. But she take him out of school because of the foolishness they stuffing in his head; so now she got to worry about him getting lick down with a lorry. And where his father, eh? Where his father. Boysie should be home teaching the boy his lessons; instead of that, he off in town somewhere. And what he doing in town anyway? He en working.

But at that same time, Boysie and the other men sitting around in the room upstairs the rumshop on Bay Street waiting for the Student.

The Student come striding into the room with a bundle of books under his armpit. Everybody quiet down.

"We've got a press conference this afternoon. It is time to announce the party to the masses," the Student say.

Boysie sitting in a corner with a folded newspaper in his hand. "You joking, right?"

And that is exactly what I thinking. For one thing, the country only got one newspaper and one radio station. He'd be lucky if anybody show up for this "press conference."

The Student look up from setting his books on the desk. "Did you say something, comrade?"

"Yes. You mean all these months meeting, having political

orientation, talking, talking, talking, and now all you have to say is, it is time to announce the party?" Boysie surprise himself. He was longing to give the Student a piece of his mind ever since his trial, when none of the comrades never show their face once in the courtroom—not even the Student. But he didn't think he would have the balls to talk to the Student like that.

Later, Mr. Thorne driving past the room over the shop on Bay Street, where the Student having his press conference with the one reporter that show up with his pencil and notebook.

These big white men from Away that operating the bull-dozer machines drinking beer like it is water. Every evening Mr. Thorne watching them, knowing from when he was in Away that the beer they accustom to in Away is like nothing compared with this local beer.

So after a couple bottles they getting drunk and keeping a whole set of noise in the shop, talking loud (they *start out* talking loud, but when they get couple beers in their head, Estelle stuffing cotton wool in her ears and *still* hearing their orders when she serving them).

They staggering to the side of the road and pissing in the ditch, something Mr. Thorne know they wouldn't do in Away where they come from.

But he en mind. This is the second time for the week that he had to leave Estelle in charge of the shop and come in town with his pickup to get some more beer and rum.

He figure he got enough in the back of the pickup to last him the rest of the week.

He stopping at Simpson rumshop, as usual, before heading back to the Hill.

Brumley sitting at a table by the front window reading a newspaper, with a pencil stuck behind his ear as usual.

Mr. Thorne take a seat at the table with Brumley. "Wha happening, Brum?"

When Brumley en in the library reading, you can see him around town with some lawyer or politician. People always wondering how he always in these people offices and walking around town, brisk, always "on business."

It is still a puzzle to me why these big-shots always confiding in Brumley, telling him their biggest secrets. It is like he's not a man to them, just a pet that they can talk to without worrying about the consequences.

Mr. Thorne start to pick Brumley, trying to find out if he know anything about the goings-on on the Hill. Mr. Thorne and Brumley is old school friends. But Brumley mouth dry, so he en saying a word until the rum come.

After the shop girl bring the bottle that Mr. Thorne order to the table and the two men fire their first shots, Brumley say, "They find bauxite."

"Box what?" Thorne want to know.

"Bauxite. But it en as much as they expect." Brumley glance at Thorne with a wry smile. "So the mining going soon stop."

"What you mean the *mining* going stop? What else they plan to do?"

Brumley lower his voice. "This is between you and me, all right?"

Thorne nod his head.

"They planning a resort."

"A resort?" That is all Mr. Thorne can say.

The group of fellas at the counter arguing about football.

The hawkers outside selling their wares.

"Cucumbers! Get the lovely cucumbers!"

"The juicy mangoes! How much you want darling?"

Finally Mr. Thorne say, "But we live up there."

"I wouldn't bet on that, partner." Brumley cupping his glass in his hands and staring at it.

"What you mean?"

But all Brumley say is, "You go see."

A little girl walking past the shop with peanuts on a tray on her head and her little brother tagging on to her skirt. Mr. Thorne would swear they look like the two children that drown on the beach not long ago.

Brumley talking low. "That is how Cynthia get kill," he say. "She know too much. I en go let the same thing happen to me. These are funny times," he saying.

A man stop the brother and sister on the sidewalk in front the shop and digging his hand in his pants pocket.

The little boy hand the man two cigarettes and a box of matches and holding his hand out. The coins dropping in his little hand, one by one.

A SLIGHT RAIN DRIZZLING AND THE SUN shining (the devil and his wife fighting). Mr. Thorne in his shop dispatching Miss Scantlebury.

All of a sudden, Patsy running past in the direction of Leroy tinsmith shop bawling, "Lord have mercy! Lord have mercy!"

Now the very sight of Patsy running would tell you something real wrong. Fat as Patsy is, she does scarcely walk fast much less run. The fellas always making joke with Leroy, asking him if he does ever let her get on top, telling him that she sit down on his head and that is why he so short.

Mr. Thorne raise the counter flap and step to the shop door to see what causing Patsy to run so.

A lorry from the Ministry of Housing in front Leroy house. A crowd standing around the lorry.

Patsy coming back down the gap pulling Leroy by his hand.

By the time Darnley come home from school, his mother and father house tear down and load on the lorry. The tin roof sandwiched between the four wooden sides and the floor. Leroy, Patsy, and Darnley few belongings strap down on top of the lorry.

Patsy and Leroy clothes spill out of the wardrobe as the men were carrying it to the lorry. Patsy struggling to stuff the clothes into a cardboard suitcase. Her hands moving fast and clumsy.

Two little boys helping Darnley chase his family fowls, trying to catch them.

"Hurry up," one of the men on the lorry saying. He sitting on the roof of the lorry with his legs dangling over Leroy and Patsy dining table. The table tied down on its back with its four legs up in the air, reminding me of turtles I used to turn over on their backs when I was a little boy, just for sport.

One of the two men sitting inside with the driver poke his head through the window. "Make haste if you coming on this lorry," he saying.

Miss Scantlebury telling Patsy, "Go along, girl. Don't worry. Whatever you can't carry I will keep for you till you get yourself straight."

Leroy saying, "Look, come along, nuh woman." His voice and the way he beckoning with his hand showing impatience, but his face looking bewildered.

Darnely look stunned.

All that week, houses tearing down, women crying, men charging at the workmen with their cutlasses and their friends got to pounce on them and hold them back, saying, "Don't get yourself in trouble, man." Because the police constables standing nearby, clapping their clubs in their palms, waiting for something to happen so they can arrest somebody.

And it is like the land on the Hill break out in small pox. The spaces where houses used to be look like scabs on the land.

The night they move Leroy and Patsy, Mr. Thorne shop full. Cephus back in there for the first time since Boysie went to jail.

He and Boysie on different sides of the shop, with the crowd of talking men separating them.

"Where they carrying them?" Claude asking nobody in particular.

"A housing scheme in town." Mr. Thorne in front of the sink wiping a glass with his back to the crowd. "The government want the land."

Mr. Thorne en know if to believe Brumley story about a hotel resort and golf club, but *something* going on. The least them bitches coulda done was *tell* him. After all these years, all these years of supporting the PLP, they doing this behind his back.

And Boysie trying to make up his mind whether to break the news about the new party he belong to or whether to keep it quiet a little longer. He has his doubts about this "People's Revolutionary Party," as the Student call it at the press conference. But what is the alternative? He made up his mind. "Fellas. I have something to say."

When he start, he had to fight the noise in the shop; when he finish, the shop silent. His last words seem to be floating in the air, soaking into the very wood of the sides of the shop. "All revolution mean is change. And none of you here can't say we don't need change."

These are the same words the Student said to the few men scattered around the room upstairs the rumshop on Bay Street the first day Brumley led Boysie up the stairs "to check out this new party a university fella forming." And Boysie sitting on the milk crate that first day with his back against the wall, with his last paycheck in his pocket, the paycheck he'd just picked up from the harbor.

The Student—goatee beard; bushy hair; thick glasses; muscular in his khaki bush jacket—talking fast, punching his words out, jabbing his hands in the air, looking at everybody in the room.

Walking down the dark staircase after the Student adjourned "until next week, brothers," Brumley asked Boysie, "What you think, uh?"

Boysie en answer till he come out onto the sidewalk, with the glare of the sun blinding him for a moment. He looked down at Brumley—specks of gray in his hair, newspaper in his hand, old enough to be Boysie father. "I don't know," Boysie said. But the words the Student used back up in that room over the shop bouncing in his head—"imperialism," "capitalism," "neoimperialists."

After Brumley walked off ("See you next week"), Boysie walking toward the bus stand really noticing what going on around him for the first time, things that he accustomed to seeing but never paid attention to: the man pushing the dray cart loaded with lumber, bare-backed, sweat running down his face, grunting with effort; the hawkers sitting on their little benches on the sidewalk, with their dresses tucked between their thighs, their provisions laid out in front them and people walking past in their jackets and ties, their high heels, stockings, and purses, with their heads straight; a girl that should be in school holding a half-empty wooden tray on her head—a bee buzzing around the few sugar cakes laid out on the tray. A bus rumbling past, belching thick black diesel smoke and Boysie fighting to hold his breath till the air clear up.

The Student made it sound so easy, talking about "the masses" taking control. Boysie looked around him, and the high spirits he had when the Student was talking earlier began to fade away.

But a couple of weeks later, after trying to work in the ground with Inez, then going out in the boat a few times with Denzil and still feeling restless, one morning he caught the minibus to town and found himself back in the room upstairs the shop on Bay Street, listening to the Student.

But over the months, it seems like all they do is talking.

The Student using the same words over and over again, but no action.

Last week the Student talked about the company from Away "cutting their losses" after discovering that the Hill wasn't as rich in bauxite as they'd thought. "So now they have a change in plans. They've come up with the idea that the Hill would be a perfect spot for a holiday resort. Yes, brother. *Your* Hill." The Student saying, looking straight at Boysie. "*Same company, my brothers.*"

But at the end of the talk, still no action. Only talk. If anybody is to do anything, it look like Boysie will have to do it himself.

The fellas in Mr. Thorne shop gone back to talking after Boysie tell them he belong to a new party. The shop buzzing with noise. It is as if they want to pretend they en hear Boysie.

Claude voice in Boysie ear saying, "Don't mind them, oui. They en ready for change."

Anger bubble up in Boysie. "And *you* ready, right? They en ready. *You* ready?"

Because when Boysie first come to Claude telling him about the People's Revolutionary Party, Claude said, "I don't know, oui. Lemme think it over." Boysie didn't expect that. He was disappointed in Claude.

But a few days later, Claude came up to him and said, "This new party you tell me about is a good idea."

So Boysie realizing now that it really en Claude he angry with. He just frustrated.

He touch Claude shoulder. "Sorry, mate," he said.

THE REST OF THE YEAR PASSED with gossip flying like hummingbirds around a hibiscus bush—hovering, zipping, darting, lighting on all kinds of topics.

— *"Girl, my earholes glad enough for this little rest now the mining stop."*

Big, yellow bulldozers that a couple months ago were growling, belching, and gouging out the earth now sitting silent up on the hill like paralyzed monsters, taking abuse from the children that playing on them, tugging the levers, making motor noises and laughing. And the watchman, a short, stocky fella that live down on the main road chasing the children, bawling, raising his stick above his head and swearing how he go break their kiss-me-ass bones if he catch them. The children scattering, frightened but laughing.

— *"Them backra up there measuring like they measuring to dig graves."*

The loudmouth, dirty-clothes white men gone; but one morning, three other white men in khaki shorts and bush jackets (is like they wearing a uniform) come bouncing up the Hill in a jeep, and every day for a whole week they walking around measuring, looking through something on a tripod, writing in notebooks.

—*"Them idlers en got nothing to do with theyself but siddown bout the place and make mischief?"*

Young fellas down by Thorne rumshop in the middle of the day, sissing at girls when they pass by or go in Mr. Thorne shop.

One of them begging Hammer-Head for a cigarette. "Gimme a fag, Hammer." That is a new practice; they en working nowhere to buy their own cigarettes but they want to look like the star boys they see in the movie pictures at the Royale on Saturdays.

"Look, go and look for work," Hammer saying, en even slowing down, with his carpenter toolbox in his hand and his hammer hooked in his dungaree pants.

—*"This going be a hard crop. You hear Drakes Plantation bringing in people from the small islands to cut canes this year?"*

When Inez pass and see Miss Slocombe boy, Victor, liming under the streetlight with his friends, she ask him if he going help her with the crop this year. "Bring some of your friends too," she say.

Victor flick the ash off his cigarette. "That is slave work, Miss Inez," he say.

His friends snickering.

Inez walk away feeling as if she lost a member of her family. From when he was a little boy going to school, Victor accustom to coming every year and helping load the canes on the lorry to go to the sugar factory. Last couple years, after his voice change and he began to fill out, he cutting canes with Boysie and Cephus. Now he telling her to her face that he en cutting no more canes.

"It is all because of Roachford and the PLP," Boysie telling Inez that night when they in bed and Inez complaining. "Running around in the elections telling people 'Not another cane blade. Massa days done.' That was irresponsible talk."

Inez fighting to keep her mouth shut. She want encouragement, sympathy, "It's going to be all right, Nez." Instead, all Boysie giving her is political talk.

She turn on her side with her back to Boysie.

Boysie talking about when the masses rise up and the People's Revolutionary Party in power, things going to be different.

Inez breathing deep and even.

Boysie rest his hand on her back. "You sleeping, Nez?"

No answer.

—*"You notice Cephus? Girl, what wrong with that boy, nuh?"*

Cephus imagining the fellas still talking his name behind his back. He think that everybody knows that he talk on Boysie down at the police station; so he stop going down by the shop.

The only time he went in the shop for a long time is the night they move Leroy and Patsy off the Hill.

All Cephus doing is working, coming home, and playing with the baby, bouncing it up and down on his knees.

Doreen between two minds. She like to see him playing with the baby—some men you can't even get to *hold* their babies much less play with them. But Cephus en the kind of man to be drawing up in a house all the time. And to make it worse, he talking to himself.

Boysie en pull him up about squealing on him to the police; en ask him why he do it. Nothing. It is like Boysie wasn't surprised. And that really hurting Cephus: that Boysie en expect no better from him. Although it really wasn't squealing—it was common knowledge that Boysie practically accused Roachford of having something to do with the Gittens girl's death—he can't look Boysie in his face. He shame to lime with the fellas.

So I get in the habit of dropping by to keep him company.

The last time I show up, it was a Sunday afternoon. Nearly everybody either at church or down at the beach.

Cephus sitting in the yard with the baby on his lap. Kwame standing up alongside him looking from Cephus to the space in front him.

That is when Doreen loss her patience at Cephus talking to himself.

"Cephus," she holler from the kitchen door, "you talking to yourself again?"

Cephus jump. Nearly drop the baby. Kwame standing up longside Cephus, looking from me to Cephus and back again.

"He en talking to heself, Aunt Reen," Kwame say. "He talking to the old man."

"Kwame, go outside and play." She turn back to Cephus. "See that?" she say. "See what you doing to little Kwame?"

But her voice en sound so certain, because she remembering what the obeah woman tell Inez. Kwame got the gift.

Kwame leave the yard, dragging his feet in the dirt and pouting his face.

"Reen," Cephus say.

"What now?"

"H-how b-bout w-we g getting m-m-married?"

Doreen can't believe her ears.

I can't neither. Especially after I just that minute finish telling him to hold off. He only doing it because he feel that he alone in the world. But he en listen to me.

Couple days later, Doreen waving her hand up in Inez face. A thin gold band on her ring finger.

Inez eyes open wide. "What that?"

But Doreen only smiling.

— *"So Cephus and Doreen married."*

— *"You lie."*

— *"Yes, soul. Brother Joseph married them. Pon the sly."*

— *"It had to be pon the sly. You see the baby? How big it is? That child en look a thing like Cephus."*

— *"What you saying? That Cephus get a jacket?"*

— *"What happen to you? You born big? You can't see that baby is the image of Boysie?"*

— *"Girl, what you saying?"*

— *"A little bird tell me they see Boysie and Doreen coming out the cane piece one time, with Doreen clothes all rumfle up."*

And every time Inez look at Kojo she seeing a resemblance to Boysie. The baby got Boysie round face, and its little bat ears got it looking just like a picture she got of Boysie when Boysie was a little boy.

What puzzling her is, she en vex with Doreen anymore. It is *Boysie* she feel like killing every time she look at the child.

She can't keep this inside much longer, even if it mean she and Boysie breaking up.

"That is you child, ent it," she say one day when she and Boysie at the table eating.

Boysie spooning the food through the opening in his beard. "What child?"

Inez put down her spoon. "How long you know me, Boysie?"

Boysie look up at her with the spoon in midair in front his mouth.

"You *know* I en no bride," Inez continue. "You *know* if you tell me *one* lie this forenoon I going pack up my things and take Kwame with me and leff you like *that*." She brushing her palms together, like she brushing off dust.

Boysie only staring at her.

"So I going ask you again. That is you pickney Doreen got?"

Boysie drop his eyes. "Yes." And he slurping his soup and staring at the food like it is the only thing in the world.

Inez turn and walk right out of the house, down to the beach, and sit on the jetty watching the sun sink below the horizon like a red ball of fire.

The raw smell of the fish market mixing with the scent of the sea. Seagulls dipping and wheeling. Waves lapping against the planks of the jetty.

On one hand, she feel like a weight drop off her shoulders now that Boysie admit the child is his. Suspicion was like a cancer in her craw.

But things never going be the same between she and Boysie. Every time she see Kojo, every time she see Doreen, it will remind her that Boysie and Doreen were two-timing her.

Something pounding in Inez head and she feeling a hatred for Boysie stronger than anything she ever feel for anybody. If she had a knife in her hand she woulda stab him right there. She can feel a pulse ticking in her neck.

Darkness creep up on Inez on the jetty. All of a sudden she realize that the sea and the sky is the same darkness. The lights of a ship burning out in the bay.

Inez get up and start walking back along the beach.

When she get home, Boysie in the verandah.

"How you could do that?" she say.

Silence is a heavy presence in the verandah. It is like all noise sucked away and leave a vacuum around Boysie and Inez.

"Everything done between me and she, Nez."

"I know. That en what I ask you."

But something in the way Boysie answer tug at something

inside her—perhaps the way his voice come out softer than she ever hear him talk before; perhaps the way his eyes can't stay on hers for the first time since they know one another.

But at the same time she telling herself, No. He can't do this to me and get off.

The pigs grunting in the pen; the turkeys gobbling; Cephus voice coming from inside his house next door.

"You en going tell Cephus, nuh?" Boysie voice rumbling low.

Inez look at him like he mad. "Cephus is my brother," she say. And just then, it is like a gear slip into place in her head and she hear herself saying something she never expect she would say. "And Doreen is my friend. All these years Cephus trying to get a boy-child, now he got one." She pause to catch her breath. "But let me tell you this," she continue. "If I catch you *looking* at *any* woman too hard, you dead. Put that in your pipe and smoke it."

And Boysie looking at Inez. In a way, he glad it out in the open. They can deal with it and try to patch up things, although he know it going be a long time before they can act normal with one another. Every time Inez see the baby, the whole thing going come up again. But it could be worse. She coulda make a fuss and walk out; she coulda wait till he sleeping and scald him. But he looking at her, and he know she en going do nothing so.

He always respect Inez. From when they was growing up together, he always like the way she carry herself. But he looking at her now with new respect and realizing how lucky he is.

For a few days after that day, Doreen noticing how Inez en smiling with her like before. Sometimes Inez might start talking and laughing as usual, then catch herself sudden. And the smile would slide off her face.

Several times, Doreen come close to telling Inez about she and Boysie and how it done now. But she always bite it back at the last minute.

—*"Me and Egbert going down by the Brethren tonight."*

—*"Them heathens? What you going mix up yourself with them for? You better don't let Pastor Wright find out."*

—*"Pastor Wright en my father. My father was a Brethren, God rest he in he grave. And I hear they getting back powerful again."*

The Brethren meeting three times a week now.

Regular meeting is still on Saturday nights. But they meeting on a Tuesday nights too—for security practice. Brother Joseph teaching the men stick licking. All you can hear down in the gully is *Paks! Paks!* as the sticks knocking against one another.

Boysie really getting into the stick licking thing; he *like* learning stick.

Thursday night is what they call Reasoning Night. That is when everybody sit down and they talk about whatsoever on their mind.

All of these are ideas that Cephus came up with when he first started assisting Brother Joseph. But Cephus scarcely going to meetings since the night Brother Joseph talk with the duppies. Every time he enter the clearing he remembering that night.

Estelle smallest boy Donald keeping watch up in the big evergreen tree near the gully on meeting nights.

Is about fifty people turning up for meeting on Saturday nights. Not as much as years ago, before the police raid them and shut them down, but Brother Joseph feeling good looking out over the crowd, seeing the flambeau flickering and smoking, watching the shadows dancing.

Kwame learning to play the drums, and it does bless my heart to see him sitting down there with the big fellas, with his little hands moving and a frown on his face, taking the music real serious.

Inez picking back up and looking good again after she had the talk with Boysie about Doreen baby.

Boysie heart nearly bursting when he look at her, he so proud. She look *regal*—that is Boysie word: "regal," with her white head tie and white robe. Course, Inez robe en just a robe. Trust Inez to do something extra. Inez robe is one long piece of white cloth that she wrap around her body and fling over shoulder, with the end trailing down to where her behind begin.

So the year coming to an end.

A new, wide tar road replace the old narrow dirt road running from the main road through the village, continuing up the hill to where bulldozers leveling the same earth that they were digging up not too long ago.

Masons building a concrete foundation on the spot where Leroy house used to be; same thing with the other bald spots that used to be places where people lived.

The rainy season getting near. It is nearly three years from the day the missionary first come, and all hell going soon break loose.

The missionary going about his business, en realizing that he going soon find out whether there is a heaven or a hell.

I EN WENT AROUND BY THE CHURCH since Pastor Wright put Lionel and his drum out of the church. And the very Sunday I decide to drop in and see what going on is the very Sunday Miss Scantlebury drop dead. Up to this day Miss Scantlebury don't think that is a coincidence. She think I had something to do with her dropping dead in church. And she wouldn't believe me when I tell her no.

The preacher voice droning on; women fanning and wiping their bosoms with their kerchiefs; old Mr. Oxley sitting upright in his suit and running his finger under his collar to loosen it up; children dropping asleep with their eyes shut and their mouths open and their head nearly breaking off every time it snap back or forward.

I notice beads of sweat pouring down off Sister Scantlebury face. What kinda idiot would keep service in the middle of the day, in the hot, broiling sun? Only a backra.

A fly settle on Miss Scantlebury face. Her face twitching, but she en knocking it off.

Sister Scantlebury en even feeling the fly. She got bad feels. Water springing up in her mouth; she feel like puking; her belly feel funny, like she want to go to the toilet; she feeling giddy; she seeing the preacher like he at a distance, and she en know a word he saying cause his mouth only moving and sounds coming out, but they en sound like words, they sound like if the preacher gargling his throat and she want to tell the young girl sitting next to her that she got bad feels and she feeling cold, like it is the middle of the night and not big, broad daylight; but she en want to disturb the sermon, cause the bad feels soon going bate down; but all of a sudden a pain hitting her in her chest and she can't breathe and she got this buzzing in her ears and everything becoming blurred and darkening and she feel herself falling forward and she can't even stop herself cause she en got no feelings in her body; she can't move her hands; she feel like she en got no legs; her head smack against the pew in front of her and this roaring sound let loose in her head like a heavy rain just done fall and her head is a giant gutter and water rushing through it; then before she black out altogether, she hearing the young girl voice bawling "Oh Jesus!" and it flick cross her mind real fast that: *Funny. I en think a thing bout Jesus all the time this happening.* Then, silence. Calm. And she floating and looking down at sheself crumple down on the floor. She feeling happy, free, like how she used to feel as a little girl when she get vacation from school, a feeling like she want to skip and jump and sing to the top of her voice. But this feeling is even better than that.

And I watching her and feeling good for her. Cause she happy. She en like some people that does dead and don't want to be dead, wanting to go back. And some of them going back and making people miserable, frightening people. But Miss Scantlebury en like that.

She look round and see me, and she en surprise, only vex.

"It is you, ent it?"

I puzzled. "That do what?"

"What you mean, 'That do what?' That come to get me."

"No. What make you think that?"

But she ignore me, and the two of we turn back to watching what going on in the church.

The whole place in a uproar. Big cadooment. People getting up from where they sitting and coming over to stare down at Sister Scantlebury body; somebody sniffling; a church brother kneeling down next to Miss Scantlebury and putting her Bible under her head to prop it up; the young sister that was sitting next to Miss Scantlebury standing up and one of the brothers got his arm around her saying, "Take it easy, sister. Take it easy." But all the sister doing is holding her hands to her mouth and staring down at Sister Scantlebury body and saying, "Just so. She fall right down, just so."

Sybil taking off Sister Scantlebury hat, raising her head and fanning her face. She look back and see the brother holding the young girl. The brother hand slide off the young girl shoulders.

Sybil feeling Sister Scantlebury wrist for a pulse. But Sister Scantlebury eyes staring open; her mouth form in a 'O', and her chest en moving.

Sybil looking up over her shoulder at the brother that had his hand around the young girl. "Hand me my pocketbook," she saying.

He hand her the pocketbook. Sybil open it and take out a little mirror and put it in front Sister Scantlebury nose and mouth.

She look up at the people standing round gawking down in her face. "She gone," Sybil say.

And Miss Scantlebury looking at all this commotion and shaking her head and saying, "There's a thing, nuh. There's a thing." Then she turn to me. "I didn't know Sybil and Brother Brathwaite was friendly." And she nod her head at the brother that had his hand around the young girl.

All this time, the pastor *now* getting down off the platform and walking toward the commotion.

His wife up on the platform standing on tiptoes and bobbing from side to side, trying to see what's going on.

And Sister Scantlebury floating above everybody and all she thinking is that she got to get in touch with her son, Darcy, in Away. She had a feeling that this was going happen. A mind tell her last week to get Inez write a letter to Darcy for her and tell him she want him come home; she en getting no younger. But it slip right out of her mind. Now look what happen.

She want Darcy to come back home and take over the property. She en want her family up in the country to get it; they never even used to come to look for her to see how she doing. And she en want the government taking it over.

And just like that, she take off. I follow her to see what going happen.

Darcy lying down in his apartment in Away, naked, sweating, listening to the street noises coming through his bedroom window. The sound of running water coming from the bathroom. Gloria taking a shower.

Six stories down, the fire hydrant open and children out on the street playing in the water and shouting; car horns honking; stereos blaring; people leaning through their windows and talking. And Darcy fuming. Big, bright Sunday and these people en know how to keep quiet. No respect for the Lord's day, he thinking. But then he realize he en know when last *he* see the inside of a church—not since he come over here to do farm work and decide not to go back. So who is *he* to talk?

All of a sudden, he feeling like somebody else in the room, but when he raise up on his elbows and look round, nobody en there, and there en no place where nobody can hide (the bedroom so small) except in the closet. But he and Gloria was here all day, so he know nobody en in the closet.

He doze off. He dreaming how he back home, over at one of the neighbors. And his mother coming in the neighbor yard and just looking at him and smiling.

That night at church, Pastor Wright announce, "Our sister's funeral will be held on Tuesday. Four o' clock. The casket will be open for viewing. . . ."

Everybody looking at one another. Tuesday? Four o' clock? But what about Sister Scantlebury family? She got family up in the country: a sister, two brothers. What about them? They doubt Pastor Wright know Sister Scantlebury family. He arranging the funeral himself? What is the hurry?

I is the last person that would defend the missionary. But fair is fair. That is the kind of fella he is. His *wife* ask him the same kind of questions when he come back from the undertaker that afternoon. *"What* are you *doing,* Bill?"

He shrug. *"Some*body has to do it."

"But what about her kin, Bill?"

"What kin?"

"Her *family,* Bill. Did you think of that? Did you? Huh?" And she sigh and flounce off.

Now, Brother Oxley stand up. He and Miss Scantlebury was friendly for years, after Miss Scantlebury man fall in a toilet pit and dead.

"Excuse me, Pastor," Brother Oxley saying. "But, anybody notify Sister Scantlebury family? And what about Darcy?"

"Family? Uh . . ." Pastor Wright look at his wife. "Ah . . . no. Ah, tell the truth, we didn't know that she *had* any family. Ah, she was living alone and, uh, we sort of *assumed,* uh . . ."

His wife roll her eyes. *We?* she thinking. Now it's *we?*

"Well, wha bout Darcy?"

"Uh, Darcy . . . ?"

"Her son in Away. You don't think he would want to come home for the funeral?" Old Brother Oxley standing up in the church in his black suit and his bushy gray hair high on his head and covering his ears.

"Well," Pastor Wright playing with his shirt collar. "That would take time."

"Time? Sister Scantlebury en going nowhere." Brother Oxley en raising his voice.

A little boy snigger.

"Well," Pastor Wright got this shamey-shamey look on his face. "Everything's already arranged. The undertaker . . ."

Somebody voice blurt out, "Already?!"

"Sealey? Sealey is a good undertaker. He know how we does do things," Brother Oxley saying. "She en going spoil."

"Spoil?" Pastor Wright eyes bug open behind his glasses in sheer shock at the image of rotting meat that flash across his mind.

Sandra Wright clap her hand to her mouth. People en know if what Brother Oxley say make her want to vomit or laugh.

"Ah, can we go on with the service, Brother Oxley?" the pastor say. "We can discuss this later."

Brother Oxley sit down, with his hand in his lap, upright, with not an expression on his face.

Later that night, Darcy having the same dream: he in a neighbor yard pitching marbles by himself; his mother standing up over him, but now she telling him, "Time to go home, Darcy."

When he wake up in the morning, he remembering the dream plain, plain. And he don't remember dreams for nothing, not if it was to save his life.

He and Gloria in the bathroom getting ready for work. Gloria sitting down on the toilet seat like he en there; he shaving in front of the bathroom mirror.

"My mother dream me last night," he say.

Gloria tear off piece of toilet paper. "Dream you?" She cock a glance at him. "You still believe in that foolishness?"

Darcy glance down at the top of her head, her wavy hair that the hairdresser does charge her a fortune to keep that way, and her light brown skin. It is times like this that does remind Darcy that if he was back home, Gloria wouldn't even be speaking to him, much less living with him. Next thing she going start doing now is calling him country buck. He en say nothing more about the dream.

Tuesday afternoon come, and women who en going to the funeral standing outside the church watching to see who come to the funeral and what they wearing.

Inside the church, Miss Scantlebury looking at her face in the coffin and saying over and over, "That en look *nothing* like me. That en look a *thing* like me."

And it is true. Miss Scantlebury never press her hair a day in her life. But now, the thick rope plaits that she used to wear wrapped around her head like a turban gone, and her hair press and curl. And her cheeks stuffed out, turning her from narrow-faced, high-cheekbone Miss Scantlebury into some fat-face stranger that look like she just come from the dentist.

The missionary making this speech about how Sister Scantlebury was a devoted Christian woman, and how she gone to be in the arms of Jesus and Miss Scantlebury sucking her teeth every five minutes and going, "Huh," because, to tell the truth, she en see no Jesus, she en see no Peter, and she *certainly* en see no "pearly gates." Pastor Wright and all them preachers is blasted liars.

"What a blasted liar," she saying to me.

"Not only that," Boysie father say.

Miss Scantlebury jump. Boysie father just appear in front her. She new to this. She got to get accustom.

"He is a kiss-me-ass thief too." Boysie father pants leg roll up to his calves. His cutlass in his hand. And he explaining that the pastor intend to sell her land to the company that building the resort on the Hill.

Just then, the little boy and girl that got drowned at the beach enter the church and run right down the aisle, screaming and laughing, naked and glistening with water, like if they just come from the sea.

The boy hop up on Miss Scantlebury coffin, sit down with his legs dangling, and start bouncing up and down, grinning.

"Get down from there, Peter," his sister say.

And Miss Scantlebury going, "Hey you! Stop that!"

"You listening to me?" Boysie father saying. And he going on to tell her about the resort: about the government having a forty-nine percent share in it, plus the politicians got their own money in it too, and if it turn out good, they plan to move everybody off the Hill and expand with a golf course and a marina on the river, and Lord knows what else.

Miss Wiggins nephew sitting on the floor in front of the altar, holding his head under his armpit as usual. He see the boy still bouncing on Miss Scantlebury coffin and he pelt his head straight at the boy. The boy duck, and the head come right back to Miss Wiggins nephew like a boomerang.

When the funeral get to the cemetery and they start lowering the coffin in the grave, the coffin wouldn't go down. It stick halfway.

The men hauling the straps and pulling up the coffin and trying to lower it again.

Same thing happen: it wouldn't go down.

Inez, Boysie, and the rest of the Brethren people standing little ways back under a tree, watching, paying their respects to Miss Scantlebury.

"That is a sign," they whispering.

Inez shaking her head when she see how much trouble they having with the coffin.

Miss Scantlebury hopping up and down (funny how

spritely people does get when they dead), laughing to see the missionary wiping his face and frowning down into the grave. The men puffing and blowing, struggling with the coffin.

"Look, give the fellas a break," I tell her. *They* en do you nothing."

But she let them fight with the coffin a little longer before she give in and let it drop.

"Wah!" one of the fellas holler out. And he scrambling back, kicking dirt down in the grave, catching to hold onto the fella next to him to prevent himself from falling in behind the coffin when it drop so sudden.

The missionary sigh; his shoulders relax. And he open his Bible, like he en even notice the fella predicament.

But all the people around the grave shuffling and whispering to one another. Everybody agreeing that it is a bad sign.

That night, Miss Scantlebury dream Darcy again.

He is a little boy pitching marbles, but now his mother hollering for him to come inside. "Darcy! Darcy!"

"Yes, Ma!" Darcy bawl out, and wake up sweating.

Gloria vex because he wake her up. "I've got to get up early for work, Darcy," she mumbling. "What're you doing?"

"I had that dream again," he say. He stumble to the kitchen to get a glass of water.

Next day he write a letter and post it off.

Days stretch into weeks. Darcy letter come from Away, but it still in the post office in town.

Darcy got a strong feeling something wrong, but he en got the money for the airfare. Besides, he en got his green card; so if he go home he might not be able to come back.

"Your mother is all right," Gloria saying. "If something was wrong, we would've heard."

Every time people pass Miss Scantlebury shut-up house,

they calling to mind Miss Scantlebury, how she used to smile and go about her way quiet, not bothering nobody, a real nice woman. Then all of a sudden, *bam!* She en there.

Then one Sunday morning Pastor Wright get up in church and make a announcement.

"Brothers and sisters, y'all've done yourself real proud for our dear departed sister. Real proud. We raised nine dollars to help with the funeral expenses. And that is real good, seeing as none of us is rich," and he smile. "Not even your humble servant."

People smiling and fanning.

"But I'm afraid nine dollars will not cover the expenses." He pull a glass of water from somewhere under the pulpit and sip. He put back the glass. "Fortunately," he continue, "Our dear sister made me executor before she passed."

He reach in his inside breast pocket and pull out a piece of paper. "This," he shake open the piece of paper, "is a letter our dear sister wrote before she died . . ."

Big mistake. People glancing at one another. Everybody know Sister Scantlebury couldn't read and write.

". . . leaving me as sole executor of her estate, in case something happens. . . ."

Now, why Sister Scantlebury would leave the lovely piece of property she got, with nuff ground and all kinda fruit trees, why she would leave that with the pastor when she got a son in Away? Why she wouldn't leave it to her family? But nobody en saying nothing. Not even Brother Oxley this time; they listening, and thinking: you would think with all the collection on Sundays, the fowls, eggs, potatoes, yams, greens, even a calf that the congregation giving him, the pastor would be satisfied. But no. He want to thief Miss Scantlebury land.

"My brothers and sisters in the Lord, I prayed long and hard, begging the Lord's guidance. Many's the night I fell on my knees saying, 'Lord, show me the way.' Many's the night I tossed and turned, hoping for a sign. And last night, praise

Jesus, it came. Came like the blinding light that struck Paul on the road to Damascus. William, he said. William, I hath need of the widow's mite."

Well, first thing, Miss Scantlebury wasn't no widow. She and Darcy father was living together, and he dead when Darcy wasn't no more than about five. But they wasn't married. So the pastor got *that* wrong.

Bright and early next morning, Brother Oxley walking down the hill from his house. The dew still wet; some people en even wash their face yet; Estelle littlest boy carrying out the sheep to the pasture.

From up on the Hill you can see the minibus coming along the main road down the valley, heading for the country; you can see Brother Oxley waving his hand to stop it and getting in.

All day the whole village talking about how the missionary take over Miss Scantlebury property.

—*"You hear the news, nuh? I always say that man wasn't no good."*

When Brother Oxley come back round midday, he head straight for Brother Joseph shoemaker shop.

That night, the Brethren sitting around in a circle down in the gully. Kwame up in the tree with Estelle biggest boy, Donald, watching out for if anybody coming. This is a big people meeting. This is the first time that Kwame get to be watchman.

Kwame try talking to Donald, but all Donald saying is, "Keep quiet, nuh. If anybody coming they going hear you." When Kwame realize that Donald serious, he rest his back against the tree trunk and looking down the hill. Donald taking this thing too serious, far as Kwame concerned. Donald must be think he's some big-time watchman or something.

Lamps burning in houses in the village, looking like fireflies in the distance. A ship anchor down in the harbor, with lights string across it like the Christmas tree Kwame see in town last year. His father say them is tourist boats that does be light up like that. It look close, but the last time he went down by the harbor with his father, they walk. And it take a long time to get there.

The voices coming up from down in the gully. Every now and again, Kwame can hear somebody voice raising above the rest, but he can't make out what they saying. Kwame know is something to do with the missionary. When Brother Joseph was at his father house, Kwame hear his father say, "We got to do something about this." And Kwame coulda tell by the way his voice sound that the 'this' his father and Brother Joseph was talking bout is the missionary.

Light shining in the missionary house, and as Kwame watching, a light in a little window flick off.

For a long time, after what happen a couple days later, when Kwame remember the missionary, his mind always come back to that night sitting down there in the tree with Donald, with a soft wind blowing through the branches, and watching that little light go off in the missionary house.

And that night Miss Scantlebury dream Darcy for the last time. He dream that his mother standing up in the middle of the neighbor yard and telling him, "If you don't come in this minute I going roast your behind!"

Next morning, Gloria call in sick and put on her clothes, telling Darcy she going to the bank and come back.

It is Darcy day off. Darcy in the bed relaxing when Gloria open the apartment door, walk in the bedroom, and toss a airplane ticket on the bed. A return ticket home. To this day, Darcy and Gloria married, with two children, and whenever

Darcy ask her why she give him the plane ticket that day, all she ever says is, "I won't tell you my story; you won't have to tell me yours."

That morning, all she say is, "Go home and see what's the matter."

The next day, Darcy in the taxi going to the airport with his head feeling like it going bust. Last night when he was sleeping, somebody fill him in on everything that going on back home.

Something about the way Gloria hug him before leaving for work making water well up at the back of his eyes.

Women. One minute she acting like he is a barefoot cane-cutter and she is a bank clerk; next minute she giving him money to go home and see his mother, and she hugging him before she left the apartment and her voice by his ear whispering, "Take care."

He hope he get back in the country; he hope he see her again.

AND WHILE DARCY ON THE AIRPLANE flying toward home, Miss Scantlebury family getting off the minibus that bring them from up in the country and walking up to the Hill to pick a bone with the missionary.

Bright and early in the morning. Women and children bringing water from the pipe; women in their yards washing clothes. A few people standing up in front Mr. Thorne shop, talking.

And these four country people walking up the main gap, now a new tar road, heading for Roachford bungalow. Two men and two women; the two men in front.

When they reach in front Roachford bungalow, the older man with gray hair showing under his brown felt hat open the palisade door and they walk up in the gallery and rap hard on the front door.

Torrectly, the pastor come to the door wearing a v-neck T-shirt. His suspenders dangling. "Yes?"

"We come to see bout Evelyn things." The older man talking.

"Who?"

"Miss Scantlebury," the younger man say. Look like the older fella son. The young fella bareheaded, with his hair cut low. He got a nice round head, a broad face, a wide nose, and lips that look like they sculpted. He is the image of the old man, without the old man moustache.

The older woman with the big straw hat push to the front and rest her hand on the older man shoulder. She got the same broad face as the two men. "We sister. Evelyn. We hear you say she left the property for you."

The pastor looking from one to the next.

"Hm," short and sharp like a hiccup, coming from the young woman. Her face look sour, like she really vex. But then again, it look like she got one of these faces that does *always* look sour.

Her sharp features en take after none of the other three people. So the people that standing up there in the gap watching figuring that she is the young man wife or something.

The missionary step back and hold open the door. "Come in," he say. "Come right in."

The four people in the gallery look at one another. The older man nod his head; they step in the door, the older man first.

Not too long after, the younger man fling open the front door, stamp down the front steps and stand up in the middle of the road, His noseholes flaring. "Where the will, uh? That is what I want to know. Where the will? *Everybody* know Aunt Evelyn couldn't read and write. Blasted thiefing backra bitch."

The other three of Miss Scantlebury family come out together, slower. The two women standing next to the young man. The older woman looking up at him and saying, "Don't get yourself in trouble. Cool yourself."

And his father saying. "Listen to your aunt. She right. Take it easy."

And the young man flare up. "If unna didn't hold me . . . !"

His wife hook his arm in hers. "Come," she say.

And they start off back down the gap.

Later, Sybil tell everybody that when she coming through her gate door, they was passing in front her house and she hear the young man say, "I going kill he. So help me I going kill he." But nobody else en hear that.

People going about their business as usual.

Twelve o' clock. A sharp shower come down sudden, driving everybody inside. Just as sudden as it start, it stop. Steam rising from the tar road; the earth smell rich. The sky clean.

The schoolchildren get let out for lunch and their voices filling the air as some of them walking home; some playing in the schoolyard.

Afternoon. The sun scorching; a little breeze ruffling the banana leaves in Miss Scantlebury ground; a dog stopping in the middle of the road, scratching itself and then going in the cool next to Miss Scantlebury shut-up house and lying down; the place quiet except for the tap-tapping of a hammer on leather in Brother Joseph shoemaker shop.

Nobody en notice the taxi that stop down on the main road where the new tar road leading up to the Hill branch off. Nobody en notice the fella that get out of the taxi, sling his long-strap shoulder bag over his shoulder and look with a puzzled expression at the chain that stretched across the entrance of the road from one steel post to the next.

"The company put that there," I say.

Darcy jump, and start looking around to see where I come from all of a sudden.

"Huh-who you?" Darcy coulda swear the road was just empty. Now this old man in khaki clothes and a old felt hat with sweat stains standing in front him. "Where you come from?" Darcy words tumbling out of his mouth.

"Never mind." I nod at the chain and padlock. "The company that building the resort put that there. Your mother en tell you about that?"

Darcy start stumbling toward a boulder at the side of the road. "I want to siddown." He gasping like a tired, thirsty man.

"Roachford bungalow," I say. "That is where the preacher live. Talk to him."

And I walk away. Because I can hear Sandra Wright moaning in the wind.

Down by the river, the preacher wife on her knees with her face down in the grass; her elbows on the damp ground; her dress bunched around her waist. And Lionel grunting, sweating, digging his fingers into her shoulders.

One hand grab her hair, like reins, and yank. Sandra Wright head snap back; her eyes closed; her teeth bared, and a cry straining from her throat.

But Lionel feeling her become more slippery. He pounding like a piston. Sweat dripping into his eyes, tasting salty on his lips. Power. Power flowing through every muscle in his body, swelling his lungs, making him strong.

Lionel at it again.

"And you turning into a peeping Tom. What you doing?" Boysie father voice is like a bucket of cold water dousing me.

Boysie father up in a tree overhead, crouched in a fork.

"Same thing *you* doing!" I say. Boysie father does get on my nerves sometimes. "Mind your blasted business and leave me alone," I tell him, and head for the village.

Hammer-Head working on Mr. Thorne shop, repairing the roof. His hammer banging.

Nobody else en stirring. Most people that en out working either in their backyards settling into their hammocks, or inside their houses out of the heat.

I head back down by the river. Dolphus gone from the tree. Sandra Wright stretched out chest down on the grass as though it weren't damp from the shower not long ago. Her face resting on her arms, eyes closed. Lionel en no where around.

Nothing to see here.

The schoolyard empty. School start back after lunch.

The children sing-song voices coming from the schoolhouse when the preacher white cat streak out from the preacher yard with its tail up in the air, meowing, bound up in the soursop tree next to the preacher house, and stretch out on a branch, looking down in the yard with its eyes wide open and its tail flicking like a white snake behind it. Then it jump up, let go another meow, rub its paw on its face, and scamper back down the tree trunk. Big foolish cat that the preacher and his wife bring from Away with them. En got enough sense to know that the soursop tree riddle with black ants.

Hammocks swinging under trees; people dozing. A light breeze rustling the leaves in Boysie coconut tree.

And this loud bawling break out. Sound like it coming from the missionary yard.

"Oh my God!" A woman voice, and you can't miss the foreign accent. And a big cow-bawling start up. "Waaaugh!"

Doors opening and people rushing out and running down by the missionary house. Doreen left the baby sleeping on the floor in the bedroom and shut the bedroom door so that he can't come out if he wake up. Inez grab on to Kwame hand and the two of them running pelting down the gap, Kwame two little feet moving like windmills, trying to keep up.

Estelle down at Mr. Thorne shop dispatching when she hear the cadooment. People running past the shop and she weighing flour but en really paying attention to what she doing. She hearing the scale hitting, *Bup!* and she know she pour out too much, but she tossing the scoop back in the flour barrel and wrapping up the package and taking the money. She turning to Mr. Thorne sitting down at the desk, with a question in her eyes.

"Yes. G'long and see what happening." Mr. Thorne want to know what going on as bad as she, but he can't leave the shop. She en wait for another word; she fling her apron oneside and take off.

Hammer-Head hammer stop pounding on the roof.

Before you can say Boo! look like the whole village standing up at the gate door pushing and peeping over one another shoulder, looking in the missionary yard.

Mistress Wright standing up by the paling, staring down at the pastor. He sitting down with his back resting against the paling; his legs stretch out straight in front him, his body sagging like a bag of flour. You can't tell what color shirt he wearing—it soak in blood.

The skin on his left arm peel down like a banana skin and the bone showing. The only part the person en chop is his face. His right hand resting on a Bible on top a tree stump; the fingers chop off clean, and the cutlass blade cut the Bible in half and sink down in the tree stump, so that the hand on one half of the Bible and the cut off fingers on the other half, like whoever do it make one last swing with the cutlass, *Whomp!* hard enough for the cutlass to stay in the wood. The missionary eyes wide open and fasten onto the cutlass blade. And the piece of cloth that stuffed in his mouth hanging down to his chin.

And the place smell like a butcher shop. Flies buzzing around the exposed meat.

When Doreen see it, she nearly faint. She had to go and prop up against the electric pole in front the pastor house and try to catch herself.

Cedric Brown bore through the crowd. "Lemme pass. Lemme pass," he saying.

"Hey! What you think you is?" a man voice bawling. "A gorrilephant?"

"Let him through, bo. Let him through," A woman voice saying. "You en see the boy massa dead?"

And people laughing.

Cedric Brown in the yard helping Mistress Wright to sit down on the back step. One of the sisters that follow Cedric through the crowd step in the kitchen and come back out with a glass of water and hand the preacher wife. She gulp it down like she thirsty and hand back the glass. Her elbows on her knees; her head resting in her hands. "Oh my God," she saying. "Oh my God."

Cedric Brown standing up over her now, looking down, looking foolish as a ramgoat, en know what to do. Then he look round and say, "Anybody call for the police?"

A man voice come from the crowd at the gate. "They coming, suh."

A few laughs ripple through the crowd. But most of the faces in the crowd serious. A woman voice cutting in sharp. "Unna en got no respect for the dead?"

One of the little boys ran down at the guardhouse soon as he peeped through the paling and saw what happened. So the sergeant and the constable pushing their bicycles up the hill.

They lean up their bicycles against the house; the people open a space to let them through. The two policemen standing shoulder to shoulder, looking down at the dead white man.

The sergeant look over to the back steps where the preacher wife sitting down—Cedric Brown and the sister from the church standing up near her. He look back toward the gate where the people standing up. The ones in front plant solid, like somebody stretch a line in front them and they can't cross it. Heads in the back moving up and down and sideways, trying to see in the yard.

"All right. What unna looking at?" the constable say. He walking toward the crowd at the gate. "Move. Move and lemme shut this gate. En nothing for unna to see."

Nobody en moving.

"Unna hear what the constable say?" This is Bumpy Green,

the sergeant. He walking towards the crowd, slapping his club against his leg. His hat push back, exposing the front of his hair. Bandy-legged Bumpy Green. He get the nickname Bumpy from when he was about fifteen, because of all the bumps in his face.

The crowd backing off. Bumpy Green just like Big Joe, the sergeant that was there before: big and ignorant. Make you wonder where they does get these people from to put in the police force.

The people at the back of the crowd en moving; the ones at the front pushing back. Bumpy getting closer and the club smacking in the palm of his hand. People eyes full of panic when he get to the gate, because although the crowd bunched a little ways back from the gate, they know he liable to whacks one or two of them with the club, just to show who is boss.

But he just stare at them, then shut the gate door.

The crowd shuffling away. A couple people peeping through cracks in the paling. The road in front the missionary house full of people standing up talking.

"Wha you see?"

"I hear they cut off he head and slice open he belly. That is true?"

And the people that see in the yard swaggering and talking important.

"I never see nothing like that in all me born days." This is Mr. Holder, Doreen father. Couple people mouth drop open. Mr. Holder does scarcely pick his teeth to anybody. But it look like the sight of the missionary got him talking all over his face. "By Jove," he saying, "A bloody mess. I say. A bloody mess." He wagging his head from side to side and tapping his cane against his shoe.

"Wha happen, Mr. Holder?" a woman ask.

Mr. Holder look round, surprised that somebody asked him a question. He stare at the woman. "Some . . . *vagabond* chop up the missionary. It en a place they en chop. If he had his *tongue* out they would've chopped that too, by Jove." He shaking his head again. "And his hand . . ."

"Wha bout his hand?" This is Estelle, with her big gold earrings glistening in the sun and her head tie looking like it got all the colors of the rainbow in it. Estelle was at the back of the crowd, so she en see in the yard.

Mr. Holder just staring at her blank. So she ask him again, "Wha bout his hand?"

"Child," Sybil fat hand waving; the bangles jingling; her left hand in her kimbo; she like a giant over Estelle. "Them brutes, whoever they is, chop off the pastor fingers clean, clean. Pon top a Bible."

"A Bible?" Estelle eyes open wide.

"Them damn brutes," Sybil saying.

Mr. Holder looking round and he spot Doreen resting her shoulder against the electric pole in front the missionary house. "Reen!"

Doreen look round. Mr. Holder raise the walking stick, nearly jooking out a fella eye ("Hey, man. Watch that stick! You want to jook out my eye or what?") and waving for Doreen to come over.

Doreen press herself from off the pole and walk over slow.

"You all right?" Mr. Holder say. His face serious; his voice brusque, so you can't tell what he feeling.

"Yes, Da." Doreen got her arms wrap round her breasts; her shoulders hunched up.

"You see what happen in there?" Mr. Holder voice still gruff.

Doreen nod.

All around them, people talking.

Mr. Holder nod towards his house up on the hill with the two palm trees leaning in front. "Come. You want a cuppa tea?"

Doreen shrug; she staring down at the ground.

"Come." Mr. Holder hold her arm and start walking home. Doreen walking, still with her arms fold in front her; her shoulders droop; even her behind en jiggling perky like it accustom to; it just sort of rolling.

Sometimes I does wish I was still alive.

The people still standing up in the gap, in front the missionary house. Everybody got an opinion about who do it.

Lionel standing near the edge of the crowd, looking from face to face, en saying a word.

Down on the main road, a minibus stopping to pick up two passengers going in the direction of town.

The minibus driver looking in his rearview mirror to see who getting on. The three benches in the back of the bus empty. Dummy, the deaf and dumb fella that does make baskets and brooms and sell to the tourists in town, pushing his baskets inside the bus. The driver don't know the other fella, a short, stout looking man with a traveling bag sling over his shoulder.

The driver changing gears and watching the fella give the conductor a dollar bill and staring through the open back of the minibus at the receding tar road. The conductor got to tap him on his shoulder to give him his change. He look preoccupied, just like the fella they picked up going in the other direction, to the country. What it is that happen up the Hill? the driver wondering.

Back up on the Hill, Inez standing in front of the missionary house watching Doreen and her father getting smaller in the distance, walking up the hill.

Kwame holding on to Inez skirt. His heart beating fast; he looking up at the big people talking, everybody talking the same time. His Ma is the only one that quiet.

He can see the backra man sitting down in the yard soak away in blood. And the flies. And the fingers. And the gray-and-white eyeballs. He know he going be frighten tonight when he going sleep. He know he going see the backra man clear, clear in the dark; same way he see Miss Scantlebury coffin the night after the funeral and swear blind she was coming through the bedroom door and calling, "Kwaaaame, Kwaaaame."

"What a little liar," Miss Scantlebury saying now. "I didn't do nothing like that."

And I resting my hand on her shoulder and saying, "Take it easy. You know how children does imagine things."

Doreen and her father in the old house up on the hill. Mr. Holder en saying much. Doreen in the front room sitting in the rocking chair. Mr. Holder moving around in the kitchen. Even after he bring in the enamel cup of steaming cocoa, he moving a chair a couple inches, dusting off the mahogany center table, glancing at Doreen and asking, "You all right?" but he en waiting for her to answer; he going to the window and looking down the gap. Is like he can't stand one place.

And Doreen blowing on the cocoa to cool it, feeling the steam warming her face.

"Sit down, Da. Rest yourself," she say.

He sitting down in the chair by the window, looking outside with his face serious. "I never see anything like that in all me born days," he saying.

"Not even in the war?"

The old clock ticking loud. The voices reaching into the house from back down the hill.

"That was different," he say. His hands playing with one another in his lap; he sitting down with his back upright. "This young generation."

Long time Doreen en hear him talking soft like this, not biting off the words. It is like he surprise, like he looking at a miracle, something he can't understand.

"It could be somebody old," Doreen say. And she thinking about this for the first time. Up to now, she en stop to think about who do it.

"No." His voice firm; his forehead knit up in a frown. "Whoever do that is a strong, strapping somebody. You see how that cutlass chop that Bible and stick in the tree trunk? That take a lot of force."

When he say that, she seeing the whole thing again, and is like she can feel *her* fingers getting chop off. She wincing.

When she finish the cocoa, she stand up. "I got to go, Da. The baby might be wake up."

And Doreen walking back down the hill, seeing her father moving around in the old house by himself. And suddenly, for the first time she asking herself, Where Cephus? She can't remember seeing Cephus in the crowd down by Pastor Wright. Come to think of it, she can't remember seeing Boysie neither. That's funny. They wouldn't miss something like that.

But right then, Cephus down by the mouth of the river sitting on a boulder near the bank, trying to get things straight in his mind.

It look like just yesterday he was happy: working his own ground, living with Doreen, firing a drink with the fellas pon a evenings. What more could a man want?

But since the thing at the police station, he can't look Boysie in his eye; he feel the fellas talking about him behind his back, accusing him of telling on Boysie down at the police station; he married—he never thought he woulda get married, but it is only he, Doreen, and the baby now, so he figure, mise well get married.

And his father saying yesterday that the baby en look like a Cudgoe, and Cephus saying, "I-it strike back."

"Strike back?" his father saying. "Strike back how far?

Nobody in the Cudgoe family ever look like that." He pause and puff on his pipe and then say. "Look like Boysie pickney to me."

His mother looking on en saying a word.

And that is when he walk out of the house. His father never like Doreen. He always thinking the worse.

But now he and Doreen married, Doreen and he living good again. He didn't realize that Doreen was unhappy because they wasn't married. He thought she was satisfied.

"You thought she was satisfied?" I say. "Boy you got a lot to learn about women."

Cephus look up. "W-why you d-don't leave me lone, Grandpappy?" Cephus voice sound irritable.

Just then, Boysie voice say behind him, "What happening, mate?" and Boysie hand rest on his shoulder.

Cephus notice that Boysie hand wet; his clothes damp, like he just come from swimming.

COUPLE EVENINGS LATER, THE RAIN drizzling light, pattering on the tin roof on Cephus house. He look through the window at the dark clouds that rolling across the top of the hills, and at the dry, thirsty dirt yard.

After the mortuary van took away the pastor body, his wife packed a suitcase in the trunk of their big American car the same afternoon and drive off to a hotel in town.

Fat Sybil poking her head in the car window and asking, "Where you going Missis?"

Missis hands clench on the steering wheel till her knuckles white. Her lips is a red line with tiny puckers around them. She en answering.

Lionel watching her drive off, remembering the last time in the bushes, feeling as though a partnership break up.

But Sandra Wright eyes red and focused straight as she driving toward the main road, scattering chickens out of the way.

Now as Cephus listening to the rain drizzling on the rooftop and watching the dark clouds, it is about a week after the pastor get killed. The village back to normal.

All of a sudden, out of the clouds come five planes, thundering over the mountaintop and shitting dark blots that billowing into parachutes where there were only dark, drifting clouds before.

"D-doreen! C-come! L-l-look!" Cephus holler.

And Doreen rushing out of the bedroom with the baby against her shoulder.

That foreday morning when Cephus came out to milk the cows, he had looked down at the harbor as usual, and he had seen three big gray ships. Man-o'-wars. But Cephus noticed during the day that he didn't hear nobody talking about the schoolchildren going to visit the man-o'-wars. Strange. Because Mr. Hutson don't miss a chance to carry them to visit every warship that come in.

Now Cephus looking at the men drifting down and landing in the distance. The planes banking and heading back out to sea.

And for the first time in a long time, Cephus walk down to the rumshop, slow and jerk-waist as usual, after he done wash up and drink his cocoa.

Doreen step next door at Inez and Boysie, but Inez over by her parents asking them if they see the parachutes.

Talking stop when Cephus step in the shop door, but start right back when the fellas notice it is only Cephus. Cephus feeling uncomfortable, feeling that everybody ignoring him. But the fellas caught up in talking about the planes and parachutes.

Cephus lean against the counter next to Boysie. "Y-you see them?" he ask.

Boysie nod.

And Cephus feeling the uncomfortable feeling of meeting somebody and trying to make friends.

And that whole night, everybody in the shop got an opinion about who the planes belong to, who the men in the parachutes are, what they doing in the hills. But Boysie en joining in the talk.

He slip out of the shop, get his bicycle out of his yard and peddle off to the main road.

And as he riding to town, couple times he had to get into the ditch with his bicycle to prevent himself from getting knocked down by the police jeeps that zooming past him on the dark road.

When Boysie get on the outskirts of town, the only thing on the streets is the stray dogs that running behind his bicycle on every street he turn on to, barking.

Boysie lean his bicycle against the palisade in front the house where the Student live.

All along the street, windows closed as though people expect a storm. A neighbor dog barking in the yard next door.

Boysie step up on the verandah and knock on the front door of the Student house.

After a while he hear a shuffling behind the door. "Who is it?"

"Me. Comrade Blackman."

The door open and outline the Student in bvds and vest. "Come in."

And whole night the Student pacing back and forth in the drawing room, his shoulders hunched, jabbing the air to make his point, drawing on his cigarette, running a hand over his bushy hair, talking, talking, quoting this revolutionary and that, talking about "dialectics," "imperialist aggression," and "armed struggle."

Boysie sitting in the low sofa with his knees nearly up by his face, frowning, concentrating to understand what the Student saying, waiting to get in the question he really come to ask.

When the Student bend to flick his cigarette ashes into the ashtray on the glasstop center table, Boysie pounce on the silence.

"What we going do?" he ask.

The Student, bent over with the cigarette still hovering over the ashtray, cock his head at Boysie. "The masses aren't ready." And the tone in his voice is like if Boysie question is the stupidest question anybody could ask.

After that, Boysie lean back in the sofa, and the Student voice droning on through the night. Rain pattering on the galvanize roof, giving Boysie a strange feeling of security inside the room with the Student pacing, and with the wind whistling through the wooden jalousie windows, bringing in a little chill and the sound of tree leaves swishing out front.

Back up on the Hill, Inez tossing and turning all night long, getting up sometimes to look out the window to see if Boysie coming.

But it en till morning—the sun lightening up the sky—that Inez hear Boysie bicycle ticking outside and bump against the side of the house when Boysie lean it up.

"Where you been all night?" Inez en even wait till Boysie get in the house good. "You know I been worrying about you all night long? Where you been?"

But all Boysie saying as he untying his shoes is, "They invading us, Nez." His voice sound tired.

"What? Who?" Inez face bland with puzzlement.

"The planes. The parachutes. Roachford send for help from Away."

"Why?"

"Bostick was getting ready for a no-confidence vote. Some of Roachford men were going to cross the floor and join the opposition."

"But why they land up here?"

Boysie only shrug.

Inez fling off her hands, exasperated.

She whirl back to face Boysie. "How you know all this?"

Boysie shrug again.

"What we going do, Boysie?"

Boysie look up from untying his shoes. "Do? . . . What we can do against a whole army? Besides." A sarcastic sneer on his face. "The masses aren't ready."

Later, the sun beginning to peep over the mountain; the grass still wet with dew; the air got a slight chill to it, and explosions going off up on the mountainside, popping, cracking, rattling, booming explosions. And if you look good you can see people moving around up there.

The road in front Mr. Thorne shop jampacked with people. Everybody talking the same time, looking up toward the side of the mountain.

Somebody in the crowd say, "Who that?"

A little boy in the distance running from the direction of the mountain towards the crowd. When he reach the crowd in front Mr. Thorne shop, he panting and holding his sides.

"He live up the mountain," a woman say.

Boysie kneel in front him. "What happen?" he asking the boy.

"They hunting gorillas." The boy panting. "They think we is gorillas."

"What?" come from a couple people in the crowd.

"They ask my father, 'You's a gorilla? Where the rest of gorillas?'"

A woman hand the little boy a cup of water. He holding the cup in both hands and guzzling. When he finish he gasp, hand back the cup—"Thanks"—then say, "My father get vex, ask them 'I look like a gorilla to you?' and when he raise his cutlass to chase them out the yard they shoot him and I run through the canes and they run behind me but I get away."

"Gorillas?" Claude looking puzzled.

Boysie look up at Claude. "He mean guerrillas. G-u-e-r-r . . ."

Just then, the *beep . . . beep . . . beep* sound announcing the seven o' clock news coming from the radio in Mr. Thorne shop. People drifting toward the shop door. The crowd quiet. But the news en saying nothing about soldiers in the hills. Some foolishness about a man that chop up his neighbor cow with a cutlass because the cow trespass on his land and—the last item—the leader of the opposition "was shot while attempting to run through a police road block." Nothing about soldiers up in the hills.

The heavy explosions stop. But gunfire popping up on the mountainside.

Mr. Thorne wife take the little boy hand and take him in her house next door to the shop.

The crowd begin to disperse, but nobody en going to work.

A couple bottles of rum on the counter; the fellas drinking slow, watching the mountain.

Eight o' clock, no news. No more gunfire.

Mr. Thorne hop in his pickup and drive down to the post office to use the public telephone.

But a woman on the phone, and Mr. Thorne saying, "Scuse me, I want to use the phone."

And the woman saying, "Wait, nuh? You in a hurry?"

And Mr. Thorne getting more impatient and saying, "Yes. I in a hurry. You don't know who I am? I am Mr. Thorne!"

But the woman on the phone acting like she en know who Mr. Thorne is. "Pleased to meet you. I's Gloria," she saying, then going on talking on the phone.

When Mr. Thorne finally get to use the phone, he saying, "I am Grantley Thorne . . . from the Hill. I am a personal friend of the prime minister."

But all the woman on the other end saying is, "The prime minister is busy. Call back later."

"What you mean call back later?" Mr. Thorne voice raising. I want to know what going on up here on the Hi . . ."

The phone click in Mr. Thorne ear.

"What happen?" Hammer ask Mr. Thorne as soon as he get out of his pickup.

"The prime minister en there," is all Mr. Thorne say.

And as he saying this, a police jeep come roaring up the road, past the shop.

Minutes later, Bumpy Green walking down the road with Lionel grabble up by the back of his pants, walking him past the shop toward the main road where the police station is.

Lionel pants up in the crease of his ass and he on tiptoes; his pants squeezing his balls; he grimacing. "What you arresting me for?" He can scarcely talk. His toes barely touching the ground.

"Keep quiet! Else I ram this stick up your ass!" Bumpy Green barking. And he thump Lionel one backslap cross his head. Lionel head jerk forward.

More police vans roaring up from the main road. By the time they reach Mr. Thorne shop, the shop empty. Everybody scatter. Mr. Thorne shut the shop doors and bolt the wooden windows.

All over the village, is policemen like peas, kicking open doors, dragging out everybody from inside their houses.

And the whole place filled with women screaming, children crying.

"Where you was when the missionary got killed?" This tall, brown-skin constable standing in Brother Joseph shop door, blocking out the light, looking nervous.

Brother Joseph just looking up at him.

"I talking to you!" the policeman barking.

But Brother Joseph sitting on the bench stitching on a shoe sole.

The young policeman face as smooth as a baby's ass. He look as if he just join the force fresh from school. He squaring his shoulders and frowning. But Brother Joseph ignoring him.

The young policeman turn away in a huff and walk up the gap to one of the police vans.

The van pull up in front Brother Joseph shoemaker shop. The young, brown-skin policeman and another stocky darker constable get out.

"Brother Joseph!" This is bandy-leg Bumpy Green with the sergeant stripes on his shirt sleeves, who also getting out of the van.

Brother Joseph look up.

"You under arrest." Bumpy Green say.

The thin brown-skin policeman grab on to Brother Joseph arm.

Bumpy Green heart beating fast. Brother Joseph used to be a stick licker in his young days. Brother Joseph can drop the young constable with one blow from his snake staff. But Brother Joseph only stare Bumpy Green straight in his face and say, "All right." He shake off his arm out the young policeman hand. The young policeman face set up and he start to raise his club.

Brother Joseph en even flinch.

Bumpy Green frown and shake his head. The young policeman hand drop.

Brother Joseph stand up slow, reach for his snake staff, and walk straightbacked to the police jeep.

The brown-skin constable give Brother Joseph a little chuck soon as he reach the jeep. Brother Joseph turn his head and give him one fierce look, then get in the back seat of the jeep.

Denzil, coming up from the river with his fishing net over his shoulder and a basket of fish on his head, see Brother Joseph and the three policemen. He turn around to cut through the bush to head for Boysie place to find out what going on. Two policemen standing up in front him.

Same time, Cephus out behind his cow pen sharpening his cutlass ("I-if they come for me it en go be like l-last time," he saying), when he hear a police jeep stop in front Boysie house.

Cephus peep round the cowpen. Next thing, Boysie coming down the front steps with his hands handcuffed behind his back and two policemen holding his arms.

Soon as the jeep drive away with Boysie, Cephus run inside the house. "K-keep inside the house," he tell Doreen. "D-don't go outside." And with that he take off for the gully. With all the bush, caves and tunnels down there, it would take a army to find him.

Soon after Cephus take off, Brother Joseph come walking up the road from the police station, right back to his shop.

And word spreading.

—"*Brother Joseph come back.*"

—"*What you mean? They let him out? Who else?*"

—"*Only he. With not a scratch.*"

And Brother Joseph sitting in his shop realizing he made a big mistake coming back. He shoulda say, "No. I staying with the rest of the men."

But what that woulda do? They would only beat him too.

But he can tell by the looks on people faces as he was walking through the village just now that they think he in collusion with the police. They suspicious.

And Brother Joseph realizing that maybe Bumpy Green en as stupid as everybody think.

That night, the Pentecostal Church down on the main road keeping service as usual. What going on up on the Hill en concern them.

But while the service going on, they can hear blows hitting and men bawling in the police station next door. When they singing, it drowning out the noise. But when the reverend praying, they hearing, "You's a fucking liar!" *Whup! Whubupbup!* "We know unna do it!"

The collection plate passing around and all of a sudden,

somebody screaming out in the police station, then a deep, rough voice shouting, "Sign it! Sign it!"

People looking straight ahead, trying to pretend they en hearing, cause this en the first time it happen. They can always tell when the police arrest somebody.

The sun gone down; Cephus come out the bush and going around the village trying to find out who get arrest.

Estelle propping open the window with her hand; the lamplight in the house got her face silhouette in shadow so Cephus can't see her expression; her big earrings glistening, though.

"What *you* want?" Her voice sharp.

The other women in the village greeting him the same way when he come to find out who get lock up. One ask him, "You come to finish the job Brother Joseph start?"

That one puzzle Cephus.

But later, when Doreen tell him that the police let go Brother Joseph, the woman question make sense.

That night, Cephus en sleeping. He staring up in the roof. Doreen breathing deep next to him. The baby quiet. And every time he think he hear a footstep outside, his heart pounding. He hearing blows down at the police station, and Boysie and the fellas hollering. But it is too far; it is just in his imagination. He begin to doze off.

And just as I there watching Cephus, Boysie father appear. "You want piece of this?"

Before I can answer, he take off.

I grab Cephus and follow Boysie father.

Cephus dreaming how he flying over the village and away. Torrectly he looking down on the rooftops of what he recognize is Cambridge Terrace, where the big-shots live.

And we in the prime minister house, a big, limestone mansion with grounds as big as a racecourse and a policeman standing with a rifle in a hut by the gates.

Roachford lying flat on his back in his bed, sleeping. His wife in her bedroom next door.

And Boysie father fuming. "See that? See that? People talk about wicked people can't be happy? Look at him!"

Roachford sleeping with a big smile on his face.

The little girl that got drowned at the beach sitting at the foot of Roachford bed, playing with a rag doll. "Politicians en human," she say.

"Ha!" is all her little brother say. He busy backing the house cat into a corner of the bedroom. The cat back curved; its eyes staring; it snarling and hissing.

Miss Wiggins nephew sitting in the rocking chair, holding his head in his lap. His head grinning and singing like a ventriloquist's dummy,

"Back to back, belly to belly
Ah don't give a damn, ah done dead a'ready."

Miss Scantlebury looking at the singing head and saying, "Boy, stop your foolishness."

Boysie father pacing back and forth, fuming because he couldn't get Roachford to wake up.

Miss Scantlebury turning to me; we is the two oldest in the room. "What we going do?" she asking me.

"Nothing," I say.

"But we got to help them," Miss Scantlebury say.

"No," I say. "They got to help themselves."

Later I should've listened to my own advice.

Boysie father glaring down at Roachford stretched out sleeping on the bed and saying, "One swipe with this cutlass. One swipe and the problem solved."

Old Miss Wiggins saying, "You don't think you and that cutlass do enough damage already?"

The little boy catching Miss Wiggins nephew head (they playing catch with it) and saying, "If you get rid of Roachford, somebody else will only come along. Politicians is a curse, sucking the people blood like soucouyant, turning them into zombies."

And my mouth dropping open to hear this coming from a little boy—even if he is a spirit.

Foreday morning, the cocks crowing; outside just beginning to lighten up.

Cephus wake up feeling just as tired as when he went to sleep. He nudge Doreen, "Reen."

Doreen mumble and turn her head to face him.

"I leffing. Before the sun come up," he say. "T-tell everybody m-meet me in the g-g-gully."

Cephus stop around by Brother Joseph shop, where he does sleep sometimes in the back. The shop shut.

Cephus head deep into the gully where Brother Joseph live with his three wives and the children they have for him.

Four huts in the clearing. Brother Joseph sitting in front the door of the one set off from the other three.

Soon as Cephus step from the track into the clearing, Brother Joseph say, "It is your time, son." His voice weary.

"W-what you saying?"

"You going to the station house." Brother Joseph say it as a statement, not a question, but his eyes locked onto Cephus face.

"Y-y-yes."

"Be careful." And Brother Joseph turn back to whittling the stick in his hand.

After Cephus notice Brother Joseph en saying nothing more, he wave at Brother Joseph three wives standing little ways off—the youngest woman with her belly big with child—and leave the compound.

Later, Cephus standing up in the middle of the clearing, in the spot where Brother Joseph accustom to standing when the Brethren holding meeting. Women standing around, shuffling, talking, glancing at Cephus. Inez, Doreen, and Violet standing up together. Granville and Doreen father, Mr. Holder, are the only two men there beside Cephus.

Kwame and Estelle boy, Donald, up in their lookout tree at the top of the gully.

At last Cephus say, "A-all right. Le-lewwe start!"

The murmuring quiet down.

"Y-yesterday, the p-police arrest everybody."

"Except you," Sybil say.

"Let the boy talk, Sybil," Granville saying.

Sybil cutting her eye at Cephus father.

"T-today we g-going down by the sta-sta-station house," Cephus saying.

Boy, soon as he say that, bacchanal let loose.

"Doing *what?*"

"Who is *we?*"

"You see what happen yesterday?"

And a voice say, "You want to turn we in like you do with Boysie?"

But some of the women going, "Sshh." The talk quiet down.

And Cephus start this long speech about how the p-police c-can't come in the village arresting everybody just so. And wh-what about the soldiers up on the mountain? Who they is? What happening?

Cephus really warming up; people listening to him. Even Sybil got her hand out of her kimbo and paying attention.

And Granville got this frown on his face because he noticing the more his son talk the less he stuttering until,

"What I propose," say Cephus, "Is that we go to the police station, together. March down there together and *demand* to know what's going on."

Cephus father jaw drop. He grab his pipe quick before it could fall on the ground.

For the first time since Cephus learn to talk, he en stuttering.

Other people notice it.

And Cephus looking taller, a different man.

When Cephus raise his arm and asking in a loud, hoarse voice asking, "All you with me? If all you with me, raise your hands!" everybody just nodding and pushing their hands in the air.

Miss Wiggins and Miss Scantlebury nodding and smiling. Boysie father sitting on a rock; his face showing grudging approval.

The sun overhead and the village quiet as Cephus leading the Brethren out of the gully. Cephus in front with Doreen, Inez, Granville, Violet, and Mr. Holder.

As they walking through the village, other villagers walking beside them, wanting to know what happening; where they going. But Cephus and his Brethren just walking silent and serious. Children tagging on behind—school closed. The crowd swelling.

Cephus en shave for two days; his shirt open, showing his jooking-board muscles and the top of his underwear over his pants waist. He walking his slow, jerk-waist walk, so the crowd following him like a funeral procession.

You look from Cephus to Inez and, had not for Cephus beard, the two of them is the spitting image of one another, with Inez short afro, their narrow faces with nose lips and features chisel like masks. In between them, Doreen walking with the baby strapped to her back.

And inside the station house down on the main road, the policemen watching this crowd of people coming down the hill.

Bumpy Green looking through the front window. "What the ass is this?" he asking.

By the time Cephus and the Hill people get off the track and onto the main road, the police line up in front the police station with their clubs in their hands, waiting.

Cephus stop in front the station house; the crowd stop behind him.

"We come to see the men," Cephus say.

Bowlegged Bumpy Green belly hanging over his pants waist. He smacking his baton against his palm. Finally he say, "All right, come."

Cephus step forward; the crowd edging forward with him. Bumpy Green raise his hand. "Only he," he say.

The crowd stop; Cephus keep walking.

But soon as Cephus get close to the policemen, two of them rush forward and grab him.

Inez make a step forward; Granville and Violet following. Doreen make a timid step forward. The crowd standing still in the middle of the road.

"Uh! Uh!" Bumpy Green hand up; he wagging his head from side to side. "One more step and I *splatter* his brains."

"Leggo my blasted brother!" Inez saying.

"You want to come for him?" Bumpy Green smiling. "Come. You want the same thing I give Boysie? Come."

And Inez lose her head. She leggo one scream and rush forward. Bumpy Green raise his baton.

I couldn't let that happen. I step between them.

And Bumpy Green eyes bug open. He swallow. His goggle begin bobbing up and down in his throat.

Same time, the other policemen backing off. Fright stamp on their faces.

The crowd seeing Bumpy Green freeze; they seeing the policemen backing off and the fright on their faces, but they en know why. They puzzled.

Same time, a noise coming from above. The crowd look up. The two policemen that heading to the side door of the station house with Cephus between them stop and look up.

Two planes roaring in from the sea, headed toward the station house.

And it is then I do the thing that got me where I am today. I figure, I interfere already, I might as well finish the job.

The pilots got the station house in their sights. A crowd of people standing in the road. They didn't expect that. But their orders are clear. Hit the police station. But as soon as they getting ready to hit the buttons and launch the missiles, the fella in the lead plane say, "What the . . . ?"

Where there was a crowd in front of a wooden police station a few seconds ago, there is now a desert. A fucking desert. No police station, no crowd. Nothing.

The planes roar past.

And down on the ground, the cell doors and station house door bang open, and Boysie and the rest of men rubbing their eyes, dazzled by the sunlight, and staggering out to the people in the road.

The crowd hearing the planes zoom past and watching Boysie and the men coming out of the station house, some with blood on their clothes. Claude got a big lump above his eye.

The policemen look from the men coming out of the police station, to me, back to the men, back to me, and they take off like jack rabbits.

Cephus watching the policemen that were just holding him. All he can see is the bottoms of their boots flashing; their arms pumping.

Get these people out of here fast, I tell him.

He en stop to argue.

"Come. Let's get out of here. Quick!" He say.

Boysie and them only staring at him.

"Come along, man!" Cephus say, and start heading for the track that lead up to the Hill.

The jet engines in the distance getting closer. People scrambling out of the road.

The pilots see the people heading up the hill away from the road, like a line of ants, but their orders were to hit the police station.

The old station house explode in a ball of fire. The flames roaring and blazing; the wood crackling and falling.

And the planes heading back out to the aircraft carriers out in the bay.

WHILE ALL THIS HAPPENING, the parliament building in town in an uproar. A group of soldiers just burst through the big mahogany door of the House of Assembly. Two soldiers gripping the deputy leader of the opposition People's Doctors Party under his armpits.

He trying to shake them off. "Unhand me! Unhand me, I say!"

And when he en getting nowhere, he looking over his shoulder and bawling, "This is an outrage! Mr. Speaker, this is an outrage! I protest this outrage!"

The speaker, a retired judge, a member of Roachford People's Lawyers Party, sitting in his high-back chair in his robe and wig, like a English judge with black shoe polish smear on his face and hands. He playing with his gavel, en saying a word, en even raising his eyes.

"Mr. Speaker." Roachford standing up holding a sheet of paper in his hand.

The speaker look up.

"I have here in my hand a signed confession from an associate of the honorable member from St. Joseph"—Roachford looking at the deputy leader of the opposition standing between the two soldiers—"which shows that the honorable member from St. Joseph plotted to overthrow her majesty's government and expel all foreign residents. The murder of the missionary, Mr. Wright, was the first in a series of dastardly acts planned by this foreign-controlled element, Mr. Speaker."

Straughn, the youngest member of the PDP, fresh from studying medicine in Away, jump to his feet. "This is absolute *nonsense*, Mr. Speaker!" Straughn is a tall, skinny man in a dark blue suit that fitting him snug; his white shirt collar nearly up to his chin. He standing upright, glaring at Roachford, his fists clench down at his sides, so tense with rage he remind you of a tight string trembling in the wind.

He and Roachford glaring eyeball to eyeball and the scene day before yesterday flashing across Straughn mind.

Roachford on his feet, leaning forward and bawling, "The honorable leader of the opposition is a bloody *communist!*"

And the government ministers and back-benchers in the PLP bellowing, "Hear! Hear!"

And Bostick, on the opposition side of the aisle, leaning against the bannister, as though he would spring over the railing and attack Roachford on the spot. "Our honorable prime minister, the member for St. Andrew, is the last person who should be calling people names. Because he is the biggest *traitor*, the worst kind of *quisling!* Inviting foreign troops onto our own *soil!*"

And the crowd up in the balcony—old men in sweaty felt hats, women fanning their faces and spreading their legs to cool themselves; younger fellas, messengers that supposed to be delivering things but sneak in the parliament to see what going on—everybody murmuring and whizzy-whizzying to one another.

The Speaker banging his gavel and bawling, "Order! Order!"

Two hours after the House adjourned that night, Bostick was dead. Running a police roadblock, they said.

Straughn remembering this and telling himself to cool down; take it easy.

He taking his kerchief out of his pants pocket and wiping his dark-rim glasses.

They had planned to call for a no-confidence vote against Roachford and the PLP.

Now, what's the use? Warships are in the harbor. Bostick is dead. Deputy Leader is standing between two soldiers, under arrest.

And Roachford looking at Straughn with a little smile on his face. "The agitators are being arrested at this very minute," he saying.

Over in Away, Gloria watching the evening news in her apartment and worrying about Darcy. The TV announcer, a white man with bat ears, eyes close together and a small face, looking into the camera and saying "We have with us here in the studio, the eminent scholar of international affairs . . ."

And he introducing a heavy-set white man sitting next to him wearing a dark suit and black-framed glasses.

"Professor, what is your analysis of the events taking place?"

But before the announcer can finish his sentence, the professor jumping right in with, "Well, as I stated clearly in my most recent article . . ." And he going on to describe Roachford as "a man of vision," and he saying how for a long time he was warning of the existence of "subversive elements in the region."

Suddenly the announcer ask, "And where did you acquire your expertise, professor?"

I blinked. I know these TV announcers en got sense enough to ask questions like that.

The *announcer* blinked, like his own mouth catch him off-guard and asked a question his brain didn't know he was going to ask.

Then I hear this giggling right behind me. I looked back. Cynthia Green have this big grin on her face, feeling real pleased with herself for what she just did.

I can almost hear the professor eyelids going *blap! blap!* behind his glasses as he blinking without saying a word. Then he start sputtering, "I, ah, in my extensive research . . ."

And Gloria sucking her teeth to hear this big expert talking about this "seminal work" and that "definitive article" he read in his "research."

But all around us in the other apartments, people taking the professor serious. They en know that the only time this man ever set foot in "the region" he is such an expert on is when the cruise ship he was vacationing on with his wife made one-day stops there around the same time Roachford was studying law in Away.

Poor Cynthia. Her face long with disappointment.

"Come," I tell her. "You tried."

And as we leave, Cynthia puzzling to her self, wondering why these people never even hear about her country until their troops invade it. After all, *she* learn about *their* country when she was in school.

BACK UP ON THE HILL, the crowd reaching the village. Down in the bay, the two planes landing on the aircraft carrier. And the policemen sitting down in the road catching their wind, watching the smoke rising from what used to be their police station.

Sergeant Green, Bumpy Green, leaning over gasping for breath. The other constables watching and some of them smirking. He en the big, bad Bumpy Green that always terrorizing people. Only a big, fat, bowlegged, out-of-breath sergeant.

"Bumpy!" I say behind his shoulder.

But just as he turning to see who calling him, I find myself rushing away, backward, like if a whirlwind pick me up and pulling me, up the Hill, into the crowd.

Next thing I know, I in little Kojo body. *Fwoop!* Just like that, kicking and screaming in Doreen arms.

What going on? I bawling. Hey! What happening? I want to know.

Of course, the only thing coming from my mouth is bawling baby noise. Doreen bouncing me and shushing me. This is ridiculous.

A cold breeze coming from the mahogany tree in the yard where they found the missionary dead a few days ago, where they buried my father years ago after the slave woman betrayed him.

My father, still in the tattered clothes they buried him in, walking alongside now and saying, "You shouldn't have interfered. You want to meddle in human affairs, then *be* a human."

And I vex, vex as hell. How I going ever get seniority if they keep sending me back in human bodies? How I going ever build up real power? The few things I do down by the police station is nothing next to what my father can do. I know. I've seen.

"You've got to learn how to control yourself," he saying to me now.

Then he gone.

And all around me people talking. Inez asking Boysie what they do to him down at the guardhouse. Estelle crying and hugging Denzil.

Pearl got her hands resting on Claude chest and looking up in his face and asking, "What they do you this time?"

But Claude en answering. The things that happen that day are too much for his mind to handle.

All he remembering is the cold wind sweeping through the station house and the jail doors opening sudden so by themselves. The policemen inside the station en wait for nothing more. They nearly trample one another trying to get through the door.

And when he and the fellas walk outside, Cephus and a whole set of people from the Hill standing up in the middle of the road. It look like Cephus, but it en look like Cephus. This man that look like Cephus leading the crowd, talking without stuttering.

Claude feel as though he standing in a fog, feeling sore and bruised, not knowing how he got here.

Hammer-Head forehead, hard as it is, got a whem on it that make it look even more like a hammer, a ballpeen hammer.

Lionel standing off by himself, watching. His eyes and mine making four. His body lying back down in the burning police station, roasting. When the policemen run out and left him there in the room, nearly unconscious, he tried to raise himself, but he en had enough strength. When the rocket hit the station house, good luck for him a beam fall down and crush his skull. He died same time.

People standing around Cephus. Cephus standing erect right next to me and Doreen. I can smell his sweat.

"What is the next move, old chap?" Mr. Holder asking Cephus.

And everybody close by looking at Cephus waiting for an answer.

Through the crowd of people I can see Boysie just staring at Cephus. Because of his thick beard, I can't tell what expression he got on his face.

And it hit me. Sudden. I en know what going through Boysie mind as he staring at Cephus.

I look around. I en know what people thinking anymore.

That's when I decide to tell this story to somebody quick before I forget it. I can't risk losing all of this.

My eyes locking with Kwame eyeballs.

I got something to tell you, I say.

Kwame start pulling on Inez skirt. "Ma! Ma!"

Inez look down at Kwame. "What happen, boy?"

"The baby talking!" Kwame pointing at me. "The baby talking!"

Inez box his ear. "Boy, how many times I tell you to stop telling stories?"

But the obeah woman standing next to Inez all of a sudden. "Don't do that again," she saying. "The boy knows what he saw." Then she gone.

Kwame staring at me.

All of a sudden, I feeling myself getting irritable. Doreen bouncing me up and down on her shoulder. Plus, I getting sleepy. So I tell myself I'll tell Kwame the story tomorrow.

But that night, everything crash.

Last thing I hear that night, between sleep and wake, lying down on the bed between Doreen and Cephus, is Doreen saying to Cephus, "You ever see anything so in all your born days?"

But Cephus sleeping already, snoring easy.

I fall back asleep.

SCREAMS. SHOUTS. Running feet in the compound. A body crashing against the side of the hut.

"See what going on outside," Mama whispering to Papa.

The slavers—-raiding the village . . .

Papa getting up from the bed and leaving an emptiness behind.

Then, a man voice outside shouting, "There he is! That is the ringleader!"

Next, a crash, like the front door breaking down, and the thud of heavy boots and a scuffling in the house cause my eyes to pop open.

And I wake up, looking up into Doreen eyes, feeling her pick me up off the bed, clutching me to her bosom.

My diaper feel wet. This is so embarrassing.

Cephus voice ringing out loud on the other side of the partition, "Loose me, man! Lemme go! What unna doing? Get out my hou . . . !"

And a thudding blow cutting his words in half.

Feet scuffling on the floor, the sound of something dragging, and Doreen heart thudding as my head rests against her bosom make me want to cry. But she clamping her hand over my mouth.

When Doreen and me get outside, headlights stabbing into my eyes. I feeling dizzy.

And time is a kitten chasing its own tail.

Because two scenes weaving in and out of my mind like the intertwining links of a chain.

Men here on the Hill in khaki uniforms and boots, holding machine guns, with the straps over their shoulders, pushing Boysie, Cephus, Claude, Denzil, and Hammer-Head down the gap toward the trucks with their motors rumbling and light beams piercing the darkness.

And it is like that foreday morning three hundred years ago, before I followed the caravan to the coast and saw the pale, hairy-faced men and their ships for the first, but not the last time: when explosions, strange voices and heavy footsteps outside the hut woke me up; when smoke, crackling fire, screaming women, crying children, and men voices outside caused Mama to pull my little brother and little sister to her pregnant belly; when Papa grabbed his knife and said to me, "Stay with the family," ducked through the door, rushed out into the night, the fire, the noise, and never set foot in his hut again; when Mama stared at me like a mother hen in the midst of a fire, and I stepped to the door with knife in hand and came face to face with a boy my age, from another village, and the rifle in his hands spat fire, pain slammed into my chest like a fist and Mama screamed as I died, never again to tease Mama as she bent over the pot, cooking; never again to show my little brother how to set bird traps; never again to lay in the grass with Abena late in the evening as the wind soothed our skins with the promise of rain and carried the aroma of cooking meals.

But now Doreen running toward the soldiers and the trucks with me bouncing up and down against her shoulder.

"What you doing?" she hollering. "Where you carrying them?" Her voice sound higher than usual, and sobs catching in her throat like hiccups.

A young soldier step in front of her with his machine gun pointing at her belly. "Stay back!"

I can feel Doreen trembling, and a hand patting her shoulder. It is Inez.

"If you do anything to them, all you going be sorry." Inez voice low. She staring the young soldier full in his face, a smooth round face that en even lost its mother's features yet.

And it is right at that moment that the gunshots let go like jackhammers.

Everybody gone silent—the soldiers; the few people standing outside in their night clothes; Doreen, and Inez.

The diesel smoke from the lorry engines suffocating me.

The young soldier in front of us looking over his shoulder at the foot of the wall in front of Roachford bungalow where the missionary used to live.

Cephus, Boysie, Claude, Denzil, and Hammer-Head crumpling to the ground.

Two soldiers standing in front of them, looking down. The nozzles of their machine guns pointing downward at the five bodies collapsed together in a twitching, jerking heap.

Doreen bawling.

Inez grabbing her short afro and letting out a wail.

Estelle, with her ear hoops glistening in the light from the trucks and her light chemise reaching almost to her ankles, just staring at Denzil lying flat on his back with his arms flung out.

Her three children standing on the front steps of their house. The oldest boy standing in front of his little brother and sister with his arms out, as if he trying to shield them from seeing their father dying in the gutter in front Roachford bungalow.

Little ways back from the road, a window that was cracked

open easing shut, closing in the timid silhouette of Sybil that was there a moment ago.

The front of Cephus pants soaking wet with piss as he lying spread-eagled on the ground. Boysie en got no face, just a mask of blood and meat.

A cool breeze blowing, clearing away the suffocating diesel fumes. But the stench of shit is like a fog in the wake of the breeze, clogging my nostrils.

"Jesus Christ," a soldier saying, "One of them shit."

The soldiers laughing a raucous man-laugh, all except for the young soldier standing in front of us. He glancing at Doreen, then at Inez, and dropping his eyes. But his gun still aimed at Doreen's belly.

I call him; his eyes fix on mine and open wide, not understanding how a baby could call his name. And amidst the echoes of the guns rattling in the hills and the death rattles of Boysie, Cephus, Denzil, Claude, and Hammer-Head, a rush of wind whipping the young soldier's uniform, pulling him from his body like a cork from a wine bottle.

And he spiraling and tumbling in a tunnel of distorted sound, like a tape playing backward—seeing bodies falling like sacks; hearing shouts, tramping boots, rumbling engines, raging fire, explosions.

The sounds speed, blend, and blur, then they stop. At the silence. The foreday morning silence of my village three hundred years ago, the stillness preceding the shots, shouts, confusion, and my mother cradling my head in the doorway of our hut as the blood oozed from my chest, with my little brother and sister standing behind her, staring over her shoulder at my dead body.

"It's all right," I said to them then.

Just as Cephus saying to me and Doreen now.

But just as no one heard me then, only I hear Cephus now, only I see him.

And Doreen throwing her head back and letting loose a wail from deep in her guts.

Inez bending over, holding her belly, not uttering a sound.

Kwame standing half-naked next to Inez, in the old short pants that he does sleep in, staring up at Boysie standing beside him. "I'm sorry, mate," Boysie saying to Kwame. But Kwame en got a clue what his father sorry about. And Boysie continuing, "Take care of your brother" and looking at me as he saying this, which making Kwame even *more* confused, because to him, *Cephus* is my father.

Claude, Denzil, and Hammer-Head walking toward Miss Wiggins and Miss Scantlebury standing in the shadows.

Granville leaning against the electric pole with his old felt hat in his hand and his head bowed by the death of Cephus, his only son, who used to be my grandson.

And I feel a sadness that I haven't felt since I followed Papa here to the Hill three hundred years ago, where I tried over the years, sometimes among the living, sometimes not, planting a name here, reviving a ritual there, trying to keep the line going, the memory, reminding people of who they are, where they came from, trying to keep them together.

But change is like a hurricane—you can prepare for it but you can't stop it. And things are changing; people are changing; and no one listens anymore.

So I look down at little Kwame standing there in a foreday-morning scene he will never forget, and Boysie instruction to him—"Take care of your brother"—is a candle flame flickering in the darkness, giving relief to my sadness and some encouragement as I pass this story on.

And as I do, darkness bleaching out of the sky, birds chirping, cocks crowing in the distance, and I resting my head on Doreen's shoulder and watching the lights of the aircraft carrier, sitting big and dark at anchor down in the bay.

Step pon the wire and the wire won't bend
That's the way this story end.